Praise for *Hold You*

"The wonderful thing about *Hold Your Tongue* is that it definitely does not hold its tongue. English, French, and Michif gallop across its pages, mingling and colliding like the fractious history of the Canadian West echoing into the present. What James Joyce did for the voices of the Irish Matthew Tétreault has done for those of his own people. This earthy, wise, big-hearted novel about a Métis community's tangled past and uncertain future shouts, gossips, mourns, jokes, confesses, and sings. Before you reach the end you'll be singing along with it."
—THOMAS WHARTON, award-winning author of *Icefields* and *The Book of Rain*

"*Hold Your Tongue* expertly weaves historic Métis (and Manitoban) events with contemporary realities in a meaningful confluence of past and present. Tétreault's approach to Michif storytelling shines: sharing stories within stories while an intergenerational history unfolds, turning painful stories into silly ones out of survival, resisting settler narratives that try to erase Indigenous presence, and re-threading forgotten truths fractured by Métis dispossession into a strengthened, collective *histwayr Michif*. Uplifting Métis cultural, spiritual, and linguistic practices, the author seamlessly incorporates Michif nicknames, visiting, harvesting, and *Franglais* colloquialisms characteristic of rural and urban Métis and Franco-Manitobain communities. This novel feels like home."
—CHANTAL FIOLA, Ph.D, author of *Returning to Ceremony: Spirituality in Manitoba Métis Communities*

"Inspired by deep knowledge of his French-Métis homeland, Matthew Tétreault has given us a rich, beautifully written novel. In this story you'll meet unforgettable characters who 'sprang from the soil.' This intricate yarn is an evocative detective story, a search for the first betrayals and deviations, a glorious patchwork of vision and memory, buoyed by love as tough and vulnerable as the land that nurtured it. The past is palpable, vibrant in these pages, full of promise, like 'seedlings'."
—MARGARET SWEATMAN, author of *The Gunsmith's Daughter*

"With cutting language, Matthew Tétreault weaves a narrative that runs us through history and love of land while simultaneously questioning a modern prairie existence. His distinctive voice brings a reader along with the narrator as he navigates the passing of his great-uncle Alfred and, with that, the loss of generations worth of knowledge. At the same time, the narrator questions a future and what it really means to lose the land you love, the question of leaving, and what coming back home really looks like. From brawls with the neighbouring small towns to being buried in your favourite camo ball cap to figuring out a future that may never really exist, this is a read that will keep you sucked into the pages like a hose pumping out the honey bucket."
—CONOR KERR, author of *Avenue of Champions*

"Witty, down-to-earth, and transformative, Matthew Tétreault's *Hold Your Tongue* sets a new benchmark for literature in Canada, folding in francophone and Métis voice and culture and navigating the tensions of family, history, self, and place. Marked both by verisimilitude and contemplation, *Hold Your Tongue* is a journey through the geography of identity that emerges speaking with a fresh, assured voice."
—CONRAD SCOTT, author of *Water Immersion*

Hold Your Tongue

Hold

Your

Tongue

a novel

Matthew Tétreault

NeWest Press

Library and Archives Canada Cataloguing in Publication

Title: Hold your tongue / Matthew Tétreault.
Names: Tétreault, Matthew, 1983- author.
Series: Nunatak first fiction series ; no. 60.
Description: Series statement: Nunatak first fiction series ; no. 60 | Includes some text in French.
Identifiers: Canadiana (print) 20220410429 | Canadiana (ebook) 20220410445 | ISBN 9781774390719 (softcover) | ISBN 9781774390726 (EPUB)
Subjects: LCGFT: Novels.
Classification: LCC PS8639.E896 H65 2023 | DDC C813/.6—dc23

Board Editor: Smaro Kamboureli
Cover and interior design: Michel Vrana
Author photo: Lisa Bergen

NeWest Press wishes to acknowledge that the land on which we operate is Treaty 6 territory and a traditional meeting ground and home for many Indigenous Peoples, including Cree, Saulteaux, Niitsitapi (Blackfoot), Métis, and Nakota Sioux.

NeWest Press acknowledges the Canada Council for the Arts, the Alberta Foundation for the Arts, and the Edmonton Arts Council for support of our publishing program. We acknowledge the financial support of the Government of Canada through the Canada Book Fund for our publishing activities.

NeWest Press
#201, 8540-109 Street
Edmonton, Alberta T6G 1E6
www.newestpress.com

No bison were harmed in the making of this book.

Printed and bound in Canada
22 23 24 25 5 4 3 2 1

For Geneviève

Author's Note

Set around Sainte-Anne-des-Chênes, in south-eastern Manitoba, this novel uses different registers of French—Standard French, French-Canadian, and French-Michif—to capture some of the cultural diversity, history, and tensions of the region. It honours previous generations through their ways of telling stories.

Translations are largely conveyed through context.

This is a work of fiction. All resemblances to persons living or dead are coincidental.

La Grotte

RAIN FELL HEAVILY ON THE STONE ARCHWAY OVERHEAD, but the boy and the girl hardly noticed over the drum of their own pulse. Months, they had stared at each other across the schoolyard, discreetly brushed fingers whenever they passed in the hallway, and whispered in the communion line. At last, they had decided to meet under the old grotto. In the dark, at the Virgin's feet, they pressed their lips together like chickens pecking at seeds. Stones groaned overhead as rainwater seeped through fissures in the mortar and dripped onto the statue. The girl frowned and glanced at the scattered pinpricks of light that flashed through cracks in the ceiling. Water ran like tears down the Virgin's cheeks. The boy flinched as something grazed his ear and thudded at his feet, and as he bent down to examine the object, lifting up a jagged stone the size of an orange, the archway slumped, knocking the statue from its pedestal. Toppling, the Virgin fell overtop the boy and the girl, pinning them underneath as the archway collapsed. They clung together as stones ricocheted off the statue and gathered at their feet, piling into a wall around them until they could no longer see light. Only after the thunder of the stonefall faded, and the stench of mud filled the darkness, could they hear each other scream.

Sainte-Anne-des-Chênes

1.

When the Wood Slats Cracked like Gunshots

THIS WAS THE MORNING ALFRED HAD HIS STROKE, BUT I didn't know it yet as I stood in the tall grass by the fence and emptied my bladder. I had awoken to the sound of cows battering the greyworn fence on the edge of Gauthier's yard. Cold sunlight swirled like wastewater through the dusty windows as I lay in the back of the Buick and knucklerubbed my eyes. I swung my legs off the seat and empties clattered underfoot. Beneath the warm stink of flat beer, sweat, and cigarette smoke, her perfume lingered. We had sat for some time in the Buick, and I could still feel the imprint of her soft lips on my cheek, but something that she'd said not long before she left had given us pause. She talked about how her mother had grown up around here, but her family had left after something happened. The woman wondered if we were related. Thinking to clear things up, I pulled a bundle of papers from the glove box.

"My tree," I said.

Someone had typed my name on the cover page. Inside, a slew of names spider-webbed outward from my own. "Branched," my sister said. Our parents, and their parents, and theirs still, going back years. She had put the package together and given it to me the last time I had been to the city. She told me to apply for a Métis card, and said it could help me find a job or go back to school, but I had shoved the package into the glovebox and forgotten about it until the woman had asked about my grandparents. In the dim glow of the roof light, I flipped through the pages, staring dumbly at the names and the dates, older than the country.

"Is that how people date out here?" she laughed. "Whip out the old tree and check the branches before things get serious?" She glanced briefly at the first page, but 2 AM, drunk, in a dirty Buick, was probably not the place to compare genealogies. The woman sucked her breath, and tossed the sheaf into my lap. Before I knew it, she was gone. Alone in the dark, I finished my beer.

Outside, the cows and I dribbled and wetted the earth. The dull sun climbed slowly over the treeline, and the cows ambled closer, curious, wet noses snuffling in the air. They jostled up against the old fence, trying to get a better look at me, and the wood slats cracked like gunshots against the posts, and the herd broke and thundered away into the pasture.

Gauthier's yard was a mess. The firepit smoldered still. Smoke curled over the charred remains of broken furniture, the blackened ribs of a cracked wooden pallet. Assorted cans, and bottles, and red plastic cups lay scattered in a wild, sloppy ring around the pit. Empties littered a path like breadcrumbs toward the farmhouse. Soiled plates and plastic cutlery peppered the grass before the foldup tables where Gauthier had brought out baloney and rye bread for a midnight snack. He had run cables from the house, across the yard, to power the amps on the makeshift stage where a country and western band had stomped time on a bale trailer. Folks had danced and jigged in the dew-soaked grass while fiddles squealed, and fireworks tore open the night. Flowering over the field, the booming, chemical crackle had driven cows further into the back pasture where trees grew and cattle trails coiled through the stocky bush.

The bonfire had swelled, fat with flames, gorging on the busted fence posts, the broken pallets and chairs, the deadwood gathered from the pasture that folks tossed in. Gauthier circled the fire. "Don't be shy now," he shouted, egging us on. "The sky won't burn!"

J.P. Gauthier had recently taken over the farm and decided to throw a party to celebrate his inheritance. His old man, li viyeu Gauthier, had finally moved to the old folks' home in Ste. Anne, and J.P. had big plans. He told everyone about them. He'd cornered people loading up on baloney and rye bread and yelled into their ears. Pigs, he explained. He ought to raise pigs. There had been little money in cattle since the mad cow scare, not enough, anyways, to make a decent living. Although his old man had scratched by on cattle, J.P. had bigger ambitions.

"Winters in Arizona," he shouted. "That's the plan."

Shuffling toward the Buick, a bolt of light in the frost-sopped grass arrested my step. I bent low and plucked a stainless-steel flask from the ground. It was empty but smelled of rye whiskey. Rising, I grunted as a hot, sharp pain seared down my leg and licked my toes. It was sometimes best not to move, I had learned, and let things settle. Ever since I started working for Uncle Joe, this pain had grown sharp and regular. Joe said it would get better. That I'd get used to it, but I wasn't so sure. Still, I figured doing nothing was worth the shot. As I stood fixed and surveyed the yard—scanning the tents under the disheveled oak and studying the RV that purred in the driveway with the quiet hum of a space heater—the pain began to ebb from my limbs.

The yard looked smaller than I remembered; the grass around me lay flat, driven low, as though someone had spun donuts with a 4x4. The yard had seemed so much larger when I was a child, when Monique and I used to tag along with Dad to visit li viyeu Gauthier. While they sat in the kitchen, chatting, and sipping on brandy, I would slip outside to play in the barn or climb the trees and the fences. I would chase the barn cats through the yard, and up the trees, and then sit up there on some thick branch, and watch J.P. work. He was my older cousin, and I admired him because he was old enough to drive and smoke and curse. From my perch, I watched him whip his tractor across the yard, skewer some round bales, and haul them one at a time into the pen to feed the heifers. Stopping every now and again to have a cigarette, he'd watch me from atop his tractor as I climbed that old oak tree next to the farmhouse. Then, flicking his cigarette butt onto the gravel, he would sweep his arms grandly along the length of the horizon, and then tell me how, one day, all of this—that vast stretch of rock-studded pasture—would be his.

I'd wondered occasionally in the years since, if he had known then just how long it would take, if J.P. wouldn't have rather moved to the city and taken up a trade. He'd spoken of all of his plans—the cattle and chickens he would raise, the greenhouses he would build, and now the pigs he would keep—while he waited for his old man to hand over the reins. He committed himself so fully to these visions that when they failed to come to pass, he grew bitter and resentful. He grew fat and mean-spirited, drinking too much as he waited for his old man to give way.

After Matante died, Dad stopped visiting le vieux—something had been said, which cut Dad up, but he'd refused to tell me what. I saw J.P. only occasionally, around town, or at the odd family reunion. He invited me to his party only because I bumped into him at the Petro last week. It had been years since I'd seen the farm, but I saw now, in the early morning light, how they had been unable to hold back the bush. How trees, wild grasses, and weeds pressed at the edges of the yard. Even the buildings looked weary, weathered, near ready to topple. Sprawled under the big oak, the farmhouse languished: crumbled stucco, and cracked windows, shingles fluttering like a bad combover; saplings sprouting like ear hair in the eavestroughs.

This land had once belonged to Pépère, so the story went, but he lost it in a spell of bad luck. Pépère sold it for next to nothing to his beau-frère. Le vieux Gauthier. I'd never heard the whole of it, just muttered bits from Dad, and from his brothers and sisters, enough to form some ghostly notion of what might have been. The idea that we might have been farmers. It was an old dream that had soured in the stomach.

The Buick started up fine. I scrounged around for a cigarette while I let the engine warm. I sifted through the ashtray, looking for a half-smoked butt, a smoke wastefully crushed when I'd carried on as though I were rich, and the pack endless. I plucked a couple butts from the tray and tore open the casings, then poured the tobacco into a rolling paper. I edged the window down an inch and lit my fresh cigarette. The first drag hit me like a fastball to the head, and I anchored my eyes to the horizon. As the smoke curled over the steering wheel, and the hand-rolled singed my fingers, I stared at that tapered edge of the Canadian Shield, beyond the pasture, until my eyes began to water.

The Buick jounced and rattled as I wheeled it onto the driveway and on toward the road where oak and birch trees loomed overhead. Sunlight spilled through the ragged, autumn canopy. I stomped on the gas and the old car surged into a clearing, where the sky yawned wide and blue, and the road unfurled like a gunshot. Rock and gravel pinballed through the undercarriage. As I tore out of the treeline, dragging a veil of dust behind me, I glanced at the rear-view and noticed that someone had knocked the mirror askew. I adjusted it, and paused as the rear-view cast not mine, but my father's reflection at me. I saw where all the creases and furrows would deepen and where laughter and sorrow would etch time on my face. And for a brief, bloated moment, I saw my life unfold: filled with labour and liquor, it was a hard path, and it frightened me.

In truth, it was less a revelation of things to come than a recognition of how I had come to be where I was. Somewhere along the way things had taken a wrong turn. The woman I loved had left for an education in the city, and the powder coat plant where I'd worked for half a dozen years had laid me off. Nowadays, I drove a honey wagon for my uncle Joe. Sometimes, standing over a gapping tank as piss and shit shuddered through a three-and-a-half-inch hose in my arms, I wondered what life in the city with Becky would have brought.

Frantic bursts from a shrill horn tore me from my thoughts, and I spotted a Dodge truck barreling down the gravel ridge toward me. I snapped the wheel and the Buick veered right, and began to skid

9

over the washboard, fish-tailing over the loose gravel. The truck blew past me with a deafening bang, spraying rocks like buckshot into the windshield. Then it was gone, and I was plunged into a cloud of dust. The rear-end swayed, and the Buick drifted sideways over the crest, and down the far side, where it finally ground to a stop at the foot of the ridge.

Trembling, with a knot around my heart, I sucked a sharp breath through my teeth. Dust swirled overhead, blotting the sun. Inside me, I felt a seething heat well up and I shouldered the door open. The side mirror clattered to the ground, and as I leaned out to paint the gravel, I saw my reflection shattered upon the road.

Crisse.

2.
When Alfred
Fell out of the Tree

THE MIRROR COULD NOT BE FIXED. KNEELING BY THE
car, in front of the house, I held the casing up and considered using
duct tape to attach it temporarily to the door and create the illusion
of a working side mirror. Would be real broche-à-foin, as Dad would
say, but it would have to do until I could afford a replacement. After
a moment, I stood and dusted off the front of my jeans. Squinting
through the sunlight now coming over the treetops, I glanced at the
garage. While I was thinking about where Dad kept the duct tape, the
door to the house creaked open and my mother stepped out onto the
landing. Arms wrapped around her waist, she stood there and stared at
me. I waited for her to speak, then frowned at her silence.

"What's up?" I said.

"T'étais où là?"

"Gauthier's farm," I said. "J.P. had a pig roast."

My mother grunted and glanced at the garage. "T'as vu ton père?"

I shook my head. "Been a few days," I said.

She grimaced and gazed out through the oak and pine trees toward the road.

"I was almost killed," I said, and I lifted the cracked casing to show her, but she seemed to look through it, and I placed the mirror down on the hood and chucked my thumb toward the garage. "Do we have any duct tape?"

"Écoute," my mother said. "Alfred had a stroke."

I frowned, and looked up at her again, not quite understanding what I had heard.

"Yé t'à l'hôpital à Saint-Boniface," she said. "Carole vient d'appeler. Yé t'en bad shape."

I slumped back on the car hood next to the mirror. "He's alive?"

Pursing her lips, my mother nodded. "Mais yé t'en bad shape là, comme j'ai dit."

"Well, we have to go see him."

"Ton père yé pas icitte, and I can't get a hold of him."

Frowning, I glanced at the garage, and the woodshop beyond, where he spent most of his time. "Where is he?"

"Yé parti c'matin avec sa chainsaw. Ché pas ou y'allait."

I looked at the woods. "Could be anywhere," I said.

She nodded, and pulled out a pack of cigarettes from her jeans. I could tell she had been on the phone all morning by the way she drew out a smoke, the way her fingers trembled like a stretch of fishing line. "Écoute," she said. "You have to find him."

Taking the Dawson Trail westward, with the side mirror on the seat next to me, I drove carefully toward town. I didn't want to get pulled over and have to explain what had happened, where I was going. Perched atop the treeline, the sun dripped light onto the road, and I squinted through the hard sheen in the windshield. I lifted my fingers off the wheel, flashing a curt wave, whenever someone in a dust-coated pickup truck or minivan flew by. I thought about Alfred, and how he had laughed the time I asked him if he knew that the Dawson Trail once stretched from Thunder Bay to Winnipeg. It had been a tortuous path that snaked over rock, through dense pine, and across lakes and rivers before it wound into the ragged and sandy bushland where the Shield tapered to nothing, then through swamp, and onto the open prairie. Before the railroad was built, Alfred said, this was how Wolseley had trekked west part ways to seize the valley. Nowadays, there was little of it left: a couple paved miles near the city, and long stretches of gravel. The old trail had fallen into disuse even before they'd blasted open the Shield and laid a strip of concrete from Rat Portage to Winnipeg.

This was often how it went. I heard something, somewhere, about the town, about the old days and, out of curiosity, I would ask Alfred. He'd laugh and set me straight. Then tell me some story that would upset everything I thought I knew about the world. Alfred was Dad's uncle, but he was more like a grandfather to me, the only grandfather I'd known.

West of La Coulée, on the Dawson, the trees fell away, and the prairie opened up. Grain silos bobbed, buoys on the horizon. Windbreaks like the anchored masts of distant ships dotted the land. The shift seemed so abrupt: one moment you were in the bush, and the next the land convinced you there was no such thing as bush. You could spot the church, and the radio tower, and the grain elevator back before they'd tore it down, for miles. The town lay about a mile from the treeline, sur les bords de la rivière Seine. Larry Lechene told me once, comment lii Michif had first built the town in the bush, and not on the bald and windy edge of the treeline. They had come to hew wood for the first Cathedral in Saint-Boniface, and then stayed to hunt and farm the land, but their presence had frightened away the game and in revenge some Ojibwe set fire to the forest. The forest had never fully regrown, held back by the axe and plough, and now the town rose from the flat prairie like a small island.

Alfred snorted when I asked him about it. "Y'aiment raconter dés histwayr, lii Léchenes," he said. He took his pipe out of his mouth and waved the stem around. "Ch'te bet que c'tait un Anglais qu'y'a mis feu à forêt pour clairer la tayr."

Every fall, as far back as I remember, I would help Alfred clean his yard. At first, I hadn't been much help. Knee high, barely ambling through my parents' legs, I had probably been more a pest than anything. Eventually as I grew up, my parents stepped back. Before I got my drivers, I would take Dad's truck to Ste. Geneviève, and give Alfred a hand with his yard. I would gather all the leaves and the branches and the deadfall that amassed through the year and pile them up in the backyard to burn. Alfred didn't want debris laying beneath the snow to snag his blower.

Alfred had hurt his back sometime before I was born. Story was he had fallen out of a tree. He'd been out hunting, sitting in a tree stand, when the weather turned sour and dumped a layer of wet snow on the land. He kept a flask with him, because you never know, and so this time, to keep warm, he sipped at his whiskey. There was a buck behind his cabin that had caught his eye, so he decided to wait for it to come around. He sipped his drink while the snow grew heavier and began to pile up in the branches and blanket the ground. Shivering, Alfred shook the snow off his coat. He wiped his gunstock, and took another sip of whiskey. The snow turned to rain, and then to ice when it landed and coated the trees and the branches and the tips of Alfred's boots. Finally, figuring the buck had bedded down somewhere, Alfred decided to head home, but as he began to descend, his boot slipped on a steel rung, and he tumbled backwards into a pile of deadfall.

"Deux pieds à gauche pis une branche m'aura crevé l'coeur," Alfred had later said.

With the wind knocked out of him, he lay there for a time, and watched the snow and the rain and the ice ricochet through the branches above. When he finally tried to stand, a sharp pain fired in his back and down his legs. He collapsed into the wet muck of leaves, snow and mud. Groaning, he rolled onto his stomach and began to crawl. Before long he realized he didn't know where he was going; he had never seen things from the perspective of a rabbit before, never mind all the wet snow whirling through the air. Thinking back on it,

Alfred probably had a concussion too. Still, he pressed on, and dragged himself toward what he thought was home.

Of course, the first time Alfred told the story, there was no flask, he said a squirrel had climbed up his rifle barrel and tickled his nose, and as he went to knock it away, he fell out of the tree. Second time, he sneezed, and fell out. The reason changed every time he told the story, but always there was singing. Dragging himself forward, through the thick underbrush, he grew tired but knew that to rest would bring death. To keep himself awake, to keep himself going, he began to sing. At first, he sang anything that popped into his head. Tattered bits of old songs, and lyrics without melody. He bellowed it out: *C'est au champ de bataille. J'ai fait crier mes douleurs! Où tout 'cun dout' se passe. Ça fait frémir les coeurs!* His toes twitched and the fiddle-itch propelled him forward. *Or je pris mon canif, je le trempai dans mon sang!*

When we were younger, with my sister, Monique, and me seated at his feet, Alfred would throw himself to the ground and re-enact the scene. We would crawl together through the living room, around the old coffee table, between the sofa and the wall, under the old stuffed deer head, and into the kitchen around the chairs and under the table, singing loudly and off key as we went. *C'est au champ de bataille!* The story grew taller with every telling. Alfred even once boasted of killing the very buck he'd been hunting, coming across it by chance as it lay sheltered under the boughs of a pine tree. He shot it from his stomach, crawled up to the body, split open its belly with his hunting knife, and huddled up against it so that its steaming heat could keep him warm while he regained his strength.

"Juste comme Luke and Han avec le tauntaun!" I said.

Monique rolled her eyes.

Alfred blinked and stared at me. "Quessé qu'tu racontes?"

A few times, Alfred tried to show us where it happened, retracing his steps through the woods, but such time had passed that the old trails were overgrown, new trees had replaced the old ones, and Alfred led us in circles before we retreated to his cabin. Monique later said it had just been an excuse to get us out of the house, and teach us some things about plants. I couldn't help but wonder, though, what had happened to the tree stand. Was there still an empty chair in the canopy somewhere?

Though the story changed with every telling, there were always a few constants: the tree, the fall, the singing, and Mémère. The details varied—how and when it happened or what song he sang—but it was always Mémère that found Alfred, frostbitten and delirious, crawling at the edge of her yard. It was Mémère who brought him inside to warm him up. To nurse him back to health.

"Une ange," Alfred said. "Elle m'a sauvé la vie." His eyes moist, and his dark, weathered face growing soft, he would stare off into the recesses of an old memory. And we knew then that the story was done.

"Le vieux pet est plein d'marde," Mémère had once said. "Il aurait fait n'importe quoi pour venir prendre un coup."

3.

Un café avec les boys

"O WAH! T'AS OUBLIÉ TON MIIRWAYR À MAYZOON?"
Perched on the small bench alongside the wall in front of the Old
No. 12 restaurant, an old man laughed and waved his half-burnt cigarette toward my car. From the road, the restaurant looked like a house,
a squat little bungalow plopped on a gravel lot. Nearly all the walls
had been knocked down and replaced with windows. The man on the
bench—un Gendron—had become a fixture of sorts, a stand-in for
the endless series of men and women now forced to tramp outside for
a smoke. Ever since they'd banned smoking indoors, Gendron spent
more time on the bench outside than inside the restaurant.

"Got clipped by a truck," I said, and I thrust my hip into the door
so that the latch caught.

Le vieux Gendron blinked. Smoke curled from the cigarette
between his fingers. "Ah bin, tabarnak. Où ça?"

"Au top du ridge, sur la ligne à Faucher."

"Bin crisse," said Gendron. He sucked on his cigarette, and smoke poured out from his nostrils. Then he leaned over and dropped a load of spit between his boots. "Shaanseu qu'c'tait pas un 'ead-on. Ta vie must 'ave flashed, comme y disent!"

"Bin, you could say that," I said, and with hands cupped around my eyes, I pressed up to the restaurant's windows to peek inside. A few heads inside turned to look at me, but I could not recognize their faces through the dust and the blinds. "Say, have you seen my dad, c'matin?"

Gendron frowned and peered up at my face. "C'qui ton payr encore?" Then, before I could tell him, he snapped his fingers. "Oh bin, that's right. T'é l'gars à Émile, hein? Bin oui. Bin oui. Y'tait 'citte c'mataen."

"He was, eh?" I swept my eyes across the parking lot, looking for a red GMC among the row of trucks. "Y'a dit où y'allait?"

Gendron shook his head. He plucked a fresh cigarette from the breast pocket of his plaid-coloured shirt, and pressed the tip to the old one before he flicked the stub onto the gravel, then he tossed his thumb over his shoulder. "Ch't'un fumeur, moé. Faut qu'tu demandes aux boys."

Inside, pod lights buzzed in the drop-ceiling, casting a dim sulphur-stained glow on the faux-wood wall panels. Cracked, chestnut leather benches bristled along the north side. A short wall, topped with a lattice screen, ran down the centre of the room—it had, at one time, split the room into smoking and non-smoking sections. Allowing my eyes to adjust to the light, I paused in the doorway. Cutlery and dishes rattled sharply in the big wash bins in the kitchen; the sound and smell of eggs frying drew a rumble from my stomach. After skipping over a handful of folks scattered throughout the room, my eyes settled on the old farmers along the south-side windows. One of them said something and slapped his hands; buckets of gravel-throated laughter spilled across the table.

"Sit where you like, Rich," said the dark-haired woman behind the counter. An old cash register gathered dust to her right. She leaned on her elbows and scratched at a crossword.

I watched her work a piece of gum, the muscles firing at the back of her jaw. She looked up from the crossword, and briefly rested her tired eyes on mine before she flashed a half smile. And in that moment, a thick, suffocating heaviness pressed upon my chest: a chafing familiarity that made me want to turn around and leave. I fought the urge to run. An echo in the curl of her lips, the tenor of her voice, reminded me of the woman I had come to love and the distance that had grown between us. The first time I felt this strange heaviness wrapped around my lungs was not long after Becky had left for the city. I had been sitting on the hood of the Buick, by the rail bridge over the Seine, south of town, smoking a joint with Joey Lafleur, when under the drone of his voice, ambient sounds—that constant, insect buzz of the highway on the edge of the horizon, the burble of the water in the culverts below, and the train whistle bearing down from the west—began to weave through memories I had no desire to revisit. Before I knew it, I had found myself unable to spend much time in any of our old haunts. Whenever I drove past our fishing hole, or past Fritz's, that bar on the edge of town where Becky used to clean tables, time would stretch before me and magnify her absence. Her empty seat in the Buick; the faded echo of her laughter. Though I tried to ignore it, this sense of emptiness spread beneath me, eating away at the soil, threatening to swallow me whole. It would snake like a river in the corner of my eye, nibbling at the bank, only to vanish whenever I turned to confront it— the ground seemingly solid underfoot. But it always came back, like the sound of water running in the night, a mosquito flitting around your ears, and it would taunt me through a flash of teeth, a turn of phrase, or crooked smile. The smallest thing was enough to remind that Becky had left.

The woman returned to her puzzle and flicked a dull pencil on the plastic guard above the lottery tickets. Tack. Tack. Tack. She'd been at J.P.'s pig roast last night—I might have shared a joint with her, in the bloated circle where folks slipped in and out for a hoot—but I was suddenly unable to remember her name. She had gone to school with Monique, and she also had an older sister with whom I often confused her.

"Dominique?" I said, testing, and I cleared my throat. The pencil stopped. The woman glanced up. "Have you seen my dad?"

She frowned.

"Émile," I said. "Short, stocky guy. Drives a red GMC. He's in here every other day."

"Oh, you mean Double Rye?" she said, and smiled. "Yeah, he was here. In the corner." She pointed with her pencil toward the noisy table.

Double Rye, I thought, was how Dad liked his toast and his drinks. As far as nicknames went, it could have been worse. I nodded my thanks and, glancing over, took a closer look at the men in the corner. They were all dressed alike: old ball caps, and plaid, collared shirts spattered with engine grease and cow shit, bleach-stained sweat rings under the armpits. Sleeves rolled up over their thick sun-burnt arms. Sun-faded denim and gravel-scuffed cowboy boots. One of them said something and they burst again into laughter. They slapped the table and roared.

These were Dad's drinking buddies. Men he had known since they were boys. Hard-drinking men who had a million stories about barroom brawls and run-ins with Mennonites. Having stepped back to let their sons and daughters take over their farms, they now spent ever more time honing their stories. Dad could kill whole afternoons with them, nursing tepid coffee, and chewing the fat. Always seated by the window overlooking the Petro across the street, they would watch people fuel up. Spying on the trucks that came and went, they developed together an elaborate theory about how the condition of one's truck was a window to the soul. New trucks meant money, which signalled some good fortune, a turn of luck, a raise, a new job, or maybe an inheritance, or even—like that lucky son of a bitch, Skinny Joe Mourand—a lotto win, but it also offered the titillating possibility of something illicit or nefarious. That was worth talking about. An older, well-maintained truck meant that things were steady: it revealed nothing new. It was simply the confirmation of a consistent level of devotion or fidelity, loyalty, and perhaps even love: that the owner had lovingly stood by their once new truck and, like a faithful spouse, had grown old with it. There was no consensus on this point though. One farmer figured it meant le pauvre enfant d'chienne never had a lick of luck or they would've already bought a new truck. Finally, a real used truck—a beat-up, rundown rust bucket—with its long miles easily spotted in the constellation of dents, scratches, and rust patches on the body meant trouble, either at work or at home. This wasn't just a lack of luck, or even bad luck. It was more than an odd, ill-turn of fortune. This was a visible manifestation of a lifelong down-spiral, a karmic echo that betrayed a rough life and troubled soul—and this was worth talking about. Their theories were extravagant and preposterous. Vile rumours mushroomed out of such fertile bullshit.

"Did he say where he was going?" I asked, and the woman shrugged. I rapped my knuckles on the counter and looked across the room. Pas d'choix. I shuffled toward the farmers and sidled up to their table. As one, the old men looked up and grinned.

"Pichenotte," they said.

As far as nicknames went, I'd had the misfortune of having this one stick.

"T'as l'air un peu pâle là. Had a rough night?"

"Un 'tchi coup d'trop là, hein?"

One farmer, with a John Deere ballcap, pried open the blinds and pointed to my Buick. "Ah bin, you still drive that boat?"

"Pourquoi tu drive pas un truck à place?" said the one wearing a New Holland cap. Their extravagant theories faltered when confronted with cars. All they understood were trucks.

"Whoa, là! Quessé qu'yé t'arrivé à ton miirwayr?" said John Deere.

"Avez-vous vu mon père, c'matin?"

"Faut mieux t'asswayr mon homme, t'as l'air comme tchu vas prendre une culbute," said the quiet one with the camouflaged ballcap. He almost looked like my great-uncle, Alfred.

"Sit, sit. Assis toé," said New Holland.

Swaying on my feet, I bumped into the table and realized a deep hunger had taken hold. The last thing I'd eaten was a soggy baloney sandwich.

With his foot, New Holland pushed out a chair at the table. I swung over into the seat. Before I touched the back, the woman from behind the counter appeared next to the table, and I blinked and, without thinking, ordered a cup of coffee and a stack of toast. Double rye. Quick as she came, Dominique vanished. John Deere released the window blinds and turned to look at me.

"Écoute," he said, very solemnly. "Un char c'peut-être assez pour faire du shopping en ville. Mais tu beat pas un half-ton pour d'l'ouvrage."

"I'm out of work," I said. "Been running my uncle Joe's septic truck on weekends."

"You're driving a honey wagon?" said John Deere.

"Ho, ho. Djis-moé pas que les Mennonites t'ont laissé aller?" said New Holland.

"They laid off the whole afternoon shift," I said.

"Les viarges!"

John Deere leaned over the table and whispered. "Did they make you pray before work?"

"Crisse, Roger, y vient d'perdre sa job," said the quiet one with the camouflaged ballcap. I'd always liked him, the one with the camo-ballcap, because, although he often seemed to blend inconspicuously into the walls, as though stalking prey and waiting quietly for the right moment to fire some devastating shot across the table, his words were always sharp, and to the point.

"That's okay," I said, and dropped my voice to a whisper. "Mais c'est vrai, t'sé. Avant qu'ton shift commence, et pis too après chaque break."

The old men howled with laughter.

"Tu voé, tu voé! Ch'te l'avait dit!" said John Deere.

New Holland wiped tears from his eyes. "Oh, that's a good one."

"Let me tell you about les Mennonites," said the quiet one.

John Deere sipped his coffee and New Holland rolled his eyes.

The quiet one began to recount a story about a run-in he had had with some Mennonites, back in the late '70s, when a group of them had come up the highway from Steinbach to look for property by the rail tracks. "I was offloading du grain at de time," he said. "When I saw dese big guys standing dere, à côté des tracks—c'est dure à manquer ça, six-pieds sept avec des cheveux comme un champ d'blé—and I said to myself, what da heck are dey doing dere?"

"Ostie d'menteur, t'était à bar en train de t'souler," said John Deere.

"So, anyway," said the quiet one. "Moé pis Bedaine Beaulieu decided to go ask dem—"

"J'pensais qu'c'était Babines Bottineau," said New Holland.

"So, we finished our beers and walked over—"

"Aha!"

"Pensais t'était à l'élévateur à grain?" said John Deere.

"On buvait dans l'truck, okay?"

New Holland and John Deere cackled.

"So, you were drinking. What happened after that?" I asked.

The quiet one shrugged. "We went over and asked, and dey told us they were tinking of building a window factory à côté des tracks."

"That's it?" I said.

John Deere shook his head. "Non, non, non. You forgot the best part. Babines Bottineau gave that big speech telling them ten ways to go fuck themselves and—"

"C'était en français," said the quiet one. "And den dese guys just stared at 'im like dey didn't understand a word of it."

"Bin, they didn't."

"That was Bedaine Beaulieu, and that happened later, at the protest," said New Holland.

"Protest?" I asked.

"Against les Mennonites."

"Quessé qu'y pensaient venir icitte pour nous achaler?"

"Bin," said the quiet one. "Fallait avertir quelqu'un, so I went and told de priest. Oh boy, qu'y'était choqué! As-tchu connu le vieux Duhamel? Calice! Y'tait un tough. Y'aurait pu êt'e un professional hockey player you know."

"Coup d'Coude, they called him."

"I've heard the name," I said.

"The Aces were playing in Steinbach, and he was digging the puck out of the corner, when this big Mennonite snapped him in half. Poor bugger never played again."

New Holland leaned over the table and whispered. "Rumour is y'a trouvé li bon Djeu while he was laid up à l'hôpital."

"Knocked a screw loose, boy," said John Deere.

"He nursed a grudge against those Mennonite boys for years," said New Holland.

"Anyway," said the quiet one.

The waitress brought my toast and coffee, and I sipped my coffee, then lathered the toast in strawberry jam while the quiet farmer recounted how the would-be-factory owners had reeled, stunned at the backlash. They'd naively mistook our languid town for job-starved and imagined a warm welcome where none was forthcoming. Finally, the Sunday after they'd visited the site, le vieux Duhamel delivered a fiery sermon fat with wild rumours and bald-faced innuendos about an immanent religious and linguistic invasion. Raining hot spittle down on the front pews, Père Duhamel shouted at his flock to resist the temptation to acquiesce; the jobs were not worth their souls! There were two irrevocable issues: the would-be-factory owners were not French or Catholic. Seems it wasn't a very big leap from there to believe that the factory owners would require everyone to pray to some orange-hued idol before work.

"Bin," yelled the quiet one. "No one tells a Catholic when to pray!"

John Deere cleared his throat. "Excepte le prêtre."

"À chaque dimanche," said New Holland.

"L'évêque," said John Deere.

"À Pâques, à Noël, et pendant l'Carême."

"Le pape."

"À naissance, à mort, et chaque nuit entre les deux. Baptême!"

"Le gouvernement."

"Jamais à l'école ou au public!"

"Pis les Anglais."

"Jamais devant les Anglais!"

Swatting the table with their ball caps, John Deere and New Holland howled.

The quiet one shook his head and continued. Le vieux Duhamel organized a big protest; he gathered all the men and the women and the children from town and the surrounding hamlets and farms—all the francophones from La Coulée to Dufresne—gathered them before the steps of the Church. With hand-sown banners and flags, and hastily crafted slogans ready to chant, they listened to le vieux Duhamel shout at them from atop a tractor on the street. Stoking their fears, he whipped them into a furor. Neighbours—English-speaking Ukrainians, Poles, and Métis—watched from their cars and their homes as the crowd marched to the vacant lot by the grain elevator. And in that empty field of ragged, knee-high grass, next to the rail tracks, the priest delivered another devastating prophecy of linguistic assimilation and cultural apostacy. Gasping, the crowd shook their banners and flags as though swatting away Protestant spectres, uncorked small vials of holy water and doused the earth and tracks, and while men working at the grain elevator gaped and looked on, the crowd chanted mis-translated slogans: Hold Your Tongue! No Jobs for Souls! In the end, deciding that rail-access was more trouble than worth, the men behind the proposed window factory built their factory elsewhere.

"So," I said. "That's why I have to drive to Steinbach for work?"

"Bin, là—"

I had heard about Mennonites all my life, about the parking lot brawls, the fist-fights at socials and hockey games. The hypocrisy as they kept liquor out of their town, but then drove to La Broquerie or Ste. Anne for booze. How they'd looked down their noses at us for doing in the open what they did in the dark. I had heard all about this bad blood. How villages and towns only a few miles down the road from each other had grown worlds apart. I had heard of folks who had tried to bridge those worlds only to be cast out by both. Dad's cousin, Laura, was disowned for marrying a Mennonite. They moved out west to Regina to raise their children and returned only years later, their kids mostly grown, having never known their grandparents.

Things had changed radically since, but every once in a while, old stories resurfaced, like distended echoes, hollow and unrecognizable. The old men stared into their coffees. Their own kids had married Mennonites.

"Écoute," I said to them. "Have you seen my dad?"

They blinked, and for a moment, while they searched their memories, said nothing. Then John Deere snapped his fingers. "Bin oui. We saw him this morning."

"Y'tait icitte," said the quiet one.

"We talked about trucks," said New Holland.

"Do you know where he went?"

New Holland and John Deere shook their heads, but the quiet one nodded.

"Y'avait pas dit qu'y'allait ramasser des parts pour sa chainsaw?"

John Deere snapped his fingers again. "That's right!"

"Y'avait besoin d'une nouvelle chaine," nodded New Holland.

"Okay. Où-ça?"

4.

The Good Ol' Game

WHEN MY DAD WAS 16 YEARS OLD, HE BROKE A Mennonite's arm. It happened behind the net, along the boards, by the painted logo for Champdeau's Hardware store. The man—he was only a few years older than Dad—had just stripped the puck from him, and, in desperation, Dad spun and swung his stick down on the man's arm.

Dad had grown into his body at a young age, and so when the Aces started looking for fresh bodies to man the blueline, he gathered all the old hockey gear that his brothers had passed down to him—sweat stained socks and cracked shin pads, des patins à-moitiés rouillées, gauze-thin shoulder pads, and a helmet too small for his round head—and he tried out, and made the team. Le vieux Duhamel, Père Coup d'Coude, was the coach, and truth was he'd spotted Dad in the communion line one Sunday, collared shirt stretched tight over his shoulders, and he thought, now there was a boy you could mold into a hockey player. Dad held out his palms to receive the host and Coup d'Coude grabbed his hands, turned them over, and smiled at the scuffed 'n' cut-up, blue-bruised mess of knuckles Dad carried around. See, Dad was a fighter. At least, he had been. Le bébé d'la famille, he had grown up with a platoon of older brothers who'd teased him mercilessly until he figured out how to make them stop. With a whirlwind of fists, knees, and feet, he threw himself at them. They would pick him up and toss him around, back, and forth, until Dad screamed loud enough that Mémère heard and came and put a stop to it. The problem was when Dad grew into his body, that whirlwind of fists, knees, and feet became a weapon. It took him a long time to realize this and change his ways.

"Défends-toé, mais fait pas d'mal," he told me once, when I was still in high school, after I'd gotten into a fight, and he was called to the school office to pick me up. "Le mal c'est comme du poison, ça reste avec toi, ça t'mange, pis ça s'répand alentour d'toi."

I stared at the aspen and the oak trees, piles of snow and the high water in the ditches.

"On récolte rien de bon quand on sème le mal, Richard."

"Whatever," I said, and rolled my eyes. He sounded like a priest, and I figured he'd been spending too much time at the Knights' Hall in town. Dad grew silent. He drove past the turn off to the house and swung north, across the highway onto the road that wound through marsh land that flooded nearly every spring. Anger clouded my eyes—it took me a while to notice that we were heading toward Ste. Geneviève. When I finally realized that we had long-passed the house, and I asked where we were going, Dad pointed down the road.

Through the woods, Alfred's little cabin appeared.

Dad parked the truck out front and told me to wait as he went inside. I stared at Alfred's cabin, at the paint peeling off the walls like sunburnt skin, eavestroughs sagging like bags under the eyes. Water pooled before mounds of snow. Then the door opened, and Dad stepped through with Alfred. They walked up to the truck and Dad knocked on my window.

"Okay, Alfred y'a accepté de t'watcher pour la s'maine."

"What?" I said. "What about school?"

"Crisse, Richard. T'as brisé l'nez à Chaput."

"Do you know what he said?"

"Open the door et sors d'là."

Dad glared through the window as I locked the door.

"Tabarnak, Richard. C'est ça ou j'appelle la police."

Alfred placed a hand on Dad's shoulder and looked at me. "Viens mon gars," he said. "C'pas 'si grave que ça. J'ai d'besoin d'ton aide quand même."

After a moment, I unlocked the door.

When Dad drove away, Alfred handed me a shovel. He told me to clear away some of the snow that had piled up by the cabin. He was worried that the melt would seep inside and into the crawlspace and eat away at the foundation. He would have done it himself, but his tractor needed a new belt, which he hadn't had the chance to replace, and he was feeling a little sore on top of it. I didn't argue. I grabbed the shovel and headed for the pile, but Alfred shouted.

"Attends là, j'ai des bottes en rubber pour tes pieds."

For an hour, I shovelled. The snow was wet and heavy, compressed by a crusted layer of ice formed through repeated warm and cold snaps, and then built up again by a monster blizzard. Beneath the surface of brown puddles, layers of ice spread underfoot. Meltwater poured from the eaves, from the branches of the trees. There'd been so much snow that year. Only weeks before, a Colorado Low had pummeled the valley. Swollen rivers like fat lips, wet and red. Only a few days from then, the Red River would burst its banks, and stretch into a sea.

Tossing my jacket onto an empty birdbath in the yard, I wiped sweat off my forehead and surveyed the area around the cabin. I'd moved the piles of snow back a couple dozen feet, but the water still had a clear path to the crawlspace. The door opened and Alfred stepped outside with a couple mugs of tea.

"Bonne job," he said.

"Thanks," I managed to say and coughed, out of breath.

"Faudra sandbagger bientôt, j'pense." He shook his head, pointed to the waterline. "Fait des années depuis qu'j'ai vu l'eau si haut." He looked at me and laughed. "Plus tard, là. Pas toute suite. Boé ton thé. J'ai pas d'sable."

As we drank our tea, Alfred led me around to the back of the cabin and on toward the tree line where water lapped at the yard through the trees.

"Holy shit," I said.

Alfred explained that there was a bog not far away and with the recent, heavy snow and the quick melt, the bog had spread out across the land. The bog usually flooded every year, but rarely did it ever reach his yard. Then Alfred led me to the side of the cabin, where he lifted an old beat-up tarp to reveal a small canoe.

"Are you serious?" I said.

"Why not?" Alfred laughed.

We hauled the canoe over to the edge of the yard, then we fetched the paddles, and I ran around to grab my jacket while Alfred locked the door to the cabin. Then we pushed the canoe through the trees, onto the water—it only needed a couple inches to float—and we climbed into the craft. I sat at the front, though I knew how to guide. Alfred pushed us out a little further and then climbed aboard. The canoe rocked as he settled onto his seat, and I grabbed a small tree to steady us. We launched forward, and took it slow, careful to avoid the clumps of underbrush and dead branches that could snag us like le diable from below. Branches clawed at the sides, raked the bottom. A few times I had to pull the canoe over deadfall—Alfred had conveniently left his rubber boots—but after a while the land began to drop off toward the bog. The water deepened, and we drifted unimpeded through the woods. We came upon some widening in the undergrowth where the repeated passing of deer had pushed the brush back, and, seeing where it might lead us, we followed the trail. After a while, Alfred cleared his throat and began to tell me about Dad, and how he too had had trouble with his temper when he was a boy.

The canoe rocked as I glanced back at Alfred, so I bit my tongue, looked out ahead, and listened.

"Petit boeuf, ils l'appelaient," Alfred said. "Y's'battait pour n'im-porte quoé."

Following the slash on the Mennonite, Dad was suspended for one game, but old Coup d'Coude congratulated him for "playing hard, comme un tough," and started him after Dad had served his suspension. So, Dad went out and hit everything he could. He crashed and banged and slashed and speared and dropped the mitts, and got his nose bloodied, his lip cut, his eye swollen shut after a punch to the face, all the while old Coup d'Coude, clerical collar showing, screamed apoplectically on the bench, and rained spittle on the back of his players' helmets, "Tue-les, tue-les!"

Dad drove a boy headfirst into the boards. As the kid lay unmoving on the ice, Dad was escorted to the dressing room; a hush fell over the crowd as cries for a medic echoed through the arena. Dad undressed and showered, changed into his clothes, and quietly left the rink. He felt a pit growing in his stomach. His brother met him outside and drove him home. They turned onto the main drag, the strip leading out of town, and passed an ambulance with its lights flashing and its siren wailing. The pit in Dad's stomach grew deeper. After a mile, he asked his brother to pull over. He opened the door and threw up on the side of the road.

At home, he ate little and went to bed early, only to stare at the ceiling all night while his brother snored in the bed across the room. He could not stop thinking about what he had done, if the boy was okay. The idea that he had broken the boy's neck took root, and grew, filling the pit in his stomach with a black, writhing mass. He clutched his stomach and groaned, then he began to sob quietly. Had he killed the boy?

The following morning, Dad rose early, before anyone else except his mother who was baking bread. She gave him a pained look as he appeared in the kitchen, drank a glass of water, and left without a word. He stepped outside and saw his brother's truck. He climbed in and saw the keys in the ignition, so he started the truck up and drove off. He drove fast, and hard, without much idea as to where he was going, trying simply to outrun the notion that he killed the boy. He still had no idea what had happened after he left the rink.

Alfred's cabin appeared. Dad slowed, and turned into the driveway, and sat there as the truck rumbled low around him. The lights were on inside the cabin, and he saw Alfred's shadow moving through the window. He stared for a time, then as he went to shift the truck into reverse, Alfred opened the door and shouted. "Émile, mon homme, tu veux des toast?"

Inside, Dad nibbled at some dry bread. Alfred lay a hand on his shoulder, and poured a cup of hot tea. Dad broke down. He confessed what he had done, what he was feeling, how some notion of harm had taken root inside of him, its grip slowly squeezing his stomach up through his throat. Alfred listened and nodded.

"Appelle-le," Alfred said.

"Quoi?"

"Appelle-le," Alfred repeated.

Dad groaned as the black roots tightened momentarily, then began to loosen. He looked up at Alfred, who had set a mug for the road next to his lunch pail, and was pulling on his work boots, and Dad understood.

In the canoe, Alfred relayed to me how Dad had gone home after that, since Alfred didn't have a telephone at the time, and began a series of phone calls—first to his coach, le vieux Coup d'Coude, who'd marvelled at the idea of an apology, then the opposing coach, who begrudgingly provided Dad with the injured kid's phone number. At the news that the kid was home and well, Dad sensed the black roots further relinquish their grip. Still, he pressed on, and as he listened to his older brother recount the terrible hit to his mother and his siblings in the kitchen, Dad dialled the boy's number in the living room.

"T'aurais du voère ça, c'tait un vrai sauvage, là, sur la patinoire."

"Non," Mémère said. "Mon p'tit Émile a fait ça?"

Dad saw his mother's face crumbling in horror, and he sensed a profound disappointment in himself as she looked through the doorway, from the kitchen to the living room. The telephone rang, and as he waited for the boy to pick up, he watched his mother's eyes grow hard. She came into the living room and glared at him, her mouth working, malformed words, tumbling stillborn from her lips. A great tiredness settled over her. She seemed to visibly shrink.

"T'appelle qui-là?"

The ringing ceased suddenly, and a voice called out, "Hello?"

Dad asked to speak with the boy, with Jonathan, and his mother looked down at him in puzzlement, trying to understand the words coming out of his mouth. She'd never pick up much English, not enough for more than a basic conversation. The boy came to the phone.

"Hello?"

"Listen, là," Dad said. "I'm de guy dat hit you last night."

The boy swore at the other end of the line. "What the hell do—"

"And I wanted to apologize for dat. See how you are."

"—oh."

"I'm sorry," said Dad. He glanced at his mother out of the corner of his eye, and saw that she recognized the word and flinched as the scene became clear to her. Her eyes softened and the great tiredness seemed to lift from her shoulders.

"That's—" the boy at the other end of the line didn't know what to say. He paused, and for a moment Dad wondered if he'd hung up, but then he heard the boy's rising breath, out and in. "I've got a headache," the boy said. "The doctor says I need to rest."

"I'm sorry," said Dad. "Rest yourself."

The boy breathed out and in. "I have to go now."

"Okay."

As Dad placed the receiver down, he felt the last of the dark roots vanish and the pit in his stomach shrink. He rose to his feet and felt light, lighter than he had in a long time, as though he could have floated up into the sky, and his mother flinched again in confusion as he threw his arms around her and laughed.

"J'veux pas suggérer que Coup d'Coude 'tait un mauvais prêtre, là," said Alfred, in the canoe. "He wasn't a bad priest, but y'en avait des drôles d'idées."

I nodded, barely paying attention, engrossed in the idea that my dad had nearly killed a boy—I wondered whether it still haunted him. We passed a towering pine tree, water lapping at its skirt of needles, and Alfred grunted suddenly. The canoe rocked as he twisted in his seat.

"J'pense qu'on devrait tourner d'bord," he said.

So, we began to turn, a slow loop through wickets of underbrush, squeezing through the bone-bare aspen and birch that jutted out of the high water. Deadfall scratched along the bottom again; we pulled ourselves over a submerged log. Then I spotted something up in a tree. It was an old tree stand, though it looked like a wooden chair which someone had knocked the legs off and nailed the seat fifteen feet up in the air.

"Regard, Menoncle," I said.

At first, I thought nothing of the silence, hearing only the gentle movement of the water through the trees. Then I felt a deep sadness from behind me, as though a sinkhole had suddenly cracked open beneath us, and had begun to swallow everything around. I glanced back and saw Alfred's face, how his eyes were locked onto that chair, and I realized then who had placed it up there. This was the place where Alfred had fallen, where he had hurt his back and his life had changed. So, in the cold maw of that silent sinkhole, I shuddered and, without a word, paddled away from that sad monument.

After breaking the Mennonite's arm and nearly breaking a boy's neck, Dad was expelled from the league, and he never played organized hockey again. The next spring though, when Dad was once again in the communion line, with his palms out in front of old Coup d'Coude, le vieux Duhamel looked him up and down and smiled.

"Have you ever played baseball, mon gars?"

5.

When the Shell Cracked

THE HARDWARE STORE SMELLED OF OIL RAGS LEFT OUT in the open for too long. Dust hung in the air and the lights buzzed and flickered dimly over long rows of cluttered shelves. Even the bells above the doorway seemed weathered—they rang reluctantly, as though their tongues had grown rusty from disuse.

The bench behind the counter was empty. Voices drifted down the aisles, but I couldn't spot anyone, so I waited by the register to ask about Dad, if he'd been here, and my eyes drifted over the fishing gear on the wall—the last time I had been here was with Becky, over a year ago, before she left for the city. I had meant to replace a couple lures we'd lost casting into the reeds and the waterlogged trees that crowded the banks of the river near our fishing spot, but she had talked me out of it. We fished on the Seine, caught undersized jackfish for the most part. We'd spent long hours casting into that muddy water, through slicks of lime-green goo, and through drought and flood. The spot was tucked at the edge of a farmer's field, southeast of town, where an ancient oxbow dipped into the earth and large oaks had been left to grow. It hardly mattered when the fish stopped biting.

I had tasted my first beer along those banks when I'd tagged along with Monique and her boyfriend, and he plied me with cheap beer to show my sister just how generous he could be. Not long after, when she left him, he took a dislike to me, and I had been forced to break his nose. He cornered me in the hallway one day, between classes, and placed his curled fist on my chest as he told me what he thought of Monique. I knew she would laugh it off, and she did later, after I told her what he had said, but in the moment, as he pinned me against a locker and vile words spilled from his mouth, I simply reacted and drove my forehead into his nose.

"Don't need you fighting my battles, Rich," Monique said once she finished laughing.

When we were much younger, and still lived on the small river lot on the edge of town, I used to sit by the river and watch for turtles. A friend had told me to watch for snappers, and I'd become obsessed with the idea of catching one. All I had ever seen were painted turtles, sunning themselves on some half-submerged log. Painted turtles were just about the size of a small dinner plate, but my friend said that the snappers could grow to the size of a small dog. Part of me knew he was pulling my leg, but another part of me wanted it to be true; the notion that small dinosaurs still patrolled these lazy waters was too great to dismiss without hope.

In the hardware shop, Becky and I stood before the pegboards: they bristled with an array of hooks and pins, loaded with lures, spoons, rigs, jigs, sinkers, and floaters, and with spools of fishing line, reels, nets, needle-nosed pliers, and red-striped bobbers. Overwhelmed, I grabbed a red devil off the wall and wondered how the jackfish would take to it.

"Too big," said Becky.

I put the spoon back and fingered a smaller, black one, peppered with yellow dots.

"Rich," said Becky.

"Uh hmm," I said, turning over the small spoon and looking at the price.

"I'm moving to Winnipeg."

I stared at the spoon and couldn't seem to add up the number of dots. As soon as I moved from one to the next, the count vanished, and I circled back and counted the same one over and over again, unable to add the numbers up. Part of me had been expecting the news. For a while, Becky had mused about going back to school. She had talked about it seriously at Carlson's the other night, but I had hoped that she'd decide to commute. Finally, I looked up at her.

"What do you mean you're moving to Winnipeg?"

"Well," she said. "I'm going to pack up my things, put them in the car and then haul them to Winnipeg with me. What the hell do you think I mean?"

She crossed her arms and frowned as I spluttered broken words. Her eyes seemed hard, though I could tell it was an act. As if she had tried tearing off a band-aid, only to have it catch on the skin and tear it open. I couldn't tell whose skin, though, hers or mine. Maybe both.

"I just," I cleared my throat, "I'd hoped you'd decided to stay. I mean, what was all that talk of moving in together?"

She shook her head.

"I do want to move in together. But in the city, Rich. I can't live out here anymore, not while I'm going to school. I can't drive to the city and back every day."

"Why not? Everyone does it. Hell. You only do it half the year. Some do it year-round."

"That's not true. And anyways, it doesn't matter. How am I going to find decent work out here? I'm not cleaning tables at Fritz's again. No way," she shook her head, then, smiling softly, she touched my arm. "Come with me, Rich."

* * *

Alfred told me to try a bit of meat. He had stopped by for a visit, and we sat on the deck overlooking the river while my parents prepared dinner inside, and I told him about the turtles. Snappers liked carrion, he said, so a bit of fish or a piece of chicken might draw them out of the water. So, the next day, without knowing much about where to get meat, I snuck into the chest freezer in the basement, plucked out a small sausage from a Ziploc bag, and brought it down to the river. I tied the sausage to some fishing line, and threw it over a branch so that the sausage dangled over the water near shore. I sat quietly along the bank in anticipation. For about a week, I repeated the process, each day tossing the thawing meat into the river after my mom called me to bed. Then, one afternoon, as I stretched my arm into the deep freezer, my feet dangling over the edge, I heard my sister.

"Quessé qu'tu fais?"

Sheepishly, I slid down from the freezer, and holding a bag of sausage behind my back, I told her about the turtles.

"That's stupid," she said. "Don't be ridiculous. Put those sausages back before Mom sees you." Then, reaching into the freezer, Monique plucked a square of Nanaimo bar from the tray of Christmas dainties that Mom prepared months in advance, popped it into her mouth, and skipped up the stairs, out of the basement.

Later that day, as I tossed bits of sausage along the shore of the river, toward the half-submerged trees where snappers might float along the surface, I saw the turtle, its wide and dark shell skimming along the surface, its snout gingerly pushing through the water and into the air. I froze and watched. The snapper sniffed and turned toward me, toward the shore littered with bits of deer sausage. The turtle drifted closer. I sat unmoving as the turtle first lumbered ashore, then snapped up the meat. After a moment, the turtle paused, pointed its sharp snout at me and raked its eyes over my small and still body; then it turned, slipped into the water, and down the river.

The snapping turtle returned the following day and lumbered ashore once more, drawn by the smell of Dad's filched sausage. I tossed small bits of meat in front of it and the turtle crept up closer, and closer, and I retreated up the hill, half afraid it would take a bite out of me or snap off one of my toes, and flee into the water. The snapper came, day after day, inching further up the hill, toward the edge of the yard where Dad had built a small pond for ducks and geese that flew over the property.

From across the pond, I watched the turtle discover this new, smaller body of water, and scan the bed and shore. The water was not deep, the pond not very large, but spacious enough to provide some respite for small creatures. My parents would sit on the deck behind the house and watch the birds come and go, Dad with the old binoculars he had brought back from the army—they weighed almost fifteen pounds—propped up on the railing. They'd never seen a snapper in the pond, I thought, and wouldn't that be a nice surprise. So, I tossed the last bits of sausage from the Ziploc into the pond, and the turtle seemed to coo and chortle happily, and it slipped into the pond to eat. After it devoured the meat, the turtle began to snap up the bits of wet, bloated bread that Monique would sometimes toss into the pond when trying to attract some duck or other bird. She tried to draw them and paint them, bribing birds with bread so they'd stick around while she sketched their shapes on sheets of paper, then filled in, and shaded the elaborate patterns of their feathers.

After it had eaten its fill, instead of lumbering out of the pond, and back down the bank, into the river, the turtle stayed in the small pond, embedding itself into the dirt below some piece of earth jutting over the water. It made itself at home.

For almost a week, the turtle lived there without fear. Then, one Saturday, as Monique was in the yard with her sketch book, tossing bread into the pond, and drawing birds down from the sky, everything changed. A duck landed in the water, and I watched from the dinning room window, at the table eating a late morning bowl of cereal, as the duck circled the small pond, its beak dipping down to pluck bits of bread from the water. Monique screamed. The duck flailed and thrashed as the turtle burst through the surface and snapped its snout over the duck's neck. Dropping my spoon, I sprinted through the door, down the steps, into the yard toward the pond. Monique had dropped her sketch book in the grass and was plucking stones from the earth and chucking them at the turtle. The duck squealed and squawked, its wings like thunderclaps on the surface of the water. Then Monique ran to the riverbank, grabbed a broken branch from the small wood along the shore, hurried back, and swung it like a baseball bat at the turtle.

"Non, arrête! Don't hurt him!" I cried, still running toward the pond.

"Y faut sauver mon canard!" she screamed and swung. Blind with fury, Monique swung and swung, the stick crashing through the pink churned-up mist of pond water and torn feathers. Finally, as her arms noodled, and dropped to her sides, and the oversized branch slipped from her fingers, Dad came running from the garage, and he froze at the scene before him. Monique stood knee deep in a red-soaked pond, a broken-neck duck bobbed upside down beside her; the snapper clung gingerly to the edge as though it had tried to climb out before Monique landed a final blow and cracked it open. Down its shell yawned a red and pulsing wound.

"Misère," Dad whispered.

Slumping into the grass, I stared, and saw that the turtle would not move again.

Monique climbed out of the pond, fell to her knees, and shuddered.

* * *

The voices in the aisles grew close, spilling loudly around me. Evelyne Groscoeur and Madame Champdeau, the hardware store owner, appeared around the corner.

"Ah bin!" Evelyne Groscoeur exclaimed as she spotted me. With her arms full of brushes and paint rollers, she sidled up to me and jabbed her elbow cheerfully in my side. "Fancy seeing you icitte! Mon doo, Richard! Comment ça va?"

"Ah, bin—" I began, and paused, unable to find the words.

"Tiens, Evelyne," said Madame Champdeau, gesturing to the counter next to the register, which she cleared of her things, and Evelyne Groscoeur deposited her supplies. Handles clattered on the glass. "Un sac?" Champdeau asked.

"Oui, oui," said Evelyne, and she glanced at me and grinned.

Evelyne Groscoeur had known me my entire life. She and my mom went way back, and I had always wondered how they'd ended up as friends. They were such different people. Evelyne was loud and cheerful and bullheaded; she would laugh if you stumbled on an icy sidewalk one minute, and then drive you to the hospital to make sure nothing was broken the next. I had never known my mom to be so loud, though I had heard rumours of it, and caught glimpses whenever I accidently intruded upon a committee meeting. See, my mother was on le Comité Culturel with Evelyne Groscoeur and a few others, and they would meet once or twice a week, open a bottle of wine, and plan out our cultural reawakening.

I'd also dated Evelyne Groscoeur's daughter, Roxanne, for a short while in high school. When my mom found out we were dating, she cornered me in the kitchen and thrust a finger in my chest.

"Richard Joseph, you treat that young woman with respect!"

I swallowed and nodded.

Then Monique, peeking in from the living room, added, "And don't forget. We talk."

So, later, under the railway bridge by the Seine, when Roxanne Groscoeur lifted her shirt, and offered me the chance to feel her breasts, my hands froze as I wondered what stories would emerge from this moment. Roxanne laughed, dropped her shirt, and planted me with a wet kiss.

"So, Richard. Je bouteillais du vin hier soir avec les girls, and on parlait de monter une pièce de théâtre. La chasse galerie," said Madame Groscoeur, and she pursed her lips. "Excepté, plus updaté. Plutôt une histoire métisse. Pour le carnaval, c't'hiver. Divertir l'attention historique du masculin—quessé qu't'en penses? J'disais aux girls hier soir que le festival obscure l'histoire des femmes métisse, alors—"

"Evelyne," said Madame Champdeau.

Evelyne Groscoeur blinked. "Oh, oh. Pardon," she smiled sheepishly, and retrieving her wallet, finished paying for the paint brushes. After she'd gathered the supplies in a pair of plastic bags, she turned to me again, and touched my arm. "Anyhoo. J'en parlerai avec ta mère. C'était bon de te voir, Richard. I've got things to do, comme y-disent!"

The bells jangled above the door, and I glanced to Madame Champdeau, who'd taken up a seat on her stool.

"Richard. About time you come by to pick up that fishing reel!"

"What?"

"Donne-moi deux secondes, là, and I'll grab it from the back."

"Wait. I'm sorry, I—" words seized in my throat like an overheated engine block. "—I don't know. I mean, I don't remember ordering a fishing reel."

Madame Champdeau frowned. "Bin, là. Je ne me rappelle pas exactement quand t'est-c'qu't'as commandé ça, mais j'ai une boîte dans l'back avec ton nom dessus."

"That can't be, Madame," I said and shook my head. "I never ordered a fishing reel."

"Bin," Madame Champdeau huffed. "Ça fait pas d'sens, là. Why do I have a box with your name on it?"

"Well, I don't know—"

The stool legs scraped loudly along the floor as Madame Champdeau stood. "Let me go check," she said.

"Non, non, it's okay, I just wanted to ask—" I began, but she vanished around the corner and down the aisle, and a sudden bout of dizziness pinned my feet, and I leaned against the cash register and shut my eyes. Whenever I had too much coffee on an empty stomach, I got this way; and the restaurant coffee must have been too strong for the toast to soak up. Besides, thoughts of Alfred kept swirling like clouds of mosquitoes, swarming, biting, draining me of energy.

After a few moments, Madame Champdeau returned with a small box, which she handed to me. I looked it over and gasped—it was a Shimano casting reel.

"I can't afford this," I said.

"Bin, good thing it's paid for," said Madame Champdeau, and she grabbed, and flipped the box over, then taped a finger on the shipping label. The date of the order—last spring, when Becky and I were last here—across the label, just above her name, and the words: Paid in Full.

And I realized now that she had known. Becky had known even before I did that I would decide to stay, and let her go, and that she forgave this bullheaded decision. As I ran my thumb over the dust-coated box, I wondered at the gift. It struck me as an open invitation, a sign that we weren't finished, and yet despite the time we had since spent together in the city, those odd visits when I just happened to be driving by, and she happened to be up, and happy to see me, she had never mentioned the fishing reel. Was she waiting on me to change my mind? How long could she wait? Our bond had thinned into a tenuous line of fishing wire. I cleared my throat, blinked away the gathering tears in my eyes, and tucked the box beneath my arm. I glanced at Madame Champdeau, who had resumed her post on the stool, and I said, "Have you seen my dad?"

6.

A Tongue Sharp Enough to Pierce Leather

"THE REVENGE OF THE CRADLE ONLY WORKS IF FOLK stick around," said Monique. "Otherwise, what's the point? You're just creating more enemies, t'sé."

We stood in the shadows, outside Alfred's cabin, sharing a cigarette, and Monique was getting riled up, like she always did whenever we somehow ended up talking about politics, and language, or whatever. Seemed she was always bringing them up too since she had gotten that computer and started reading things over the dial-up. She went from listening to *Rage Against the Machine* and reading *Adbusters* magazines, to trawling the web, quoting from some Royal Commission, and spitting fire about Métis history. I tried to steer clear whenever she confronted our parents about their lack of knowledge.

"You've never heard of scrip!?" She would yell at the dinner table.

She had come by that evening to drop off some clothes and deliver a message.

"Mom's disappointed," she said, and laughed as I grabbed the bag of clothes and tossed it onto the small cot that Alfred had set up for me.

Alfred invited her inside and Monique stayed for supper. We sat at the kitchen table and peeled potatoes while Alfred fetched deer sausage from the chest freezer. He had been quiet since we returned from canoeing, and so I was glad that Monique had decided to stay for a while. It was funny watching her work. She seemed so out place in Alfred's cabin; decked out in a Che Guevara t-shirt and punk-patched jean jacket, with short-sheared purple hair and a nose stud, she clashed with the stuffed deer on the wall. With that knife in her hand, she seemed more likely to stab someone rather than peel potatoes. But when she got it into her head to do something, she did it with every ounce of her being; flayed potato skin rained onto the table. After skinning a half-dozen apples of the earth, Monique looked up at me. "So," she said, "What happened?"

"I don't want to talk about it."

"I heard you broke Martin Chaput's nose."

"It was an accident."

"Weren't you fighting?"

"Well, yeah. But I didn't want to break his nose."

"Second nose you break this year," she said.

Alfred slipped into the kitchen, carrying an over-sized Ziploc bag full of sausage. He placed the bag on the counter, then began rummaging through the cupboards for a frying pan.

"I was just trying to drive him back, you know. Make him stop talking. I guess his nose got in the way."

Monique nodded. "You should have kneed him in the balls. A quick thrust, comme ça," she said, and yanking her fists down, she fired her knee upwards. "He would have gone down."

"That's not how men fight," I scoffed.

She lifted her eyebrows and scoffed back at me. "You mean smart?"

Alfred chuckled and I dropped my eyes on the table.

Monique had taken Tae Kwon Do lessons in La Broquerie and for a while she'd relished the opportunity to test her skills on unsuspecting school bullies. She once goaded Justin Leclair into throwing a punch at her, then knocked his clumsy blow aside and dropped him with a quick leg sweep. Although everyone knew she had goaded him—Monique was a straight-A student, a bright star in a dim field, an exasperated teacher once said—and so the principal gave her a half-day in-school suspension, while Justin Leclair was sent home for the rest of the week.

"Quessé qu'y'a dit?" Alfred said, lifting himself from the ground and placing a cast iron frying pan on the stove. He limped over to the table and sat across from me. Monique tossed the potatoes into the pot. Alfred grabbed his tea—he always kept a mug of tea at his fingertips—and he took a quiet sip. "Bin," he said, afterwards. "Quessé qu'y'a dit?"

"Qui ça?"

Alfred sipped his tea, and he seemed to disappear for a moment, hidden behind an old, camouflaged ball-cap, tinted eyeglasses, and his mug. Monique glanced between us.

"Le gars à-qui qu't'as cassé son nez," said Alfred.

"Menoncle," I said. "I don't know if I—"

"Geez, Rich," Monique snapped. "Just tell—"

Alfred gently touched her arm and she grew quiet. Then he turned to me again and after a long moment, nodded. "Une fois qu't'é prêt," he said. He placed his tea down, pressed his hands on the table, and lifted himself out of his chair. Monique brought the potatoes to the stove. Once the potatoes started boiling, Alfred dumped the sausage into the frying pan.

We ate quietly, listening to Alfred explain how he'd harvested the deer. Where he'd seen it, how he'd stalked it, how he shot it. Apparently, la biche had been coming around the cabin all summer, eating his plants, the flowers he grew in the stopped-up tops of old milk cans, and in the sill-trays that hung beneath his small windows. He grew herbs—garnishes, medicines, he said—and la biche had gotten into them, and had taken a bite out of a couple of the plants. The flowers were one thing—it hadn't much bothered Alfred that they'd ended up in the deer's stomach—but the herbs were another matter.

"I can taste the rosemary!" said Monique. Alfred chuckled. Then he grew serious again, and explained how he set about hunting the deer. He plonked himself by the window, rifle by his side, and waited pour qu'la biche revienne.

"Drette là," he said, pointing with his fork to the small window by the doorway.

At first, he had watched her out of the corner of his eye as she breached the treeline not far from the cabin. La biche meandered through the yard, its ears rigid, flicking back and forth, and scanning for sound. Dipping her head into a bucket, she tasted and drank still water. She ambled over to a bunch of weeds sprouting through an old, rusted farm tractor that Alfred had set out as a decoration. La biche stood there and chewed for a while before retreating into the forest. Day after day, Alfred watched her come and go. Nearly a week passed before she stood centered in the window. In the early evening, as light came through the clouds and the leafy tips of birch and ash trees, Alfred saw her. With the smell of rain in the air, the stink of mulch rising from the tray on the windowsill, Alfred lifted his rifle, and brought the sight up to his eye.

"Bang!" Alfred shouted, slapping the table. Monique squeaked and I choked on my food.

The deer tumbled, then righted herself and dashed into the woods.

"Mais j'savais qu'j'l'avais eu."

"Because it almost fell over?" I said.

"Bin ça, oui," Alfred said, and he laughed. "Pis l'paquet d'sang par terre itou."

La biche didn't make it far. Alfred followed the deer into the bush, trailing the snapped branches and splotches of blood on the leaves and in the grass. When he came upon her under an old maple tree, la biche 'tait morte, so he set about bleeding her carcass. The next problem was finding a butcher in the middle of summer. "Mais ça," said Alfred, "C't'une aut'e histwayr."

After we helped Alfred clear the table, clean the dishes, and boil some water for another pot of tea, Monique and I slipped outside to share a cigarette. I'd only recently started to smoke. After scrounging through Monique's purse to borrow twenty bucks, but coming up empty, I had swiped a couple smokes and lit up behind the shed. Monique found out—I thought I had been clever, chewing some mint gum so she wouldn't smell it on my breathe, but I'd forgotten about my clothes. She punched me a few times, then invited me out for a smoke.

"You know," Monique said, pausing to drag on her cigarette, then blowing smoke out of her nose. "We really should speak French more."

I smirked and plucked the cigarette from her outstretched hand. "What the fuck are you talking about?"

Monique frowned, then glanced at the cabin. "Bin, you know. Menoncle Alfred. Mémère. Mémère barely speaks a lick of English—"

"En français ça se fait-ait-ait," I began to sing.

Monique pinned me with a glare. "You're an idiot, Rich. I'm trying to be serious here. C'pas fair d'toujours les parler en anglais."

"Sure," I said, passing the smoke back to her. "But come on."

Monique cleared her throat, straightened herself up, and then, squeezing every last drop of wisdom from her seventeen years like juice from an orange, said, "The revenge of the cradle only works if folk stick around. Otherwise, what's the point? You're just creating more enemies, t'sé?"

I stared blankly. After she explained to me what the revenge of the cradle—la revanche des berceaux—was, a sort of baby boom to buoy our dwindling numbers, I nodded sagely, and flicked the cigarette butt to the gravel, crushed it with my sneaker, dropped a noisy loogie, and squeezed out a short, squeaky fart.

"You're fucking hopeless, Rich."

"Oh, come on, it was a joke."

"No," Monique shook her head. "You know what? This is why people leave, why people stop talking to each other, why we're all losing our French and our culture and—"

"Wait," I said. "Are you telling me I'm killing our culture one fart at a time? Holy shit! Is that my superpower? I am fucking Thunder Butt!"

Monique scrounged through her handbag and pulled out her car keys, then she looked up, and needled me with her eyes. "Grow up, Rich."

7.

La terre alentour d'icitte

IN THE BUICK, I SQUEEZED MY EYES SHUT AND LEANED back in the seat. My jaw ached with a constant, urgent desire to yawn. A weepy sentimentalism washed up relentlessly behind my eyes and seeped like floodwaters through a spring dike. I scrubbed the moisture away and looked out over the town, surveying the half-shorn trees, and the brown, wizened grass on the boulevard, the parked cars and trucks, coated in a fine gravel dust. Someone trudged along in the distance, and I wondered at their purpose.

Not long after she graduated from high school, Monique had moved to Winnipeg. She'd came back to the country eventually to visit, but her visits were infrequent, and they grew further and further apart, the time she spent out here shorter and shorter, until she finally stopped coming altogether. Once she had children, Monique started coming around again, but by then something had changed. Something had been lost. Some measure of intimacy that we once had had became frayed, as though the threads between us had withered and wasted away.

Thing is lots of folks left, and it wasn't just language or culture that kept them around or drove them away. I kept thinking about the old guys at the restaurant and their stories. How folks had clung so hard to the idea of French they'd been unable to see what was happening. Seems to me that a bunch of French folks working at an English-speaking factory might have better kept a community together than those same folks scattering like sands on the wind. Some that left went to Montreal or Ottawa, but most went west—to Winnipeg, Calgary, Vancouver—and those folks tucked their childhood tongues away in a closet or an attic somewhere like some dusty, forgotten guitar, with rusty strings, and an out-of-tune twang that they rarely ever practiced. Missing words like absent notes.

Then I thought about Dad and his family, and all the aunts and uncles and the dozens on dozens of cousins that dotted the towns and villages from here to the Rockies. So many had left, and yet so many remained. Monique counted them all up once, but I quit paying attention after fifty. Fifty first cousins on Dad's side alone. I didn't even know half their names. I'd never met some of them; they'd moved away before I was born.

Cracking open the door, I spat thickly on the street.

Becky's fishing reel rocked on the seat next to me. I hadn't dare open it.

"Chez son frère," Madame Champdeau had said. That's where she thought Dad was. At his brother's. She didn't know which one. Had mentioned clearing fallen trees.

Dad had a handful of brothers scattered across the southeast—Ste. Geneviève, Richer, St. Labre, La Coulée, Giroux. One in Winnipeg and another further out west. Most had bush on their land, and any of them could have used Dad's help with a chainsaw.

Pulling the ashtray open, I sifted through the ashes, and remembered with disappointment that I had already cleaned it out of butts this morning. I knocked the ashtray shut, and glanced in desperation in the cup holders.

As I combed through my thoughts, I figured Dad was at Menoncle Dave's. Not long ago, Dave had lost a couple toes to diabetes and though he still hobbled around his land, cleared trails and fixed fence to keep the deer out of the garden his wife had kept, and generally puttered about as he tried to keep himself busy, he had come to rely more seriously on Dad's help. Dave's kids had moved to the city years ago and although they still came out once a year to get a deer—Dave had installed a couple permanent tree stands some years ago in the back, where his land edged some hay fields and deer always came through—their visits had grown far and fewer in between.

I flicked open the glove box and scrounged through the papers in search of an old joint or a discarded cigarette, anything to take the edge off and dampen that creeping sentimentality. At one time I'd kept a small Altoids tin in the glove box for my roaches, but Becky had discovered them, and she'd tore open the blackened, oily bits, and rolled a new joint out of the remnants: a rezzy, multi-generational, super joint. It tasted of oil, like sucking on an old, black-stained glass pipe, but it did the trick. I'd have taken a hoot of resin now too if I hadn't lost my pipe. Truthfully, I suspected Becky had taken it. In another bout of drunken sentimentality not long ago, I had come to accept this theft as a sort of parting gift, as a remembrance of our time together. But, staring at the Shimano fishing reel on the seat, it seemed like a poor trade, and I pondered once more over the implication, and the inherent invitation. Did it still stand?

Anyway, the Altoids tin was gone, the pipe was lost, and the glove-box was filled with all the wrong kinds of paper. I shut the box and spotted on the floormat the flask I had picked up in Gauthier's yard. It must have fallen when the truck smashed my mirror. I grabbed it, wincing again as another shot of heat flashed down my leg. Turning it over in my hands, examining the smooth steel casing, I tried to ignore the pain by studying the flask. Wiping flecks of dirt and grass off of it, I could see myself in the steel—a dark, amorphous blot, hints of my brown hair, my dark eyes, and the scruff along my jaw. Unrecognizable. I twisted the cap off and held the flask under my nose; it smelled of whiskey. A few drops swirled around the bottom as I shook it, so I tipped the flask back and let the drops fall on my tongue.

"Starting a bit early there, Pichenotte?" said J.P. Gauthier. I heard his muffled laughter, and I coughed, and dropped the flask between my legs. Bent in half by the window, J.P. Gauthier peered into the Buick.

"The hell are you doing here?" I said as I rolled down the window.

J.P.'s hot breath curled into the Buick. With a grunt, he straightened, pressed his hands into his lower spine, and arched backward. I flinched as his belly thrust forward, and I averted my eyes from his navel, visible through his thin shirt. Buttons strained. Wisps of black belly hair wound through the gaps. J.P. leaned forward again, and he stuck his head through the window.

"Did you know your side mirror's missing?"

"It's not missing, J.P. It's on the seat, there."

J.P. craned his neck and frowned. "Don't see it."

I glanced over and saw that it too had fallen to the floor.

"Had a bit too much to drink last night, eh?" J.P. laughed. "Saw you sitting in this piece of shit with a girl last night too. How'd you manage that? She polished your piton?"

"What? No. I think she's my cousin."

"Your cousin?" J.P. frowned. He stood and glanced over the Buick. "Not on your dad's side, she's not," he said. "She's from the city, eh. New teacher at the school here."

"She told me her mom was from around here. Moved away when she was a girl though. So," I shrugged. "You know. Chances are."

"Ah," J.P. nodded, and grinned again. "So, you tried kissing your cousin, eh? That what happened to your mirror?"

"Fuck sakes." I shook my head and told him about the brown Dodge truck on the road this morning. He nodded, and rubbed his chin, as though falling into deep thought.

"That might be old Krawchuk's truck, but you won't get a penny out of him," he said, and he clapped his hands. "But a roll of duct tape should do it anyways. Lucky you're sitting in front of a hardware store! Wouldn't want to get stopped with a broken mirror like that, you'd get towed for sure!"

"Seriously, J.P., quessé qu'tu veux? Why are you here?"

"Bin, le vieux voulait voir son beau-frère," he said, throwing his thumb over his shoulder. Glancing in the rear view, I saw J.P.'s truck parked behind me. Somehow, the diesel monster had snuck up on me. Tufts of white hair peeked out over the dashboard; le vieux Gauthier had shrunk a lot, I thought. "Anyway, là, we spotted you here, and I thought I'd come and see what you were doing. Thought you'd be à l'hôpital by now, t'sé? Didn't you hear about Alfred?"

"Of course, I did," I scoffed. "Do you think I'd be sitting here if I hadn't?"

J.P. peeked over the Buick's roof again, to Champdeau's Hardware store, and frowned.

"I'm looking for my dad," I said. "To let him know. He forgot his cell at home again, and I'm trying to find him."

"Oh," J.P. said, slowly, and nodded. "Gotcha." Groaning, he straightened his spine, and thrust his belly into the window once more. Then, bending low, he punched me on the shoulder. "As-tu checké à bar?" he said and laughed. "They might not let you in with those bloodshot eyes though, eh!"

"Crisse, it's a bit early to drink, non?" I said.

J.P. lifted his eyebrows. He glanced at the flask that had fallen between my legs. "You don't say," he said, with a chuckle. He suddenly frowned. "Is that my flask?" He reached down and grabbed it. "I've been looking for this!" he cried. "Mon ostie d'voleur!"

I huffed, managed to say I'd found it in the grass this morning, but not before J.P. landed another punch. I rubbed my shoulder and glared at him. "It was just laying there, all wet and full of muck. You're lucky I found it. It could've rusted by now."

"It's stainless steel, mon homme."

After a third blow on the shoulder, and following a hearty belly-laugh, and a painfully drawn-out two-faced act of generosity, in which he forgave me for my trespasses, J.P. clutched his flask, waddled back to his truck, and clambered inside. The engine growled to life, and with a flash of J.P.'s fingers, the truck peeled out from behind the Buick and tore up the street toward the highway.

Absolution throbbing in my shoulder, I started the Buick, spun it around, and drove east toward the treeline—past that strange, protestant church on the edge of town, past empty fields, and sheep farms, past the rusted junk yard, and into the bush, toward La Coulée.

A blue pickup swept by, heading west, and the man at the wheel flashed his fingers, and I lifted mine in return. I recognized him from my hockey days, when I manned the blue line for the Aces, back before the registration fees became too expensive and Dad moved us out to the bush.

Funny that. For all the talk of leaving, some purposefully came back. Mom and Dad did. They'd met in the city, and after they'd married, they moved back to raise a family. We'd started off in town but, after a dozen years or so, Dad bought thirty acres of oak and birch on the side of a gravel ridge, and moved us out there. I never did get a straight answer, but I suspected it had to do with small town bullshit—nosy neighbours, prying eyes, high taxes, and the inability to fire your rifle out the window whenever you damn well pleased. Monique was furious. She felt she was being punished for something. Spirited out of town in the dead of night to start a new life in the middle of butt fuck nowhere, she complained. She wasn't even changing schools, our parents told her. But it was too late. She couldn't adapt. As soon as she could, she packed her things and left. Moved to Winnipeg.

The other thing was some never left. And as I watched the trees and the houses and barns zip by me, the sheds full of skidoos, quads, tractors, trucks, bush cars and deer antlers, I began to glimpse at that singular chemistry that kept folks around—that complex and heady mélange of circumstances and passions. It was an ever-shifting and amorphous formula that weighed family, career, hobbies, lifestyle, language, and culture together. But the crux of it all was land. Whether or not you had some. For all of his frustrations, J.P. Gauthier had never left because he'd stood to inherit the farm. And I wondered, deep down, if for all of my miserable luck—my aborted career and shitty jobs, lost friends, and failed relationships—if I too stuck around for the possibility that I might inherit some land, that my parents might one day pass along to me that piece of bush they called home.

Unlike Monique, I had grown familiar with and had to come to love that land. Spending time outdoors with Alfred whenever he visited, or quadding on the old cattle trails with our dog at my side, drinking somewhere in the bush with my buddies, the land had impressed itself upon me. Roots had wormed into me, coiled through my guts, and fused themselves to me, until I was unable to envision myself apart from this place. Unable to voice the depth of my attachment, I had been powerless to explain to Becky why I could not move to the city—just as she had been unable to understand my reluctance. But as the fishing reel rattled in its box, I snorted. Maybe Becky did understand. Maybe she knew me better than I knew myself.

8.

The Tracks
in Tinker Town

ALONG THE DAWSON, SOON AFTER THE ROAD PENETRATES
the treeline east of town, past that place known as La Coulée—la
vallée des voleurs, as a few old-time French guys still called it—where
the land suddenly dips away from an otherwise pancake-flat, glacier-
scraped landscape, rests Lake Riviera. Creek-fed and man-made, that
little body of water had always seemed out of place, like some misfired homage to the French Riviera, plonked on the edge of the prairie
amid scrub oak, aspen, birch, and pine trees. Nestled between Agassiz's
ancient sand bars, the lake appeared without warning. No one remembered who built the Riviera, or why. It had been a public beach for
a while—Dad had some stories of swimming there as a boy—and
there'd even been a music festival at one time. Rock bands and folk
musicians from the city had congregated one weekend for a wild orgy
of music, liquor, and ditch weed. Legend has it, Burton Cummings
showed up to play a set and, in keeping with local tradition, rode in on
the back of a pickup truck. That beach had closed before I was born,

and the land around the lake was subdivided, bisected, halved, and quartered to be sold off to folk who'd build large, lake-front homes, but like most plans around here, it too flopped. Nowadays, other than a scattered handful of houses, Lake Riviera sat mostly empty, a weather-worn "For Sale" sign rising crookedly next to the gravel-rutted road leading into the *estates*.

I only knew this because one of the homeowners who lives around the lake told me. We stood outside her home, admiring the way the sunlight filtered through the trees and painted the surface of the water gold. Uncle Joe's septic truck droned on behind us, the pump whining now and again, as a slurry of piss and shit drained from her septic tank, and swirled through the three and a half inch, steel reinforced, hose by our feet.

"The water gets pretty stale in the summers," she said. "Sometimes you get these big green slicks that cover the whole thing."

"Those happen on the Seine too," I said. "Too much duck shit or something."

"Fertilizer," she said. "Spring runoff carries it into all the creeks and rivers, unbalances the nutrients."

"That's it," I said. The hose jerked at my feet and as I bent down to adjust it, the pump engine whined louder. The tip broke through the surface of the wastewater and a burst of air rushed through, causing the hose to buck in my arms. Squeezing it as it kicked my ribs, I forced its tip back into the tank.

The woman grimaced and recoiled. I couldn't tell if it was the smell or the sound that drove her back. The smell was what you would expect from a tank full of sewage, but the sound was something else: a chorus of children sucking on Slurpees.

"It's a live one!" I laughed. The woman had lost colour to her face, gone grey around the ears. "The hose sometimes has a mind of its own," I added.

She nodded, then turned her head and coughed.

"Tell you what," she said, her voice thin, stretched. "Come by the house for the cheque when you're done."

I watched as she retreated up the hill, paused about halfway, leaned forward, and with her hands on her knees, gagged and spat. I thought she'd done pretty well, overall, to ignore the stink and chat with me. I had only been doing this for a couple weeks now, helping Joe with a few odd jobs, ones he couldn't squeeze in himself. First job, I almost puked on the grass after I removed the tank lid. End of the first week, though, I had hardened myself to the odour, hardly noticed it anymore. I wondered occasionally if I had grown accustomed to it, or if the accumulated stench had already eradicated my sense of smell, except that later in the car, or at home, I would notice suddenly an undercurrent of manure in the air. Days later my nose would wrinkle at the smell, as though the stench of old shit still clung to my clothes after each wash. By the second week, I'd taken to washing my clothes twice before I wore them again. I'd tossed an extra pit stick and a spray can of Febreze in the car too. I'd even seen the woman last night wrinkling her nose after she kissed me on the cheek, and feared I had offended her, and wondered briefly, as my family tree fluttered in my lap, whether it was the smell of shit that had driven her away. I was almost ready to go naked under the coveralls, but it was mid-November, and though there was no snow yet, it wasn't getting any warmer. Standing over the tank, with the fumes drawing water from my eyes, I convinced myself that it was really the sound that got to me, and I began to hum old songs to mask the noise: *en roulant ma boule roulant, en roulant ma boule...*

Despite the obvious nuisances, I'd come to like working for Joe. What I enjoyed was the travel. I'd spent years working indoors, locked in a small painting booth as pieces of metal were dangled and paraded before me on a conveyor belt. Now to be suddenly out in the world, plying the backroads, under the sun and the clouds, was a revelation. Seeing a piece of land from a new perspective after years of driving by a place and wondering what the property looked like, what folks kept hidden behind their houses, away from the roads—and besides, I got a kick too out of telling people I drove a honey wagon.

"Ça va pas durer," Dad said one night over dinner. "Éventuellement, ça va t'écoeurer." He glared over his mashed potatoes, and I glanced at my mom. She rolled her eyes and shrugged. I didn't understand what he had against Joe's business. When I'd first told him that I had run into Joe and that he had offered me some work, Dad discouraged me from working with him.

"Ça va t'écoeurer," he repeated.

"C'est compliqué," Mom said when I asked her about it, after Dad had retreated into the living room and fallen asleep on the couch. She smiled sadly as I stared at her, then gathered the soiled plates and utensils from the table and brought them over to the sink.

Finally, I asked Joe. I had just dropped off the truck at his place south of town. He had a couple acres by the rail tracks, on Seine Road, enough for a large workshop, and a place to park his septic trucks. We stood outside his house, a modest, raised bungalow with a long wraparound deck. He had landscaped his property with small, grass-covered hills, and crescent-shaped flower beds. Seven young oak trees dotted the yard. Dad had once asked him why he planted oaks—oak trees took ages to grow—and Joe shook his head, told Dad to read a damn history book. Joe took pride in his property, his land. When he wasn't emptying septic tanks, he was in the yard pulling weeds, tilling soil. He had a flagpole installed in front of the house too, and he cycled between a couple different flags: the red maple leaf and the Franco-Manitoban flag, that one with a weird tuft of weed on it, even though he barely spoke a lick of French. The flag that he flew most often though was the infinity symbol. He would often, at the end of the day, sit beneath that flapping figure of infinity with a big cigar wedged between his lips and watch his oak trees grow.

We were inspecting the truck I'd just dropped off, walking around the back, making sure the hoses were secured, and the medieval-torture tool looking, shit-busters—heavy steel spears bristling with small hooks—were latched to the truck deck, when I brought up Dad's comments.

Joe scratched at his wispy beard. "Your dad's funny like that," he said.

"I don't think he was joking."

"I don't mean ha-ha funny."

"Oh."

"I mean weird."

"Gotcha."

We circled around the back of the truck and looked up at the release valve. Above it was a large, jolly honeybee: *#1 with your #2!* it shouted in a speech bubble. A couple figure eights, as though blowing in the wind, were painted in the corners. Joe had visions, he told me. He wanted to expand the business. Add a couple more trucks. License out the name. He envisioned himself as the King of the Southeast.

"Just lord over the busy-bees in their honey wagons," he laughed, snorted, and spat.

If I'd had Monique's tongue, I would have told him that bees don't have kings.

We stood at the back of the truck, looking over the paint job, when Joe pressed a thumb to his nostril, and with a quick and loud huff, blew mucus from his airway, onto the gravel, then he wiped his thumb on his jeans, and cleared his throat.

"Your dad ever tell you about the Tinker Town job?"

"You mean that amusement park on the highway just outside of the city?"

"That's the one."

I shook my head.

Joe nodded. He reached into jeans and pulled out a crumpled pack of cigarettes, and with a swift flick, drew a couple smokes out. He passed me one, and then reached into his jeans again for a pack of matches.

"Well," said Joe, sparking his match and lighting his cigarette, "Not long after your Dad and I started the business, we undercut some other guys and landed the Tinker Town job—"

"Wait, what? You started the business together?"

"That's right, but I bought him out after a year and half," said Joe. He offered me the cherry-red end of his cigarette, and I pressed mine to his until the tip began to smoulder. "You didn't know that?"

"Well, I knew he worked with you for a bit. I didn't know he'd started the business too."

"You were always an ignorant little shit," said Joe. And he began to laugh. "I mean that in a good way."

"Okay, then."

"Like you were happy, off playing with your toys, or some shit. Anyways," Joe waved his cigarette around and pointed to the truck.

"We used to have to swing by Tinker Town every second day or so in the summer. They had these huge tanks in the corner of the park, and those tanks filled up fast—guess a thousand kids and their parents slurping juice and pop, then getting spun around, upside down, and back again will make you need to go—so we'd spend half a day there, hauling their waste from the park to the treatment plant on the south perimeter there, just east of St. Norbert. It was steady work, though it didn't pay that much. Anyhoo, the thing was, there was this railway track, like the little kiddie-ones, you know, with a miniature choo-choo train, and whistle, and little train-cars with seats on them to carry kids and parents around—"

"I know, Joe. I've been there."

"Well, the thing is the tracks run next to the septic tanks, right? Every so often, we'd be pumping sewage and the train would come around the bend. You'd hear the little engine, at first, maybe the whistle too if the operator felt like it."

"You sound like a damn country song."

Joe snorted, and continued.

"Thing is, then you'd hear the kids. See, those tanks were huge, and they put out a lot of gas, not like these small single-family homes. You think those are bad. Christ. Those tanks were awful. So, as that train goes by, the kids would just start pissing and moaning—ewwww!— and some of the smaller ones would even start to cry, you know, like maybe they're wondering why their eyes are melting or something, and then they'd see us there, in our overalls, holding these fucking hoses, and they'd put two and two together."

"Damn, that seems funny."

"You'd think, right? The thing is—first time it happened was fine. We smiled and waved. Then they come around again, and again, and some kids are crying now, others are pointing at us and laughing, you know, just pinching their noses shut—and we just start anticipating their cries, now, like a fucking train whistle—ewwww! Ewwww! I guess it started to really get to your dad you know. Couldn't stand all these kids and their parents seeing him there, like that, cleaning out shit. Like he was too fucking good for that kind of work."

"He was embarrassed?"

Joe sucked on his shrunken cigarette butt, then, realizing it had burned down to the filter, tossed it away and nodded. "Still pisses me off thinking about it," said Joe.

"That's fucked," I said.

Joe shrugged. "What broke the camel's back, though, was when I had that stenciled on the back of the truck," he said, and he pointed to a small cluster of print beneath the honeybee: *Métis Owned and Operated.* "That set your dad off. Guess he's always been a bit fairweather, eh? He cares too much about what other people think."

The cigarette turned to ash between my fingers as I thought about it. Something didn't sit right in the way that Joe told it. I knew part of it was true. Mom and her family—Joe included—had only really discovered they were Métis back in the 90s, when a few of them finally followed up on some family rumours. Joe took to it like a fish to water. Went out and bought a sash, a fur hat, and a half-dozen flags. But Dad had always been a bit funny about things like that. Back in the day, when we still went to church on Sundays, Monique and I had to dress just so, our hair combed just so. Mom would do a fine job, but then Dad would glance at us in the rear-view, and turn to Mom to complain about some wrinkle in my collar or some wild tuft shooting out from Monique's hair. Once, after a few glasses of wine, Mom had suggested Dad's mother had "raised him funny," but she caught herself, quieted down, and never elaborated.

But I also remembered how, when we were young, Dad had told Monique and me about les Métis, how so many had retreated west, or were pushed to the edges of the settlement, as les anglais flooded in from Ontario. How Pépère had lost the farm. How, when growing up, Dad's older brothers and sisters had been teased, bullied, ignored, and shunned, and other things that he couldn't bring himself to talk about, and how back in the day they had had trouble finding work, and opening bank accounts. Dad muttered about les calices d'anglais, pis les français too qui sont venus après, qui charriaient leur bigoteries avec eux, et comment nous on l'était michif itou, but then, out in the world, every once in a while, when someone asked him where he was from, Dad would say that he was French.

Dad was white enough to get away with it. Brown hair, blue eyes, and a tan he explained came from working his whole life outdoors. Folks would stare for a moment, some maybe raised an eyebrow, but most would nod and accept this fact, and Dad would tell a joke, and the moment would float away. Later, in the car, Dad would confess, "It's easier like that."

Joe was right, mostly—Dad was "funny"—but there was something he had missed. I had heard Dad talk openly with his brothers and sisters about getting their Métis cards, and how they were all following some big court case about hunting rights—a guy had challenged the province after being charged for hunting ducks near Turtle Mountain, and folks across the province were waiting on the decision. With others, though, Dad clammed right up. Like he'd rather talk about anything else. And that was the crux of it; some things were simply not for others.

When Monique finally went back to school after a couple years bumming around the city, she came home first to ask Mom and Dad about it—to get their birth certificates and family tree. She wanted to get her card. She didn't need a fucking card to tell people who she was and where she was from, she said, but she explained how she might be able to get some help paying tuition from the Manitoba Métis Federation; but as we sat around the kitchen table talking about it, Dad was reluctant. He clung to his stories, holding them closely to his chest.

Monique patiently peeled his fingers away from what she needed, explaining how things had changed, how it was safer now—relatively. People were talking again, gathering, and getting to know each other once more. People were dusting off the old stories, the ones mémère had kept wrapped up, or pépère had stuff into a box and shoved into the attic. People were reaching out to those who'd never gone anywhere, those who'd never hidden, who'd never been able to hide and who'd suffered to keep the dream alive. Monique went on, but Dad wasn't so sure. It didn't feel right to be so open. What if the Government got hold of the lists? What if they decided to round up the Métis? Ship them off somewhere. They'd done it to others before. Not even that long ago.

Mom rolled her eyes, but said nothing.

"Dad," said Monique, shaking her head. "That genie is out of the bottle."

"Quoi?"

"If they want to know, they just have to look it up in some archive. It's all there."

Dad grunted, but then he loosened his grip, and stories began to seep out.

A few years after Monique got hers, Dad applied for his membership card. When it came in the mail, he stared at it for a long while, running his thumb over his name, over the small cart-wheel, and rifles, and bison head embossed on the corner. He showed it to me that first morning, and with bleary eyes, I looked at the card.

"Cool," I said, disinterested.

He grunted, took the card back, and placed it carefully in his wallet.

Thinking back, I saw now that brittle pride, like malnourished bones growing stronger through care and attention, and as I listened to Joe ponder aloud about Dad's passion, my dad's words echoed in my ears, and I wondered then if Dad had not meant something entirely different when he said ça va t'écoeurer.

Mom was right. C'est compliqué.

9.

Dans La Coulée

PASS THE CREEK THAT FEEDS LAKE RIVIERA, SUR LA LIGNE à Faucher, there's a road that turns west towards La Coulée. Some years ago, Menoncle Dave bought land close to that corner. He built a house and a shop and cleared some trees to cut out a network of trails through the woods for him and Matante Louise to enjoy their retirement. Then Matante Louise died of a heart attack before he ever finished. After that Menoncle Dave found it hard to be in the house—everything reminded him of her—and so he spent almost all his time outdoors. Without his wife around, he stopped eating well; he drove to town almost every day for a cheeseburger and a side of fries. He gradually lost control over his diabetes, then lost a couple toes. Dave bought a four-wheeler after that, and booted around his property, up and down the road, visiting neighbours, friends, family. When a windstorm knocked trees down across the trails, he would try to move them himself. He would slip a cable around the trunk and then hook it to the winch nestled on the front of the four-wheeler, and yank the tree out of the way.

For the really big ones though, those towering aspens caught half-fallen on some shorter oak tree and rotting in the middle of the air, Dave needed a chainsaw. Waiting for help, Dave started drinking. Only a few beers now and again, but that turned into a six-pack a night. Then he would show up on his quad in the yard in the evenings with a slight slur to his speech, and Dad would give him a look, but never said anything about it since Dave was older. The six-pack turned into a two-four on the weekend, and eventually the beers turned into hard liquor. Cheap whiskey and diet coke, because of the diabetes. Over this last summer, Dave had taken the quad out to visit someone après un coup trop de whiskey, like he does, and drove it into a culvert. He near tore the front wheels off. Broke his arm too. I had last seen him a few weeks back, just before I started working for Joe. His arm was finally out of the cast, but he had grown thin, gaunt. Dark bags sagged under his eyes.

The driveway snaked out of the treeline near a rise in the land, and you'd miss it if it wasn't for a pair of reflective markers sticking out from the ground. You couldn't see the house from the road, only a few plastic deer through the trees. A once brightly painted wooden cut-out of an old lady, bent over—presumably gardening—and crookedly stuck into the dirt appeared as you neared the house. Peeking out beneath her dress, her once white gitch now grey and peeling.

Dad's truck sat in front of the garage. Wind rustled through the tops of the trees, tearing leaves from the branches, and peppering the ground. The air was warmer here, heavier, recently exhaled. Laden with the scent of deadfall. Chainsaws growled in the distance, and I spun around, trying to pinpoint their origin, but the sound ricocheted through the trees, echoed, and then faded as the wind passed, then started up again from another direction.

The underbrush was thick, so I stuck to the trails, backtracking once or twice as I turned and tracked the chainsaws down some offshoot. Through the years, Menoncle Dave's network of trails had radiated out through the woods like a spider's web. Some paths led to small clearings, and piles of drying wood, or small benches carved out of logs, simple places to sit and be. Others circled back and spat you out onto the road, down from the driveway. One led to a small pit he'd had excavated, filled with water, and stocked with fish. The fish were gone now, and the pit bred nothing but des quenouilles et des maringouins. The chainsaws grew angrier, and their pitch rose sharply as their teeth chewed through bark and moist-green wood.

"Sacrament!" I heard. "Watch out, là. Tu vas péter la chaine!"

Wood cracked and snapped, the sound spilling like water across the ground. The treetops shuddered.

"Donnes-y du gaz!" Dad barked, and Menoncle Dave's quad suddenly roared, and wood cracked again, louder. Trees swayed, branches rattling above, raining desiccated leaves.

"Fucking marde, y'é stuck!" Dave shouted over the engine.

"Papa," I shouted, but neither he nor Dave seemed to hear.

The chainsaw wailed and clouds of wood dust shot up through the trees. I pushed through the underbrush, quitting the trail, and cutting across to the next one, when another crack sounded. Before me, the woods opened up momentarily, and I saw Menoncle Dave sitting on his quad and looking at me, his eyes growing wide as the woods closed up, and a tangle of trees crashed down on top of me.

* * *

When my dad was twelve years old, he was buried alive with a girl under a pile of rocks. He had snuck out from the house after dark one evening in late spring, and biked over to the park behind the church to meet a girl. They'd caught each other's eyes at school and circled warily for a time, inching closer as their nerves grew, and desire drew them together. They brushed against each other in the hallway as they passed slowly and veered into different classrooms. At the time, the boys and girls were kept separated by the nuns. Even outside, they played at opposite ends of the yard as vigilant nuns patrolled the boundary in between. One day, however, the girl breached that line, purposefully tripping and falling into Dad. Picking themselves off the ground, hurriedly whispering as nuns bore down on them, the girl suggested that they meet somewhere after dark.

"Où ça?" Dad said.

"La grotte!" she suggested.

The nuns swooped and dragged them back across that thick, invisible line.

In the park behind the church rose an old grotto, an archway, cobbled together from large stones and mortar to create a cavern of sorts that housed that bright white statue of the blessed Virgin. People would come from afar—from Giroux to Dufresne—to pray before her, to fondle her toes and rub her feet, as though her holiness was somehow transmittable, an infectious virus that could root out and destroy the devil's influence. In summers, the priests would occasionally hold mass outdoors, the Virgin looming over their shoulders, unblinking, staring at the prostrated crowds while the priests droned on in Latin.

That night, as Dad pedalled toward the centre of town, he hardly noticed the air pressing down on him. Humid and heavy, pregnant with moisture. Storm clouds massed out west, in the valley over the Red, flickering with distant, silent, lightning.

Dad lay his bike next to the girl's on the dais where the priests would set up an altar, and he stepped toward the grotto. The girl stood in the shadows, watching, her silhouette illuminated by growing forks of light. They could hardly hear the thunder over their own beating hearts. Dad neared, and they touched, gently, lacing their fingers together. They stood under the archway as rain began to fall. The world faded away as they embraced and pressed their lips together, or so it must have been.

The story was stitched together from a dozen half-tellings, some whispered innuendoes, and drawn-out echoes of local lore. It had become legend. Dad was the boy who had been buried alive. He and the girl had been in the papers afterwards. *Miracle!* Headlines shouted. Beneath the headlines spread sordid rumours of their romance. The family became uneasy and eventually the girl moved away, and her part had been gradually forgotten, but Dad remained, and so his story lived on, told and retold, changed, until it was hardly recognizable and hardly possible. He never talked about it—like many other things—and folks had learned to not bring it up in front of him, not after he'd clubbed a man in the head with a bottle of Labatt's for mentioning it.

The only way it made sense was that Dad and the girl were so enamoured, enraptured, by their first kiss that they didn't notice the rain, and didn't notice how the deluge had started to eat away at the mortar holding the stones above their heads. As though kneeling in supplication, they crowded at the Virgin's feet, their lips pressed together, and the Virgin blessed them. When the stones gave in and the archway crumpled, the rocks knocked the statue forward, and the Virgin crashed down overtop Dad and the girl, creating a pocket of air between the ground and pedestal where they huddled in shock and fright as stones piled up around them.

They weren't found until late the next morning, when un petit vieux from La Villa, the newly built old folks' home nearby, out for a walk, happened to spot the bicycles on the dais. He approached and realized that the grotto was gone, replaced by a pile of stones.

"Miséricorde!" he exclaimed, and as he came closer and pressed his hands to the stones, spotting slivers of the Virgin through gaps in the pile, he heard a gentle sobbing.

Soon a crowd gathered as men rushed to remove the stones, carefully peeling them from the pile and placing them aside. They shouted through the gaps, asking who was there, and Dad and the girl shyly gave their names, no louder than a whisper, forced through chattering teeth and incipient stages of hypothermia. Police came and pushed the gathering crowds back, and firemen replaced the workers, methodically removing stone after stone. Old Coup d'Coude walked down from the church and had the crowd pray to the Blessed Virgin; a few men placed bets on how long it would take to rescue the lovebirds. Mémère appeared, having hitched a ride with the neighbour, and ploughed through the crowd to the front, where she yelled and screamed at the firemen to hurry. Someone took a photo as firemen lifted the statue to reveal Dad and the girl, mud-covered and shivering, curled up against the pedestal. The statue a bit scuffed up, but still gleaming behind them. Weeks, the photo would be splashed across the province—front page of the *Carillon*, *La Liberté*, and the *Free Press*.

Dad hid out at home for a while, resting, recuperating, away from all the attention. Some newspaper men tried to get a word with him, clambering onto the porch and peeking though the windows into the house, but Mémère met them at the door with a large wooden spoon, smacked them across the hands, and chased them off the property.

Eventually the story died down, folks' attention faded, and Dad finally returned to school only to discover that the girl had moved away. I don't know if he ever knew why she'd left, or been forced to leave, or where she went, but Dad developed a sense that her folks blamed him. Dad tended to accept blame for nearly everything that went wrong around him. He shouldered everyone's mistakes though they were not his—as though he might somehow redeem some miserable course of events, or atone for his own short-comings.

* * *

Light knifed through the trees, and the ragged ceiling of the grey-tinged leaves, mottled with brown and orange. Clouds of warm breath frosting before me. The smell of earth so near.

"Tabarnak! Y-é-tu mort?" Dave shouted.

Blood trickled down my cheek, along my jawline, dripping from my chin. I was sitting on the ground, my hands, and fingers, pressing into the cold dirt. Heavy birch trunks lay only a few feet away, scattered branches like a bone-stitched dome around me.

"Richard!" Dad shouted.

"I'm here," I said, and glanced up at Dad who was busting branches with his feet, trying to reach me. "I'm okay." Lifting myself up, and wobbling to my feet, I surveyed the tree, how it had narrowly missed me—deux pieds à gauche pis ça m'aurait fendu la tête.

Dad pulled a branch aside, stepped over the birch trunk, and swallowed me in his arms. Then he held me by the shoulders and glared. "Christophe, Richard!"

"Enfant d'chienne!" Dave exclaimed. "J'ai besoin d'un drink, moé," he said, and hobbled back to his quad.

"Tu saignes de la tête, Richard," said Dad.

I touched my forehead, wincing as fingers brushed my hairline. "It's just a scratch."

Dad led me to Dave's quad and had me sit on the fender while he scrounged through a small trunk for a bottle of water.

Dave shook his head. "Ostie d'shaanseu." He pulled a small flask from the saddlebag astride his four-wheeler, and took a sip, then he held it out towards me. I tipped it back against my lips, then passed it back to him.

Dad glanced over and glared again. He tossed me a bottle of water, which I opened and drank to wash the taste of cheap whiskey from my mouth. "Quessé qu'tu fais icitte?" Dad said. "You could have been killed—"

"Écoute," I said, holding my palm up in the air. I took another swig of water, shuddering as the cold flowed through my chest, my stomach. I leaned forward and spat on the ground, then looked up at Dad. "Menoncle Alfred had a stroke," I said.

Dad's face crumbled, blood draining away. Dave grunted in surprise and reached into the saddlebag once more.

"Yé t'à l'hôpital," I said. "À Saint-Boniface."

Saint-Boniface

10.

À quatre pattes

"THEY FOUND HIM À QUATRE PATTES, SON TÉLÉPHONE dans main. Can you believe that?" said Dad in the passenger seat of his little half-ton truck as it hurtled down the highway. He held out the Motorola Razr—the one he had left at home that morning—away from his body and squinted at his contacts. Mom nodded behind the wheel. Curled up on a small bench behind the passenger seat, I groaned as heat zinged down my leg. Pins and needles erupted from my toes.

"Is that your back again?" said Mom. She frowned in the rear view. "I've told you before to get that checked out."

"À quatre pattes. You told us already, Dad," I said, ignoring my mother.

"Oui. Trois fois, déjà, Émile," said Mom.

"Bin. Imagine that," said Dad. "Having the presence of mind. À son âge, itou."

Despite my reluctance, Mom had insisted I accompany them in the half-ton. I protested, but she grabbed my head and pulled me down so that she could have a look at the cut where the tree had caught me. We were at home wolfing down tomato soup and grilled cheese sandwiches before heading out for the city. I felt her thumbs brushing hair away from the cut, and I winced. Her grip tightened as she examined the wound. With her warm hands around my head, and the soft sound of her breath in my ears, I closed my eyes.

"Don't start snoring now," she said, her nose wrinkling. "You need a shower too." Then she grunted. "Misère, you got lucky."

"Deux pieds à gauche, pis—"

"Yeah, yeah. Go put some peroxide on that."

When I argued over hopping into the half-ton with them, my mother laughed.

"Ta pas d'miroir, là. La police va t'arrêter sur l'highway, and then what are you going to do? Walk?"

So, I squeezed in behind my dad and settled on the little pullout seat. Dad didn't want to drive, too upset; also, he had been calling his brothers and sisters non-stop on his cellphone.

"Quoi?" he said into the phone. "Ils l'ont trouvé à quatre pattes?" He turned to Mom and said, "Ils l'ont trouvé à quatre pattes!"

"I heard, Émile."

We shadowed a CN train down the highway, and I stared out through the side window at the train cars. Electric poles whipped by. The train cars were covered in graffiti, busy rainbow-coloured splotches and bubble letters that overshadowed dull tags. I counted the cars with those big tufts of wheat on them, and my mind wandered, remembering the time, some years ago, that Becky and I had driven through Saskatchewan. We had decided spur of the moment, and drove 14-hours to the mountains. We took pictures in front of that lake on the 20-dollar bill. The Buick overheated on our way back and we spent the night in Swift Current, waiting for a mechanic to replace the radiator hose.

"*Saskatchew-on, and on, and on,*" Becky sang endlessly as we crossed. Her feet up on the dash, flashing her thighs at me, she laughed whenever I complained about the damn rhyme or her feet, or how she hadn't paid me a cent for gasoline. It felt as though we were hardly moving at all—ants on a boundless table-top.

Dropping my head into my hands, I groaned in the backseat, unable to stop my thoughts from pinballing between Becky and Alfred. The last time I'd seen Becky, maybe a week after I lost my job at the powder coat plant, before I started working for Joe, we stood in her kitchen, doing dishes, and I told her that I couldn't afford to keep visiting her in the city. She dropped a plate into the sink and wheeled on me, jabbing a finger in my chest.

"There's plenty of fucking work in the city, Rich."

"Beck—"

"I mean, fuck. Don't you want something more?"

I stood tongue-tied, holding a damp towel that dripped dishwater over the scratched-up linoleum floor. Becky sighed, and she turned to the sink. She lifted the plate from the water and began to scrub, her arm moving up and down like a piston, furious and intense, peeling layers of grime with each scrape, polishing that dish like new, moving ever toward a sense of finality.

"À quatre pattes, Edmond. C'est vrai!" said Dad again into the phone.

I sighed and closed my eyes and lay my head back to rest, but the truck kept rattling, up and down, bouncing on the frost-heaved highway.

"There's Deacons," said Mom.

Winnipeg wasn't far now. Not that it was far to begin with; half hour trip from town and you were there. C'était pas comme dans le temps, Dad liked to say when, before the government built the Trans-Canada, his dad used to take a horse and buggy along gravel roads into the city. It would take him half a day to get there, and then another half-day to run errands. They'd stop into Lorette on their way back and spend the night with Mémère's brother. Trips to the city back then could take two days. Dad told me how his father had refused to buy a car until his horse died; he had spent too much time breaking in the colt, training it to pull, but then Pépère died before the horse did. I always thought that was pretty bullheaded of him, though I never told Dad. He spoke of his dad and the horse with such respect.

The highway narrowed down to one lane as we hit the floodway construction. Crews had begun expanding the bridge deck to add an extra lane; the whole bridge was being redone since Duff's ditch was being widened to handle ever more floodwater. Staring out over that vast ditch with only a string of water curling through it now, I wondered about the decision to build it. Not the reason behind it; that I knew. I had heard the stories about the big one, the flood of 1950, and how it had rolled through the city, the Red rising faster than anyone could remember. Faster and higher than anytime since well-before this place was Canada, when folks had packed their things up in Red River carts and drove their animals to high ground near Birds Hill and Silver Heights. No. What I wondered about was the path that ditch took; how the floodway had cut off the Seine. Larry Lechene once told me how they had built that floodway over our little river. I'd wondered how in the hell do you make two rivers cross and keep them true. Larry said that they diverted the Seine underneath the floodway using a siphon.

"So, the river just disappears?" I asked.

"Yup, goes underground."

For some reason that just rocked me. We sat in his mom's basement getting high, talking about canoeing to the city, just to see if we could do it. Making plans we'd never follow through with. The idea that every spring they split the Red in two, sending half its waters around the city, overtop of our little river, seemed incredible and outrageous.

"It's like a fucking moat!" I shouted.

"A what now?" said Larry.

I shook my head, thinking about how that stretch of prairie had been dug up and gouged so thoroughly—a wound never allowed to close—that no one could recognize it.

"They moved more earth than the Panama Canal, almost," said Larry.

Larry was an odd duck. First time I met him he was shooting beer bottles off fence posts at the Fleurettes' place outside of Marchand—he held a .22 rifle in his hands and offered to buy my Buick. I refused, but we got along fine anyway. He offered me a warm beer and we struck a wild and unhinged sort of friendship for a time; one moment we shot traffic signs from the back of Al Verrier's old pickup truck, and the next we delved into the philosophy of existence over a fat joint in his mother's basement. You might not have known it from looking at him—what with his torn-up jeans and his grease-coated hands—but Larry was a reader. Back before he killed the Fleurette girl in a rollover accident, Larry had been happy and curious, and he'd told me all kinds of things about our town and our history.

"Is it even the same river, when it pops up, on the other side?" I asked, holding the joint out for him. He took it between his fingers and nodded.

"Well, apparently. Same water anyways," he said.

"Sure, but is it the same river? I mean, can the fish get through?"

"I'm not an engineer. Just telling you what I read."

I shook my head again. "Sounds to me like they killed the river."

"Maybe," Larry shrugged, and he pulled on that joint.

Dad stared at the road workers and the cats and the excavators, the stacks of rebar and the mounds of gravel. "Ça c't'une job, là," Dad said.

"What?"

"Ça c't'une job," he said again, and pointed to the road crew on the bridge deck.

I snorted, and glanced back as we passed. "Ça va pas durer," I said, and I grinned as Dad glanced over his shoulder and frowned. "It's true," I said. "Once the work is done, then what?"

"Roads always need fixing, Rich."

"Not like we're going to run out of shit," I said.

Dad snorted, and then silence filled the cab as we retreated into our own thoughts and stared out at the horizon. Not long after we crossed the Perimeter, I spotted the Ferris wheel rising through the trees along the highway, the colourful gate topped with bright flags. The parking lot empty, the season finished.

"There's Stinkertown," said Mom.

"Ewwww!" I said, and felt a sudden, sharp twist in my guts. Holding my breath, I waited until Dad grunted and he said that he wouldn't mind stopping somewhere for a coffee. I dropped my head between my knees and groaned.

"There's a Tim's in the hospital, Émile."

"Oh, that's right," he said and nodded.

Mom cleared her throat, raising her voice suddenly.

"You okay back there?"

"I'm fine," I said.

"What?"

"I said I'm fine."

Mom sniffed. "Just let me know if you want me to pull over."

"I'm fine."

We crested the overpass coming into the city. Symington Yards— CN's big rail depot—fanned out below us like a dried-river delta, stitched, and scarred. Train engines clattered on the tracks, shunting back and forth. Mom turned up Lag, towards Marion. Dad wrinkled his nose. I could tell by the way he grunted and shot Mom with a series of side-eyes that he wasn't happy. He hated taking this way. He always complained about the smell. At the corner of Marion and Lag was a meat packing plant always spewing thick smoke, and the air around was perpetually ripe with fuel exhaust and burning carcasses.

"T'as l'nez fin," said Mom.

"Bin, tu fais exprès."

"Je m'en crisse de ton nez, Émile. I'm trying to get us there quick."

Dad grunted again and glared out the window. Sirens wailed in the distance. Dad's half-ton bounced over the pock-marked streets, all zit-scarred through years of frost and thaw, and we flew over a series of rail tracks. Teeth rattled inside our heads.

I began to laugh.

"Tu trouves ça drôle?" Dad asked.

"That's not it," I said, and Dad snorted.

There was something about being crammed together that always seemed to drive us to each others' throats; it wasn't just bickering over pig shit, or where to stop for coffee, or which road to take. It wasn't any of that, but the arguments themselves. The way it always came down to some absurd little thing. It was as though when we sat for too long, we searched for things to argue about. That same chafing familiarity I'd begun to experience after Becky left had already long infected us, like poison, transmuting our comfort into misery. Somehow, when we were all together, a force began to accumulate between us, like strong and opposing magnets, pushing us apart. The more of us together, the quicker it grew, the stronger it got, until we could no longer hold it back and we began to yell and spit. Often, we would never let it get that far, and one of us would leave before sparks flew, defusing that volatile energy; but every once in a while, it would explode and one of us would say something that we'd later come to regret.

11.

Cigarettes

THE ROOM WAS DIM, QUIET, EXCEPT FOR THE GLOW AND hum of machines at Alfred's bedside. He lay unmoving, his eyes closed, his chest rising and falling steadily. A web of tubes and wires sprouted from his arms, chest, and head, feeding the machines with numbers they spit back out at us—numbers I read without understanding. Dad stood at Alfred's bedside and stared at his uncle; I could see a lump of muscle contracting, jumping around, at the back of Dad's jaw. Gingerly, he took Alfred's hand in his and squeezed. I stepped back and fell into a chair along the wall.

Mom stood in the hallway, chatting with a few matantes who'd stuck around once they'd heard Dad was coming. All day, apparently, there'd been a steady stream of visitors—an endless parade of nephews and nieces, des petits-neveux et des petites-nièces—stopping in to see Alfred and pay their respects. Seems a lot of them had figured this was Alfred's last moments, and they wanted to say goodbye, but then

Alfred, avec sa tête de boeuf, clung stubbornly to life, and some time after noon, said Matante Yolande, he turned a corner.

"He opened his eyes, for a second," she said.

"Ah bin," said Mom. "C'est positif."

"Doctors said it was a reflex, so not to read too much into it," Yolande paused, and I could almost hear her purse her lips in that way she always did, "Mais, oui. Not a bad sign."

On the small table at the side of Alfred's bed, someone had placed flowers wrapped in blue and white ribbons. There were a couple get-well cards propped up against the flower vase. There was also a small picture of la Vierge, with a new rosary draped over the corner. Someone had stuck a small infinity flag onto the headboard above Alfred's head. I spotted a pair of loose cigarettes on the table and wondered briefly why they were there, but then figured that it was an offering. Though I couldn't figure who had left them.

Alfred never much talked about his spirituality. I'd always seen him as a sort of laissez-faire Catholic who'd preferred speaking directly to the Saints, rather than through a priest. Then again, whenever he came to one of our rites, our first communion or confession, or confirmation, whatever it was, there was Alfred in the front pew with Mom and Dad, and afterwards cracking jokes with the priest.

"Menoncle," I heard Dad whisper. And as though he knew I had heard, he leaned closer to Alfred, and lowered his voice, whispering inaudible words. The room suddenly felt too small, my presence too large, and so I quietly rose out of the chair and slipped through the door.

Mom glanced at me.

"Papa wants to be alone," I said.

Matante Yolande nodded. "Allo, Richard."

"Hi, Matante."

"Give me a hug," she said, and she squeezed me hard, then she held me by my shoulders and studied my face. "What happened to your head?"

"Oh, that's nothing," I said. "Just a cut."

Matante frowned, but nodded. "You look tired. Are you sleeping enough?"

Mom snorted softly under her breath.

"It's been a long day," I said, and my legs agreed, suddenly buck-ling, and causing me to flinch and sway. Matante steadied me and she offered me a soft smile that did not touch her eyes, then she pointed down the hallway with her chin.

"Menoncle devrait être dans la waiting room là, avec une couple d'autres," she said.

Slipping from her grip, I nodded my thanks, and headed down the hall.

In the waiting room, I saw my uncles. Menoncle Frank et Menoncle Roger. They greeted me with a heavy handshake and a word when I entered. "C't'un maudit temps!" they said, and I lowered myself into a chair and we sat in silence for a time. After a while Roger turned to Frank and told him about his new card. Their eyes lit up like kids and not old men in their mid-sixties.

"This one's a harvester card," he said, taking it out of his wallet and passing it for Frank to see. Frank held the card out, away from his body, and squinted through his tinted eyeglasses.

"Faux que je m'en poigne une comme ça itou," he said.

They talked for a bit about how the deer looked this year—they were both semi-retired and lived out east of town, closer to Giroux than Richer, and had time to watch deer come and go. Like most of their siblings, they had spent a lifetime working, offering their hard labour, for the chance to retire near where they'd grown up, and to take in and enjoy the land a little before they passed.

"So, j'l'ai promis une hanche de chevreuil pour une chaudière de saskatoons et un seau de pembinas. Figured c'était un bon trade."

"A deer haunch for a pail of berries? Pas sure c't'un bon deal, là."

Roger shrugged, "Y'avait pas d'fruits chez nous c't'été. Mais y'a des biches en crisse."

They talked of hunting and fishing, and gathering wild fruits and plants, and trading for things they could not get. Listening to them speak, I wondered how they knew these things. How many ducks for some moose meat? How many saskatoons for walleye or pickerel? Occasionally a pail of berries would show up on the doorstep at home, and I figured that someone had dropped them off, but in exchange for what, I wasn't always sure. Some woodwork from Dad, probably.

Menoncle Roger took his card back and slipped it into his wallet.

"Vas-tu t'poigner un moose c't'année, Menoncle?" I asked.

Roger looked up and smiled, then shook his head.

"J'pense qu'j'ai fini d'chasser les orignaux, c'trop dur sur le dos, t'sé."

"À moins qu'tu veux venir à chasse avec nous," said Roger. "Pour charrier la viande."

Scratching my chin, I studied my uncles. The invitation seemed genuine, if off-hand, and I wanted to accept, but something held me back. Shaking my head, I confessed.

"I've never been hunting."

"Quoi?"

"Dad never taught me to hunt," I said.

"Baptême! Vraiment?"

"Bin, we'll have to fix that—"

"Roger, mon enfant d'chienne!" J.P. Gauthier's voice boomed across the room. He stood in the doorway and waved, his father, le vieux Gauthier, a half-step behind him, peeking around J.P.'s belly. "T'é t'encore icitte!?" J.P. waddled over toward us, his father trailing slowly. "Bin, I thought for sure you'd be gone by now," he said, and he placed his hands on his hips and smiled, teeth splitting open his round face as he looked down on us.

"Bin, we were talking about grabbing some dinner in a little bit, after seeing how Alfred was doing, t'sé," said Roger. Frank nodded beside him.

"Pas besoin de s'grouiller, là."

J.P. nodded. "Le père wanted some lunch, eh, so we popped over to the Chicken Chef on Marion, there," said J.P., and he made a show of licking his fingers. He glanced over at his dad. "Hey, 'pa, what d'you think about that chicken? What? La poule, j'dis. Wha'd'you think about it? Quessé qu't'en pense, ostie?"

Le vieux lowered himself delicately into a chair and, trembling slightly, looked up at his son. "Hein?" he said.

"La poule, crisse. Quessé qu't'en pense?"

Le vieux blinked, and worked his lips up into a word. "'Tait sèche," he said.

J.P. batted the word away, and he glanced around, and grinned in my direction. "Ah bin, Pichenotte!" he said. "You finally made it."

"J.P.," I said.

"Did you know this son of a bitch slept in his car last night?" J.P. said to Roger and Frank and began to laugh. "First thing he does this morning, I saw because I was up making coffee, you know, was take a piss with my cows. Ah bin, can you believe it? Pissing all over my fence! What a hell of a show!"

Roger chuckled and Frank threw me a quick glance.

"Isn't that what people usually do after a night of drinking?"

"Harass cows?"

"No, take a leak," said Frank.

"Sure, sure."

Roger leaned forward. "J'ai entendu you had a big party last night, J.P."

"Ah, you should have seen it, Menoncle," said J.P., and he waved his hand as though displaying some fantastic gameshow prize. "We had fireworks and a live band, and—"

"I guess nos invitations got lost in the mail, eh?"

J.P. paused and blinked, his red face growing a bit darker. "I guess so—sorry about that." He turned toward his dad and said, "Hey, 'Pa, are you ready to go?"

"Hein?"

Glancing at Frank and Roger again, J.P. threw his thumb over his shoulder. "Le vieux veut faire des traces," he said. "We should pop by Alfred's room again. Voère le beau-frère une dernière fois avant qui crève." J.P. stepped over to his dad and helped him up out of his chair.

"Salut, Menoncle," said Roger. Le vieux Gauthier turned slowly, and lifting a trembling hand, waved, until J.P. grabbed him by the elbow and led him out of the room and down the hall. We leaned forward, watching them go. Then Roger sat back and shook his head.

"Misère," he said.

"Si c'était pas parenté—" Frank trailed off and sighed. What started as a moment of repose, a quietness to gather our breath in the wake of the whirlwind that sucked the air from the room with the Gauthiers' presence, stretched into a weary, meditative silence. J.P. always did that somehow. His presence was not so much a magnetism, as a gravity well, which at the centre boomed and cracked a hot, volatile sun, and a tongue that dripped fire. Frank kicked his feet out into the aisle and stared at his boots. Roger reached into his jacket and retrieved a cellphone. He held it outstretched as he tried to make out some of the words or numbers on the screen. After a few long moments, I cleared my throat, and my uncles glanced up.

"Have you cleaned out your septic tanks yet?" I asked.

Roger blinked, pausing as though it took him a moment to register such as a wild change in the conversation, and then he nodded. "Called a guy last week," he said.

"Reason I ask is j'ai poigné une job avec mon Menoncle Joe; ma mère, son frère," I said. "Doing the odd tank when he's too busy."

"Ah bin," said Frank and he rubbed his chin. "Maybe I'll give him a call then."

"Appreciate any work," I said, but I sensed he was humouring me. Seemed a septic guy was like a barber, and after you got used to one, and built trust with them, you would rather stick by them than risk a new one. Wouldn't want to switch and then find a torn-up yard by accident, or shit on your lawn. Silence fell again, like a wet snowfall. Thick and heavy. I found it odd; Dad's brothers were usually easy-going—sometimes loud and rowdy—and to see them quiet and with-drawn felt strange. As though I'd crossed into some intimate space reserved for their grief.

After a while, Frank looked up. "So, where's your sister?" he said.

"Monique? I don't know. She must be around somewhere. Mom said she was working."

Frank nodded, and I wriggled on the waiting room chair, feeling a pinch shooting down the nerve in my leg. Toes tingling.

"Boy, J.P. makes me want to drink," I said.

"Moé itou," said Frank, and he laughed.

Roger cleared his throat. "Here come the women."

We turned and saw my mother coming down the hall with Matante Yolande and Matante Carole. Yolande was Frank and Roger's sister, and Carole was married to Roger. Frank had been divorced for a few years now, though no one could still really believe it—un catholique comme lui. Story was when he wanted to move out from the city, to a plot of land on the Seine, his wife had refused to come. She did not want to move. They tried to work it out, but in the end it came down to this irreconcilable difference: Frank had grown tired of the city, and Matante Elizabeth had grown accustomed to the city. Eventually, they agreed to part ways, and Frank moved out to the country and built himself a small home—a cabin really, no bigger than Alfred's—while she kept the house in the city. After some time apart, they made it official. Now no one talked about it; whenever Elizabeth's name came up, no one really knew what to say, or do, and so we tended to drop our eyes and stare at our shoes.

As the women approached, I stood and greeted Matante Carole, who promptly threw her arms around me and planted a wet kiss on my cheek. Carefully, I extricated myself from her grip and, with an apologetic smile, I excused myself, and as my mom and aunties and uncles started to discuss the possibility of getting some dinner together, I slipped out of the room.

Dad stood before a coffee machine down the hall, jabbing at a button repeatedly with his forefinger. Stopping at Alfred's door, I threw a quick peek inside and saw that the Gauthiers had gone, and so I stepped into the room and inched toward Alfred's bedside. My eyes kept slipping off Alfred like water, pooling on the ground. Up close, the intricate array of tubes and wires was harder to stomach. Not to mention Alfred's pale and gaunt face, his sunken eyes, and his brittle cheekbones. His long, gravel-flecked, snow-coloured hair draped wildly around his head like a knotted halo.

"Menoncle," I managed to say before the foundation holding my words together gave way. I cleared my throat, but when I tried to speak again, I discovered that my throat had locked itself tight. A frog inside had grabbed hold of my tongue and I spoke soundless words. Sighing, I grabbed Alfred's hand, careful not to knock aside any tubes or wires, and squeezed his fingers. Then, as my eyes began to sting, I angrily wiped the gathering moisture onto my sleeve. Though we knew it had only been a matter of time for Alfred—that he could not go on living forever in that little cabin of his—I found myself wholly unprepared for the reality of his end. Alfred had always been there. And it had been a comfort to imagine that he would always be there. And now confronting that crumbling fantasy, that veil crumpled in the snow, I was powerless. A dense and deep sadness filled my stomach, churning meltwaters and rivers surging over banks, flooding the land. Weeping quietly, I let the floodwaters drain from my eyes. Then, like a toddler, I wiped my face on my sleeve. "Menoncle," I said. "I've got a story to tell you once you get better."

Releasing Alfred's hand, I glanced around the room and frowned. Someone had knocked the infinity flag off the headboard and onto the ground, so I reached down and picked it up, then as I wedged the small flagpole into the flower vase, I noticed that the cigarettes were no longer on the bedside table. Kneeling, I peeked under the bed, behind the wheels, and along the electric cords running across the floor, but saw nothing. Peeking between the table and the wall, I spotted an old pen, but no cigarettes. Then, with my eyes darting like water bugs on a river, I scoured the room. At first, I could not bring myself to consider that someone would have taken them, but as I thought of who had been in here last, and I recalled J.P. Gauthier's callous bullshit in the waiting room, I wondered if he or le vieux had scooped them up on their way out. I vividly imagined J.P. knocking over the infinity flag as he pocketed the cigarettes. The shock of the idea weighed upon my chest, heavy and wet, smothering me. Falling back in the chair along the wall, I tried to think, but my thoughts kept bolting out ahead me, veering off into the unknown.

"Fuck," I mumbled. "Fuck."

Shivers cascaded down my arms and legs, a tight trembling like fishing wire pulled under by unknown pressures. I stood and began to move my arms, punching the air before me, trying to break that growing tightness in my chest. I kicked my feet out, brought my knees up to my chest, one after the other, over, and over, and my chest began to loosen, and finally like an elastic band, the heavy, wet pool of shock snapped. Warmth flooded back into me, and I found myself over by the bed again, staring down at Alfred, weeping once more.

"Motherfucker," I mumbled. And I turned aside and yanked the door open—light washed into the room—and I stepped through the doorway.

"Watch it," said Dad as I bumped into him, and he spilled coffee to the floor. "Hey!" he called out as I walked away. "Where're you going?"

"Out," I shouted. "I need cigarettes."

12.

La Vérendrye's Relief

WHAT I REALLY WANTED WAS SOMETHING TO DULL THE sharp thoughts knifing through my mind. However, when I shouldered open the door to the street, I decided to settle for a cigarette. I asked the first person I saw on the sidewalk if she had a smoke to spare.

"Pardon?" she said.

"Avez-vous une cigarette," I repeated.

"Ah, non," she said, shaking her head, walking away. "Je ne fume pas."

Grunting, I turned and looked down the sidewalk. Joe still owed me from last week and I didn't want to spend what money I had on cigarettes. Not with a broken mirror sitting inside the Buick at home. With an eye out for a smoker, I headed for the sidewalk, along Taché, toward the park down the street. Traffic rumbled around me, ripping up Goulet. The sounds grew louder as I rounded the hospital, and stared out at the Red. A stiff breeze peppered me with deadfall. I could smell the water, the mud, whiffs of raw sewage and rotting plants—a thick, pungent, sickly scent oozing through the air. Bells rang urgently and I stepped aside as a line of cyclists zipped by next to me. Sirens wailed across the river, the cries ricocheting in the gullies between buildings. Train wheels squealed and clattered in the distance and the towers across the water shimmered through the frost in the air. I felt as though I was drowning amid the flood of sights and sounds. Sunlight cracked through the sky, shattered, and reconstituted by shrouds of falling crystals; ice and snow floated softly above, melting as it fell, evaporating before it hit the ground.

Spotting a man sitting on a small bench overlooking the river, I paused on the sidewalk and called out to him. "Buddy, bum a smoke?"

The man glanced over his shoulder and glared.

"Get a job."

"Well, fuck you too," I said and kept walking as he hurled insults. I spun around, walking backwards, and threw him the finger. "Hey, fuck face," I yelled. "Suce ma bine!" The man stood, and still shouting, thrust one arm like an uppercut underneath the other. I spun, stabbed my arms up into the air, and waved my middle-fingers.

After a few steps, I darted across Taché, toward the park. Someone waved from a bench and shouted. The sun dropped low behind me, falling into the city, and shadows erupted from the trees, stretching across the dry, brown grass. I briefly wondered who knew me here as I returned the woman's wave, and kept walking up Taché, but the woman at the bench waved again, more briskly, and then I heard my name on the wind. Stopping, I squinted in the fading light and tried to make out her face.

"Fuck sakes, Rich! Come over here!"

"Monique?"

My sister waved again. She was sitting at a picnic table in the park, under a pair of big elms. As I neared, I saw she was in her nursing clothes, white shoes, and hair back in a ponytail. There was a half-eaten sandwich covered in Saran Wrap on the table. Monique glared at me as I sat across from her.

"What the hell is the matter with you?" she said before my ass hit the bench.

"What?"

She thrust her hand toward the bench across the street. "Were you trying to pick a fight with that guy?"

"You saw that?"

"Half the fucking street saw that."

"Bin, là," I said, dropping my eyes onto the table, finger tracing the outline of someone's carving, a rough heart around some faded initials. "Got a bit out of hand, I guess." I looked up at my sister and shrugged.

Snorting, Monique grabbed her sandwich, flipped the Saran Wrap off, and took a bite. Her eyes drilled into my head as she chewed. I recoiled slightly, leaned back, and stretched my arms up over my head.

"Look," I said. "I'm sorry. I just saw Alfred."

Monique took a sip from a water bottle she produced from the bag at her side. "Yeah, I hear you. Just don't go picking fights."

"I know," I said. "That was dumb."

Monique nodded, and took another bite of her sandwich.

"So, how come you're not in there?" I said.

She frowned, and holding her hand to her lips, spoke out of the side of her mouth, "I'm on a break."

"I mean up with Alfred," I said, chucking my thumb over my shoulder.

Monique chewed some more, then swallowed. "I'm working today."

"But you're on a break."

With her sandwich still in her mouth, Monique paused and pierced me with another look. She put her food down. "Are you messing with me? I saw him earlier, before you got here."

"Oh," I said, and I shook my head. "No, not messing with you."

"Good."

"Hey, Mon. Do you have a cigarette?"

Her eyebrow crept up, and she studied me.

"Mom cut you off?"

"No," I shook my head.

She snorted, then pulled a pack of smokes from her handbag and tossed it to me. I flicked a pair of cigarettes out, held them in the air, and raised my eyebrows. Monique rolled her eyes, but nodded, so I slipped one behind my ear, for Alfred, and stuck the other between my lips.

"Marsi."

"You owe me," Monique said, mumbling over the food in her mouth.

"I'm good for it," I said, tossing the pack into her handbag. I lit, and took a drag from the cigarette, then blew the smoke upwards, through the branches.

"You know those will kill you," said Monique.

"Okay there, nurse."

Monique smiled and reached into her handbag. She plucked a smoke from her pack, then held it out towards me, and I pressed the red tip of my cigarette against hers.

"How are you, Rich?"

"I'm okay," I shrugged. "Started working with Joe; 'til I find something better."

"I heard. That's good."

We sat for a time without speaking, smoking our cigarettes, and listening to the city. I could fall asleep, I thought. And I closed my eyes and focused on the distant clattering. I could tell a train was winding around the ballpark down the river, coming into Union Station. Wheels screeching. Always the screeching. Such a familiar sound. The elms above trembled in the cool autumn breeze, their mostly bare branches knocking together in a rattle-clatter of spoons. A car alarm wailed in the alley. There was a constant, insect-hum of traffic. The rattle of carts and the smell of bison shit. In the distance, rhythmic chopping. A squadron of helicopters. It was all too much.

"You ever notice that statue?" said Monique, she dabbed her cigarette on the table, then pointed with the smouldering tip. Opening my eyes, I followed her fingers toward the centre of the park, and landed upon an old copper statue that looked like some weird pop-out comic book frame against a wall of stone: three men in relief, one holding a cross, looking at the horizon. A third kneeling beneath the two.

"Who's that?" I asked.

"La Vérendrye," said Monique. "The great explorer," she added, with a snort.

I studied the statue for a moment and sniffed. "He doesn't look all that."

"I think it's the crowd," said Monique. "See how there's a priest pointing the way? And that Native guy kneeling in front of him. Like the statue itself seems to admit that without these other guys, this bozo wouldn't know his way to own his ass."

Laughing, I looked closer.

"Funny that the guy who actually knows the way is barely in the picture—"

"Like an afterthought," said Monique.

"—with these other two guys towering over him."

"Some bullshit there, eh?" Monique stared at the statue. "Undermines its own narrative. Like, right there, in their own story, is evidence of how it's all built on a lie—"

"It's a shitty statue," I interrupted.

Monique glanced at me and nodded. She rolled her sandwich wrap into a ball and tossed it into her handbag, then lifted herself off the bench. "Well," she said. "I gotta get back to work."

"Okay," I said, looking up at her.

"See you in there in a bit?"

"I don't know," I said. "I might pop by Becky's."

Somehow, facing Becky, and asking her about the fishing reel seemed easier than going back into Alfred's hospital room. My chest tightened at the thought.

Monique stared at me for a moment, and then nodded. "Okay, well. Take care," she said. She turned, and started toward the hospital and I looked over at the statue again, letting my eyes wander over its dark shapes. The more I looked at it, the more it annoyed me. I felt like punching La Vérendrye in the nose.

"Oh, and Rich!" Monique yelled. I glanced over my shoulder as she retraced a few steps, then stopped and pointed down the road toward Provencher. "Watch out for the army!"

"What?"

"The army," she repeated.

"Ok-ayy," I said.

"I'm serious," she shouted.

"What?"

She walked back over. "I said I'm serious. Watch out for the army. They're training now, in the city. Bunch of them going around with guns and tanks."

"Are you fucking kidding?"

Monique grimaced. "You didn't hear about this? Operation Charging Bison—if you can believe that shit. They set up a command post overtop Le Canot—sniper nests and all. Fucking go check it out if you don't believe me. Just be careful; they might forget why they're here and start terrorizing your Métis ass."

13.

He Was a Soldier Once

DAD SERVED IN THE ARMY BEFORE HE MET MOM.
We didn't know a whole lot about it, since he hardly ever mentioned
his time there, but we knew he'd been in Europe during the Cold War.
He had bounced around between Germany, France, and Cyprus. He
kept photos of his army days in an old album in his bedroom, where
Monique and I had been reluctant to venture as kids. He brought them
out once or twice to show us pictures of himself in camouflage fatigues,
streaks of dark paint around his eyes, combat rifle slung over his shoulder, and his young face etched with determination and bravado. There
were photos of men in barracks, sprawled on identically made beds.
There was one of Dad atop a tank, clutching a six pack of beer. Another
of Dad curling his bicep, duck lips kissing the air. He had presented
these photos to us without comment, without a story to string them
together. What he did talk about, at length, was the motorcycle he'd
bought in Germany, and how he'd rode it across the Old World.

Monique tried to reconcile Dad's past with her vision of the world. She recast his time in Europe as an "anti-imperialist" revenge fantasy, as if he was part of some righteous, Native-led, peacekeeping brigade that kept, she said, that "decrepit Old World's perpetually-warring factions from murdering each other."

"An anti-what?" I asked. We sat on torn-up lawn chairs in the back yard under the oak trees. A small fire crackled in a pit at our feet. Monique was rolling a joint. She glanced up at me and shook her head.

"Anti-imperial," she said.

She painted a picture for me of a world in which there was no war, no racism, no rich or poor, no colonialism—

"Like that song by Lenin," I said.

"Uh, yeah. 'Imagine.'"

"Imagine what?"

"That's the song."

"Oh, that one!"

We smoked that joint for a while, then I frowned. "So," I began. "How does this guy go from leading a revolution in Russia, to fronting a hippy-folk rock band in Britain in the 1960s? I mean, shit, wouldn't he have been like eighty years old or something?"

"Fuck sakes, Rich."

Laughing, I threw myself back in the chair, avoiding Monique's fist as she reached over and tried to punch me. The chair teetered, then toppled backwards onto the gravel and knocked the wind from my lungs.

"Serves you right," said Monique.

I lay there for a time, looking up at the stars through the branches and the leaves. I heard Monique sigh. She carefully tipped her chair back, lowering herself next to me, and together we stared up through the trees at the powder of stars dusting the sky. Interrupted by the occasional wink of a satellite. Embers rising, clambering upward like the dead toward some heaven.

"I'm going to get bugs in my hair," Monique complained.

"What hair? It's shorter than mine!"

She passed me the joint, barely the size of a Tic-Tac now, and said. "It might be out."

I tried hauling on it, but got nothing, so I flicked it toward the firepit.

"You know, Rich. You're probably right. It is a fantasy," said Monique. She shifted on the ground, and pulled a stone out from underneath her back, and then, briefly checking to see if it was a bone, she tossed it into the bush. "It's all just the same old bullshit over and over again. Same old fucking white guys thinking they know best."

"Dad was just a poor boy, with a big family," I sang, then grunted as Monique elbowed me in the side.

Then she started to laugh. She sat up, wrapped her arms around her knees, and glanced at me. "You know, you make a good point."

"What point?" I said. "I was being an ass."

"I know, and a big one too. Still. Even a broken clock's right twice a day."

"Huh?"

She leaned toward me and planted a kiss on my forehead. I grunted and rubbed her spittle from my skin. "What the hell, Mon?"

She lifted herself off the ground. "I'll see you, Rich."

* * *

I sat on the bench in the park for a time, staring at La Vérendrye. After a while, I flicked my cigarette butt at the statue and stood. I glanced at the hospital, then north toward the museum and la Cathédrale, getting my bearings. Becky lived over past the collège, rented the top floor of a house. It was only a short a walk, so I figured I'd pop in, say hello.

The sun had dropped behind the buildings across the river, turning the sky the colour of young fire. Leaves crunched underfoot as I walked. Armoured vehicles clanged. I saw a column of men in fatigues curling around a corner up the road—those soldiers Monique had mentioned. Someone shouted. Others yelled. I veered away from the noise, taking a side road instead toward Becky's. I wondered if Dad had ever done anything like this. Thinking back, I realized Alfred had been the one to tell me the most about Dad's time in the army. After he left the forces, Dad spent a few months living with Alfred, remembering how to be in the world.

"Did you ever kill anyone?" Monique once asked Dad when we all still lived together.

Dad coughed, choking on his tea; he shook his head vigorously and with a wounded look said, "How could you think that?"

"Well, you were in the army. That's what they do there, no?" Monique had sharpened her tongue to a fine point; she could have pierced leather if she had tried. Mom tended to stay out of these arguments, unwilling to take sides, ignoring Dad whenever he glanced to her for support.

"The army helps people too, Monique," said Dad.

She snorted and said. "A few good deeds don't make a saint."

* * *

The morning after Dad dropped me off at Alfred's for breaking a boy's nose in school, I awoke to music. Bernie Elastic and his Rubber Band. Fiddle music burst from the little boombox in the kitchen, causing the cutlery that Alfred had set out for breakfast to rattle on the table. The walls juddered and the picture frames trembled above me as I curled up underneath the bedsheet on the small cot in the living room.

"Es-tu réveillé, mon homme? On a d'l'ouvrage en masse aujourd'hui."

Alfred wanted to build a new woodshed, just a small, covered space where he could keep firewood out of the rain. The old one sat in a half foot of water in the backyard, swallowed by the lake growing out of the bush behind his cabin. I peeked out from under the bedsheet. Alfred was dumping sausages into a frying pan again. He seemed happier this morning, perhaps cheered by Monique's visit last night, when she had dropped off my clothes, stayed for dinner, and amused him with her quick tongue. That earlier surfacing of sadness was now gone. At least, it was well-hidden, submerged. I began to doubt my memory of yesterday. I could not imagine Alfred in that way, distraught and broken. He was the man who sang his death away while he crawled out from the bush with a shattered leg. The man who through delirium had found his way to warmth and comfort. I would not imagine him as broken. I wondered if this was why I hadn't mentioned it to Monique.

"Okay, mon homme. L'déjeuner est presque prêt."

Alfred dumped the cooked sausages onto a pair of plates. A bowl of scrambled eggs and a small tower of toast were on the table. Kicking off the bedsheet, I swung my legs over the side of the cot and dressed.

We ate quickly enough, stuffing our mouths while the boombox blared with fast square-dancing and fiddle-jig tunes. The sun was barely visible through the windows, still half-covered by the trees. Alfred poured me a mug of tea and we sipped slowly, waiting for steam to dissipate. We took our mugs outside and set them on a small table behind the cabin, next to the shed where Alfred hung and bled deer he hunted. It had started as a small lean-to he'd built against the back of the cabin, with a thick frame and a four-by-six crossbeam, but he had added walls and doors over the years, shelves and drawers, and two big opposing countertops, until the shed grew larger than the cabin. Inside, he kept an old trike and his snow machine, which he moved out of the way whenever he needed to bleed an animal. There was a pair of sawhorses in the corner, and he got me to fetch them into the yard. We kicked snow out of the way and drove the sawhorses' legs into the ground to form a solid base. Then we fetched two-by-fours from the tarp-covered pile of wood by the treeline, our feet growing damp in snow and melt-water. The ground sunk beneath our feet, oozing water.

The air was chilly, but after moving the wood, I felt warm, and was starting to sweat, so I began to take off my jacket, but Alfred told me to keep it on, so I wouldn't catch a cold. He told me to drink my tea, since it had probably cooled down enough by now. Taking a few sips of it, I grimaced—Alfred always made it too sweet—and I surveyed the yard. I had grown familiar with this patch of land over the years, ever since my parents had dropped me off for a weekend. I had been six or seven years old the first time and Monique had a ringette tournament in Grand Forks, and I guess my parents thought I would be bored, or a pain in the ass to watch. After they drove away, and I began to cry, Alfred took me by the hand and led me around his little cabin, showing me his yard. He took the time to name everything and explain to me what these objects were and why he had them. Each had a story, a purpose.

Sipping on my tea, I glanced at the cabin and at the weathervane on the roof. It was still there. Alfred had told me how it had been a gift, a belated birthday present from his late brother, Alexandre, when he had gone overseas to serve in the war. He had fought contre les Allemands. Alfred too had tried to join the war, but after the doctors had looked him over in the recruitment office, they said his feet were too flat and they told him to go back home. When Alfred hanged his head in shame and disappointment, the doctor slapped him on the shoulder and told him to buck up—the country needed farmers too. But the land between Richer and Ste. Geneviève was no good for farming, too saturated with gravel, covered in scrub oak and thick underbrush, and swollen with swamp water to do much of anything except ranch. Alfred never became a farmer.

"Richard," Alfred said. "Viens m'aider, icitte."

I set the mug down and walked over to Alfred, who had brought out an old circular saw and placed the two-by-fours on the sawhorses. He'd already marked his cuts with a pencil. I held the wood down as he ran the saw and sawdust flew up and swirled around us.

It didn't take us long—Alfred had it all planned out already—to build a small, open-faced woodshed. Alfred wiped his brow and grinned; then he threw his arm over my shoulder and said, "J'apprécie ton aide, mon homme."

"Yeah," I said.

He glanced at the old woodshed, now sitting in water. "You know," he said. "It's funny. Ton père helped me build that old one. Quand yé revenu d'l'armée."

"Really?"

"Yé resté pour un temps, you know. While he figured out what he wanted to do. J'pense qu'y'était un peu perdu, t'sé. Comme un cheval dans une tempête."

Not knowing what the hell a horse in a storm was like, I frowned. "What do you mean?"

"Comme y'était, peut-être, un peu épeuré," Alfred said, and glanced at me; and his eyes flicked away. He sighed and shook his head. "T'sé qu'y'a vu des morts hein? Friends killed."

I swallowed a rising uneasiness, and looked at Alfred. "What happened?"

"'Ché pas exactement, mon gars. Mais ça lui a affecté, sans doute. Biggest change was his self-discipline. And that was for the best. T'sé y'en avait d'la misère avant, hein, keeping that temper in check? Oh, y'essayait. Y'essayait. For a while, ç'avait d'l'air comme y'achevait. Mais, de temps en temps, tout d'un coup, bang," Alfred clapped his hands. "Quetchose l'écoeure, puis y jette des coups de poings dans face d'un gars." Alfred reached into his pants for a handkerchief and he wiped his brow. The sun had gained some strength, and snow was melting quickly around us. Despite his efforts, Dad's temper had flared, burst like an elastic band, when pushed or pulled too far. The army cured Dad of his temper, had taught him to control it, but at what cost? Alfred shrugged and shook his head, "Anyways, là," he slapped me on the shoulder, and pointed to the old woodshed, "You'd better start hauling that wood before it floats away."

While Alfred went inside to make another pot of tea, I began moving firewood across the yard. The wood was a mixture of ash, aspen, oak, some pine, and Manitoba maple. It was mostly dry, light enough to load a half-dozen pieces in my arms. The pieces had been cut down to about sixteen inches—typical cord wood. After a few trips, and with sweat streaming down the sides of my face, I removed my jacket and tossed it aside. Alfred came around the corner with a fresh pot of tea, glanced at my jacket on the bench and grunted, but said nothing. He sat, poured himself a mug, and watched as I continued to haul wood.

"Good job, mon homme," he shouted and sipped noisily. "There's more tea icitte."

Dumping another armload onto the ground in front of the new shed, I glanced at Alfred and squinted. There was something sticking out over his shoulder. Lifting my hand to block the sun from my eyes, I peered at him.

"What do you have there, Menoncle?"

"Oh, ça?" said Alfred, and he twisted slowly in his chair, and then swung a rifle from his shoulder. "C'est ma *grande* carabine!" he said and grinned; he waited for me to laugh, and after a long moment where I just stared at him, he frowned. "*La grande*," he said.

"Ok-ay," I said, not catching the reference.

"Tabarouette," he said and shook his head. "J'pensais qu'on pourrait avwayr un p'chi peu d'fun après avwayr mouvé l'bois, pis 'tchiré la carabine."

"Sounds good," I said, then, dropping my eyes and kicking at a tuft of grass sticking out from the snow, I admitted I didn't know how to shoot a rifle.

"Djis-quoé?"

"Dad never taught me."

"Tabarnak," said Alfred. He ambled over, lifted the rifle up, and held it out for me to see. "Tchiens," he said. "Prends-le."

Hefting the rifle, I brought it to my eye, as I thought I should, but Alfred grunted, and he placed his hand on the barrel, lowering it so that it pointed to the ground. He told me never raise it except when ready to shoot, then told me how to raise it to my eye and hold it steady—how to breathe before firing. He pointed out the various parts, naming them, and their purpose, and then told me how to care for them.

Then he taught me how to shoot.

14.

A Second-Story Apartment Suite in Saint-Boniface

"OH FUCK, THAT'S IT. RIGHT THERE," BECKY MOANED. I grunted, willing-away an itch, and like a pig snuffling in its trough, tongue sawing her in half, I drove my nose into Becky's pubes. Her thighs clamped around my ears as I slipped my fingers inside her. Grabbing a handful of my hair, she held my head down. We'd barely said hello before our clothes came off.

Atop a landing overlooking an overgrown backyard in Saint-Boniface, I had knocked at the door of Becky's second-story suite where music wormed through gaps in the doorframe and the windows. Horns blared over acoustic guitars, and moaning musical saws. A straining voice howled strange lyrics. Finally, Becky answered the knock, swinging the door open, and stared. Her mouth worked through a few soundless words before she said, "What the shit, Rich?"

"I got your fishing reel."

Now my head was buried in her crotch, her thighs a vice-grip. The voice on the record player wailed about his love of Jesus Christ.

"Fuck, fuck, fuck," Becky moaned. Her nails dug into my scalp, twisting hair from the roots. Breathing in her scent, filling my nostrils like a swimmer surfacing after a near-eternity underwater, I felt more than comfortable, sustained. There was something serene, intoxicatingly familiar within her folds—a well-trodden path, from the house to the well, that you could follow with your eyes closed, where a cool wind tickled your skin, drew hairs on end, and sucked away your breath—and an electrifying, life-giving intensity to the touch. Becky and I had been together, on and off, for years, and when she'd upped and left town, and moved to the city, it was as though a part of myself had somehow gone with her. Though I'd visited her here, occasionally, I had never quite felt the same. It wasn't only that that physical distance between us had infected our love, like black mold creeping in the walls of the edifice of our relationship, but that the distance had gradually tempered and re-shaped that part of myself that she carried so that it no longer seemed to fit with the rest of me. Whenever I saw her again, I could not reconcile the me that remained out in the country with the me that I was when I was with her. But now, with my tongue driving Becky to ecstasy, the touch of our skin firing electric in our minds, that distance collapsed, and the heat melded the pieces of me back together. I realized how much I had missed her. It wasn't just this act of love. What I missed was her presence, her being, that sharp sense of self that she drew out of me.

Tears sprang from my eyes, running down my cheeks, and I dropped my gaze from her eyes into her mound, where I drove my face deeper, and pressed my lips to hers. Becky moaned and shuddered, then with the tips of her feet began to pry the pants off my hips.

Twisting, and swinging her legs up and over so that she straddled me, Becky took me into her mouth. On the wine-stained carpet of her second-story apartment suite in Saint-Boniface, we consumed one another.

Afterwards, as we lay together, atop a small afghan Becky had pulled off the couch, we wondered at our naked bodies, like old maps of terrain we'd once traversed, echoes of homeland, tracing lines with our fingertips. I lay my head in her lap, and looked up at her, touching the red scars on her pale skin. Becky had explained once, how years ago, as a child, when visiting family up north in the Interlake, she had chased some of her older cousins around a ranch—I guess they had wanted nothing to do with her, and tried to get away—jumping over fence. Becky followed and had gotten tangled in the barbwire. The sharp teeth had bit into her, and torn her open in multiple spots; doctors sewed her skin shut, and it healed after a fashion, but the physical and the emotional scars of that event remained.

"Don't," said Becky, laying her hand atop mine.

"I'm sorry," I said, and I sat up and shuffled over. Leaning against the couch, I wrapped an arm around her, and she dropped her head on my shoulder. We stared into space, breathing in each other's sweaty, spent scent. The music blared and echoed; the singer half-shouted about an airplane dropping ash from the sky.

Becky began to shake, and I looked down at her with worry, then realized that she was laughing. She lifted her head and looked at me.

"Do you remember the first time we did this?"

"What?" I said.

"This!" she said, and I shrugged. "You told me you wanted to perform Cunning Lingus, and I thought you meant to recite romantic love poetry or some shit, but then before I even knew what the hell was happening, you yanked my pants down and slid your tongue up my noosh!"

"Up your what?"

Becky laughed again.

"My 'noosh," she said. "I learned that word from a girl in my Native Studies class. She's from north of the city, you know." She waved her arm over her head, northward. "St. Ambroise," she said. "Along Lake Manitoba."

"Ok-ay," I said. "But what the hell does that mean?"

"Oh," she said, and grinned. She playfully slid her hand down along her body, curling her fingers up in between her legs. "This is my pinoosh."

"I—uh, I see," I said, and somehow, despite what we had just done, the brazen inhibition caused my face to grow red.

"And this, Pichenotte," Becky laughed, reaching over to grab my penis, "Is your pisett."

"Ah," I said, sucking in my breath. "So, this—" I slid my hand through her bushy mound, slipping in between her thighs, to rest my fingers along her warm, wet folds, "—is a 'noosh?"

Becky edged her hip against me, her grip tightening as I grew between her fingers.

"And this," my muscle pulsed in her grip. "Is a pisett?"

"Ton boute," she said, slipping her tongue into my mouth, and she drew my tongue out like a spoon between her lips.

Her hand drifted up, and down—the music played, the voice moaning over the speakers.

"What language—is that?" I asked, my fingers in turn delving between her legs, peeling her like a mandarin.

"That's—" she shuddered. "Michif, boy."

* * *

Becky was Métis on her dad's side, though she'd grown up never really knowing much about it. He was from up north somewhere, the Interlake, and he'd moved to the city in search of work, where he had met Becky's mom. Becky's mom was Polish, and German, and French, and yet she spoke only English. They lived in the city for a few years, around Wolseley, before they tired of neighbours siphoning gasoline from their vehicles at night, and they moved out into the country. Becky's grandparents passed when she was young, and her dad had never been all that close with his cousins, and so visits up north grew infrequent, reserved for the odd wedding, or funeral. That time with the barbwire just made things worse. Becky never learned French—she went to the English school—and so we met at Fritz's bar, where she started bussing tables out of high school. It was a few years before we hooked up. I'd had a few girlfriends, women I fooled around with, but nothing serious. The woman behind the bar at Fritz's had caught my eye, and for a time was the reason I kept going back. Becky was cleaning tables one night, and she started chatting me up. She knew I was French, and was trying to learn a bit of French herself. At first, it was mostly so she could speak with other locals at the bar—half the town was French after all. She also had distant family in France, on her mom's side, that she thought about visiting one day.

"No shit?" I said, tossing back the last few drops of beer before handing her the empty.

She tucked it in the large plastic bin she carried on her hip. "One day, I'll go," she said.

So, I did what I could to help her. I taught her the essentials: Tabarnak, d'Calice, d'Ostie, de Sacrament, Trou d'Cul, d'Enfant d'Chienne, Suce ma Bine, Guidoune.

"Beautiful," she said. "What does that mean?"

I laughed, and apologized, and taught her how to pronounce my name. She loved the way it came off the tongue. Reee-shaarrd. She struggled to roll her Rs and always added the D at the end. I thought it was funny. She made such an effort.

"You like the D, eh?" I laughed and she'd grow red in the face and punch my arm.

We'd slip out together on her breaks and share a cigarette, huddling close for warmth, our heads knocking together as we shivered in the cold.

"Crisse, y fait frette," I'd say and she'd study the way my lips moved.

"Frette," she'd repeat. Once, after I tossed a spent smoke, she reached up and kissed me, and I wrapped my arms around her waist. "J'aime ta langue," she said.

"You love my tongue?" I laughed.

After a while, I found I kept returning to Fritz's not to eye up the woman tending bar, but to see Becky, and as she came to clear my table of empties, I grabbed her hand and confessed to her that I couldn't stop thinking about her. She blushed and glanced away, tossing the empties in a plastic bin. Then, pausing as she stepped away, she looked at me and smiled. On her break, we ran to the Buick and fooled around in the back until someone knocked on the foggy window and said the tables were crowded with empties.

Becky was sweet, smart, and funny. She had grand plans that I couldn't understand—she wanted to see the world, visit museums and art galleries and distant family, she wanted to meet new people from elsewhere, anywhere that was not here, who didn't think that the epitome of a good time was a 12-pack by the river—and she rolled her eyes at my ignorance.

"What's wrong with a 12-pack?"

"Nothing, Rich. But there's got to be more, no?"

"I don't know," I said about her plans. "Seems extravagant."

"Backpacking Europe is not extravagant, Rich."

When she came back from Europe, we got serious. The other people orbiting our lives, those few others we sometimes fooled around with, dropped away. And for a time, I thought we were happy.

* * *

We washed up after we'd made love on the floor again, and as we dressed, Becky offered me a beer and a smoke. "Fuck it," I said, and accepted. We crawled out through the window onto the small roof over the porch and sat overlooking the street. Becky lit a smoke while I twisted the metal caps off a pair of pale ales.

"Getting fancy," I said, looking at the label. "Fort Garry, eh?"

"Better than that shit you drink," she said, between puffs.

"I drink anything."

"Exactly," said Becky.

Snorting, I lifted my elbow, tipped my arm back, then snapped my fingers and sent the cap flying into the street where it bounced on the asphalt between parked cars.

"Rich," said Becky. "Stop that."

Blinking, I glanced at her.

"We're not in the country," she said.

"No shit."

We sat there atop the roof, amid the dying canopy, and smoked. The music had looped around. I lay back on the shingles, leaves crunching under my weight, and I stared up through the thin clouds at the growing pinpricks of light above—mostly satellites, this time of evening. Dark pinks and purples oozed like syrup across the sky.

Becky tapped her cigarette and ash fluttered onto the shingles and into the eavestroughs. She pulled her knees to her chest, and wrapped her arms around her legs. Then she looked over at me and frowned.

"What are you thinking?" I said.

"Just wondering what you're planning."

I shook my head. "No plans."

"Not tonight—I mean. I have work to do still. Trying to write a paper. Still not used to it, you know, and, well," she drew on her cigarette, "Fucking pain."

"Yeah?" I said, and sat up. "How's school going?"

"It's hard," she said. "I'm so much older than everyone else. It's a bit strange," she tipped her beer back and swallowed a few sips. "You know I'm a mature student?"

"Immature?"

"Right?" She shook her head. "No, it's hard. But I like it."

"Of course, you do," I said, and laughed. "I mean, shit. You fucking went to Europe, for how long? By yourself too. This is nothing. Christ. I've never even left the fucking country."

"I asked you to come."

"I know."

Becky flicked her nails on the bottle, a quick and nervous rhythm, and looked over at me. "Why didn't you come?"

I would have said I had been broke, but at the time I had a decent job. Enough for a trip if I hadn't smoked and drank most of it. Truth was the idea of leaving the country was paralyzing. I glanced over, and shrugged.

Becky sipped at her beer and looked down at the street. Then she swung her head left and right. "Where's your car?"

"At home," I said, and then I told her about Alfred, and how I spent the morning looking for my dad to tell him about the stroke. How I had almost been killed twice. The truck. The tree. And how I'd finally gotten a ride into the city with my parents.

"Jesus," said Becky. She grabbed my head and brushed my hair away, focusing in on the cut my mother had cleaned earlier. "I hadn't even noticed."

"Well," I said. "In fairness, you weren't really looking there."

Becky snorted, and released my head. "So, they're at the hospital now?"

"Maybe," I shrugged.

"And you were here—doing that?" Becky tossed her thumb toward her window.

"Alfred's in a coma," I said. "My folks are probably over at the Chicken Chef."

"Jesus, Rich."

I grabbed her hand. "Listen, Becks."

She turned and stared.

"I had to see you. I mean. I got your fishing reel this morning, for chrissakes, and when I saw Alfred and everything started to spin, like—nothing was right anymore. You know?"

She sighed, and took her hand from mine, then slipped her arm around my shoulder.

* * *

When Becky moved to the city, she asked me to help her out. So, we packed her things up in cardboard boxes and suitcases, and stacked them up in the back of her dad's pickup truck. We squeezed in her dresser, bed frame, desk, and her night tables as if playing a game of Tetris. Then we strapped her mattress atop the pile with bungee cords and yellow poly rope. I tossed a couple things into my Buick—a garbage bag of clothes, her acoustic guitar, and milk crates full of books—and I followed her dad down the highway. Wind caught the mattress, lifting it into the air like loose shingles on a roof. One of the bungee cords snapped and the mattress rose higher. The wind began to drag it out from under the remaining cords and ropes, and with visions of the mattress flying onto the highway, causing a multivehicle, I raced up, moving the Buick alongside the truck, and honked. Becky's dad looked over and I pointed to the box. He slammed his brakes, skidding to a stop along the shoulder.

"Good eye, Rich," he said after I'd parked and walked back to help re-attach the mattress. He showed me the frayed end of the bungee cord. "Never saw one of these snap like that before."

Becky pulled rope through a welded ring in the box and tossed it over the mattress to her dad. He looped it through a second ring, then tossed the rope across again, toward me, so I could attach it next to the tailgate. Becky sidled up to me and planted a wet one on my cheek. Then we drove into the city without another problem, and carried her things up into the apartment suite. I sat around afterwards, with her and her dad, and we shared a pizza and had a couple beers, then her dad left, and Becky and I lay on her mattress and shared a joint. She opened the window and we blew the smoke out through the thick elm canopy. I asked why she'd chosen to live in Saint-Boniface. She'd been accepted to the U of M—half-way across town.

"You're not even on the right side of the river, here," I said.

Becky shrugged. "Reminds me of home," she said.

"How's that?"

"Half the folk around here are French people who don't speak French anymore," she said, and smiled as I frowned. She laughed and shook her head. "No, I'm kidding." She stared out the bedroom window, at the canopy of leaves overtop the backyard. "No, there's just something here I like," she said. "Like, this is where it all started, you know. At least, where things coalesced." Becky shrugged as I stared up at her. I didn't know what she meant. "This place is full of history, Rich. I like that—besides," she said, grinning suddenly. "My cousin, Jeremy, owns the place and he's renting the top floor cheap."

"Now the truth comes out," I laughed, and pulled her down onto the mattress.

I'd popped in to visit her a few times since, but these times grew further and further apart, until finally long weeks, that turned into months, passed without seeing each other. I visited once when she had company, a few kids from one of her classes, and they were working on a poster board about land treaties or some shit, and I sat awkwardly in the corner, rolling a joint everyone, even Becky, refused to come outside and smoke with me.

When I came back upstairs, eyes red and heavy, Becky made a point of telling her friends that I was Métis too. They looked up from the table, as though they wanted me to say something, and I grunted and slipped into the kitchen to grab a beer from the refrigerator, then I crawled out onto the roof and left them to work in peace.

After they left, Becky came onto the roof and sat next to me.

"What was that?"

"What?" I said.

"That."

"You mean how you blindsided me?"

"Blindsided?" said Becky. "I just thought you might want to say something. Share a story about your family or—"

"It's none of their fucking business, Becks," I snapped, and she blinked and leaned back, away from me. Truth was, I didn't know what to say. I didn't have a story to share. Only tattered bits of truth and rumours. Like Dad's army photos. Pieces without a story. Monique knew more than I did about our family's history—she was the one pushing me to get my card. Alfred had a few stories, but I didn't know what made them Métis. Where was that line between the French and the Métis who'd grown up together, neighbours, who'd married each other, over the years, families intertwining like threads in a fucking sash? I didn't want to start figuring it out in front of some randos in a second-story apartment suite in Saint-Boniface. I glanced at Becky. "Why don't you tell them your story?"

Becky sighed, twisting her sun-coloured hair slowly in between her fingers. "I did," she said. "I don't think they believed me."

* * *

Train cars clattered down the street, the sound of their passing washing over the house. I glanced toward Provencher, but couldn't see.

"Did you know rue Des Meurons is named after Swiss mercenary soldiers?" said Becky.

"You writing another history paper?"

Becky shrugged. I went to sip my beer, and discovered the bottle was empty, and I fought the urge to chuck it into the street. Instead, I began to peel the label, rolling bits of paper between my thumb and forefinger, then flicked the little balls into the yard.

"Monique says the army is in town, training or some shit," I said.

"Yeah," said Becky. "It's fucked up. I saw a bunch of them in front of the old post office the other day, crouching against the wall like they were under fire or something, fucking rifles up and pointed at the street. One of them was lying there, moaning like he'd really been hit. Fucking weird, I tell you."

"Do you have anything stronger?" I said, and showed her my empty bottle.

Becky glanced at me, then crawled back into the house. She reappeared, after a moment, with a bottle of Jack and a joint tucked over her ear.

"Here," she said. "Take it. I don't want any."

"You've got work to do," I said, grabbing the whiskey from her outstretched hand. I spun the cap off, and took a chug.

"That's right."

Wiping my lips, I said. "Don't let me stop you."

"Well, it's kind of hard with you sitting here."

"Oh," I said. "Guess this isn't a good time for you."

"Don't do that. Not now."

"I didn't ask for this, Becks. With my Menoncle, and—"

"Don't you blame him," Becky snapped, and I recoiled. "This is always about you," she said. "I just—I can't."

"What the hell does that mean?"

Becky glared at the shingles between her knees for a while, then glanced up, and leveled her eyes on me. "I can't believe you're making me say it. Fuck sakes. I mean, it's time to fish or cut bait, Rich."

Gripping the bottle of Jack, I tipped it back, and let it spill down my throat.

"I thought when you showed up and mentioned that fishing reel—fuck that was so long ago already—that it meant you'd finally decided to come. But no. You're just popping by, and then taking off again, aren't you? No. I can't have you coming around whenever you want like this, not anymore—hold it," she said, lifting a hand to cut me off as I began to splutter, "—just let me finish. I want more than that. I need more than that, Rich. What the hell happened to that guy I met at Fritz's? The guy who was always up for something, eh? I want more for you! So, either you're in, or—" She cleared her throat, the words caught there.

"I—" Squeezing my eyes, I fought a wave of dark heat. "Do you want to get married or something?"

Becky frowned. "Are you really asking me that?"

"Well—I don't know. I don't mean now, Becks. Like, maybe some day."

"Then, maybe some day," she said.

I nodded.

"Do you?"

I tipped the bottle back again and Becky grunted.

"I see."

"I didn't say anything," I said.

"You didn't have to, Rich." She dropped her eyes onto the shingles.

Sliding closer, I tried to put my arm around her, but she shrugged and sloughed me away, then she lifted eyes—I could see in the growing dark that they were red, wet—and with her chin, she pointed to the street.

"I think you should go, Rich."

15.

When the Waters Broke Loose

THOUGHTS SWIRLED LIKE RIVER EDDIES IN MY HEAD AS I drifted away from Becky's. I stumbled down that gradual, almost imperceptible slope toward the river. The Cathedral rose to my left, its old, fire-scarred limestone walls glowing yellow in the gathering dark. Like a moth to flame, I felt drawn to it. I climbed the steps into the courtyard, and stood overlooking the cemetery that stretched outward, toward Taché. Riel's grave sat there, in the centre of a short parapet of stone. Lépine's. Provencher's. Alfred had once told me a story about the big flood of 1950 and how the cemetery had saved the city. The dikes around old Saint-Boniface had been built too short for the record levels of water that spring. As the waters rose, the dikes sagged and leaked and threatened to give way. Finally, as water lapped the dike's edge, and with no crest in sight, the men holding back the river went to ask the Bishop for help. They needed dirt. At first, he refused, unwilling to desecrate the cemetery, but after it was pointed out to him that if the dike gave way, the river would not only sweep away the cemetery but his church as well, he relented. So, the men, dirty and weary reserve soldiers, and volunteers, quickly removed the headstones, and stacked them in a pile along the side of the Cathedral, then they scraped a layer of dirt, two-feet deep, and pushed the dirt onto the dike. The dike seeped, but held. Afterwards, once the river crested and receded, the men asked to see the cemetery plans, so that they could place the headstones back down, but the Bishop confessed that there were no plans. The headstones were replaced on memory.

"C'est pourquoi Lépine a deux pierres tombales," Alfred had said. We sat around a small fire that Alfred had built after dinner. We stunk of sweat and mud and gun smoke, and I clutched a bottle of OV that Alfred had offered me—he said I'd earned it, but not to tell my dad. I sipped quietly and listened to Alfred's story. He explained to me how after the waters had receded, and as the men laid the tombstones, they set down all but one: Ambroise-Dydime Lépine's. No one around could remember where he'd been buried. Someone suggested they place his headstone next to Riel's, since Lépine had been his right-hand man during the resistance. Some years later, Lépine's family returned and quietly installed a modest headstone over his true burial plot.

Alfred tossed another log onto the fire, and the fire crackled and embers twirled upward into the dark, clear sky. Over the burning wood, you could hear water lapping through the bush. Alfred reached into his thick, red flannel jacket, and retrieved his pipe. He filled it with tobacco from a small pouch he kept in his pocket, then brought the pipe to his lips and lit it with a match. His cheeks quivered as he drew repeatedly on the stem, sucking in quick, short bursts, allowing the tobacco to catch fire. Then great billows of smoke poured from his nostrils.

I took a sip of beer, and cleared my throat. "T'sé," I said. "Monique would say that la pire flood est v'nue de l'est."

Shadows danced across Alfred's face, the hollow of his cheeks.

"Comment ça?" he said.

My voice dropped, like Monique's when about to stir the pot, and I said, "Les Anglais!"

Alfred nodded and turned to the fire. Sinking in my chair, I tipped back the bottle of beer. My cheeks and ears felt warm. Then I heard Alfred chuckle. "Ça c't'une bonne," he said. "Elle a du feu, Monique. J'te bet qu'elle aurait fouetté Mair, itou."

"Huh?"

Drawing on his pipe, Alfred looked over. "When Annie Bannatyne horsewhipped Charles Mair? Non? Sacrament, quessé qu'y t'apprennent à l'école?"

The cathedral's courtyard glowed as the piss-coloured floodlights washed over the old limestone ruins. I stood there for a time, leaning against a doorway, staring into the sky where the ceiling once spanned. Starlight needled through wisps of thin clouds. Wind whistled through the narrow windows atop the ruins. I could hear a tank rolling down the street, the cart-squeal of gears, the grinding of its track on the asphalt. Soldiers shouting. Tucking briefly into the corner, where a tower once stood, I sparked that joint Becky had given me, and drew and held the smoke in my lungs. Releasing, I watched the smoke twirl upwards, caught in the currents of air as if in a chimney. You could feel the weight of history in this place. It intruded into the present. Walking through the courtyard, my footsteps echoed on the cobblestones. Each step seemed to take effort, as though sinews and nerves shot out at every footfall, rooting me to the ground, and each step forward was a tearing of roots. The wind picked up, hissing through gaps in the stone walls. This place hummed with ghosts—and the sound of electric wires below my feet that powered pillars of light in the courtyard. A confluence of past and present, where rivers meet, where streams curl back on one another. Didn't matter if you believed in le bon Dieu or not; this was a place where lives gathered, collected, rested. Drifting through the archway, I sat on the steps overlooking the cemetery, the river, and the city across the water. Thoughts racing like a herd of cattle breaking at the crack of a gunshot, I wondered at the persistence of it all. How had the dikes held? Had too much been lost to rebuild? Was language enough?

Becky's words echoed in my mind: this place was full of history.

Pain threaded down my leg, fire licking my toes and sheared my thoughts again. For a moment, I saw the crowds gathered on the road, weeping, and jostling atop le Pont Provencher, and I could almost feel the glow of the flames blooming above, the sky obscured by thick black smoke. The crowd recoiled as heat burst upon us in waves. Weeping. The shattering of the great rose window; the shower of glass on cracking stone. Weeping, the final twisted gong when the bells crashed— and then crowds replaced by men shovelling the graveyard as the river tore north behind them. Then a rhythmic chopping caught my ear, drew me out from my mind. I spotted a helicopter hovering over the far bank, and, as I watched it, the joint canoed between my fingers.

The helicopter drifted overhead, veered northward, and tracked along the river. I flicked the roach onto the cobblestones and lifted myself up, skipped down the steps and hurried through the cemetery toward Taché where I turned to look across Provencher. The helicopter hovered on the far side of the boulevard, and a searchlight stabbed earthward, and swept the riverbank. How many times had the army visited this city? No waters threatened it now, yet here they were again. Training for war. I could almost feel my sister's anger, her outrage radiating like sun flares from the hospital. Alfred's words floated along the surface of my mind: faut que tu les watch.

Qui ça?

Les Anglais.

"The first time the army came to this place was not to help," Becky read. She sat in bed, holding her term paper. I lay on my side, and ran a finger up her thigh. She frowned and pushed my hand away. "Listen," she said. "Does this sound good?" The sound of her voice grew serious as she went on. "Soon after the Métis agreed to join Canada, forming the province of Manitoba, Canada sent an army to exact vengeance on a people who dared stand in the way of its imperial ambitions, who had simply resisted the wholesale expropriation of their homeland. Spoiling for a fight—Rich, stop it," she said, as I traced my finger along her hip, feeling where underwear had bitten tightly into her skin. "Volunteer soldiers of the Red River Expeditionary Force assaulted, raped, and murdered aboriginal people across the valley. Horses and cattle were shot. Barns and homes set afire. People as far away as Toronto, Montreal, and New York called it a 'reign of terror'—" as Becky read her paper, and I smoked one cigarette after another, I listened as best I could. My fingers quivered with a tight energy, like a fist rolled up and ready, and I concentrated on the smoke that curled upward and filled the room. In the dimness of the cloud, I saw Becky, a naked silhouette through the smoke, her voice growing distant as my thoughts drifted through the spaces around us—Becky paused, frowned at the pages, and she took a deep breath. The air was heavy, pressing down on us. I stared at the ceiling as she glanced at me. "What do you think?"

Around the fire, Alfred listed the litany of horrors. His hands trembled as he spoke. I sat quietly, listening, clutching the empty bottle of OV, sinking deeper into the chair. Alfred cleared his throat and spat. "Connait tu l'histwayr d'Elzéar Goulet?"

Reluctantly, I shook my head. I'd never heard it before. What little that I had learned in school was a pile of horseshit. Something unseemly, dropped and forgotten, where nothing but flies gathered. Alfred leaned forward—firelight etching hard lines into his face—and spoke.

"Elzéar Goulet y'était Michif."

A postman from Pembina, he had served in Riel's Government. He was Lépine's second in command. That fall, après qu'lii anglais took over le fort, when Goulet ventured into a saloon in Winnipeg, he stumbled into trouble.

"Y'a trouvé un paquet d'orangistes," said Alfred. "Quelqu'un la reconnu, pis y'ont djit qu'y'avait condamné Scott à mort."

Recognized, Goulet fled. He hoofed it toward the river as Orangemen spilled out of the saloon on his heels. They chased Goulet down to the riverbank where he threw himself into the Red. He swam for the east bank, hoping to make it across to Saint-Boniface, to safety, but these Orangemen, all volunteers from Ontario, hurled stones at him from shore, and one stone struck Goulet in the head. He lost consciousness and sank into the water.

"Pis y'é noyé."

Staring at the embers in the belly of the fire, I tried to ignore the flame growing in my stomach, slithering through my guts, and circling up around my heart, like a snake constricting. I didn't understand that hatred, and I couldn't imagine what would cause someone to hurl stones at a man in the water. That sour, rotten feeling boiled hot in my belly, feeding budding thoughts of revenge, and sweat burst from my pores, but I swallowed the turmoil down. With my throat gone bone-dry, and my tongue heavy and lethargic, I glanced at Alfred.

"How do you know all this, Menoncle?"

Alfred shrugged. "J'écoute, j'lis."

Stumbling over the cobblestones, I caught myself on the wrought-iron fence and emptied my belly. Hot whiskey and beer splashed over my feet. Groaning, I shut my eyes and focused on the sounds around me. Train cars shunting like a cannonade of shells cracking; a series of falling dominoes; the clop of hooves; the clatter of a cart; wheels screeching. I staggered across Taché and down the steps toward the small dock on the river, where men and women sometimes cast lures into the Red. I stood at the water's edge and swayed. Mist rose from the water, obscuring the far shore. Higher on the bank, streetlights flickered like torch fire. Light splintered through the mist and smoke and washed the fort's stone walls in amber. Men on horseback shouted, and with rifles in hand, herded a crowd toward the gates; the crowd trudged through banks of snow, under the watchful eye of horsemen, hands over their heads as wind whipped snow around them. One of them yelled obscenities, some angry, hateful words, but their meaning was lost across the distance. Muskets and muzzle loaders erupted along the walls, and a cannon boomed, the report echoing over the water. Carts rolled noisily down Main Street, like semi trucks, toward Portage, where the buildings had receded into the ground. Union

Station was gone. Bridges had winked out of existence—the rue Marion bridge, le pont Provencher—and in their place floated barges and cables, swinging in the soft current. Boats ferried 300 men toward the fort. Then the stone fort was gone, and heavy wood walls sprouted like poplars on the banks where the Assiniboine spilled into the Red. Glancing over my shoulder at the burned-out husk of that place where great grand-mère was baptized, long before fire ravaged the walls and gutted the pews and the rafters, and the bells came crashing down in a death knell that signalled the end of French in Manitoba, and I saw not ruin but, for an instant, fire bloomed, and receded, then the full, round, twin-spires of la Cathédrale towered.

A horse and cart creaked by, and the man at the reins tipped his cap at me, and when they passed, I saw that the Cathedral was but a small church built of hand-hewed wood. I turned again to look across the river, and saw but a village. Wind swept sound across the water; shouting and wild cries floated in the air. *Le commerce est libre!* Snippets of fiddle. A rumble of feet stomping in time over a creaking floor. *Vous aurez beau bal!* A horse-whine as an engine turned over, the shot of a musket like the backfire of car. *You damned rascal, you have destroyed our fort!* More fire. Flood. Musket smoke curling over palisades. Grandmothers picking medicines on the banks.

I spat the last drops of hot whiskey from my mouth and wiped clean my lips. The vision shimmered; towers and bridges glowing for a moment like some bright spot burned into the back of my eyelids after staring at the sun. Forts and tipis and cabins and taxis. Then like the thrum of an approaching train, voices returned, frantic, urgent, shouting, and I saw across the water a man rushing down the riverbank, others at his heels in pursuit.

"Connais-tu l'histwayr d'Elzéar Goulet?"

Alfred tapped his pipe on the dock, ash drifted into the water and was pulled northward toward the lake. He brought his pipe to his lips and gestured toward the far shore. Faut que tu les watch. The pursued man across the river shouted, but his words were lost to me. He leaped into the river, and I staggered backwards, realizing who he was, what he was trying to do. I sprang up and raced downriver to try to guide him across. I ran stumbling over unseen rocks and trees both sprouting and vanishing instantly before me. Voices chatted overhead, on that flickering bridge, a subtle woven mix of French and English and something else, a language at once familiar and foreign that sprang from the soil like the grasses in spring that nourished the animals that in turn nourished us: some La Broquerie in the drawl, a bit of Notre Dame in the vowels, a touch of St. Laurent on the tongue. I glanced across the river again, at the men on the shore. Stones sailed from their hands, plopping inches from the man in the water. I scrambled along the embankment, through the mud along the shore, reaching out with my hand to grab him, but he was too far, and then suddenly the man in the water was nowhere to be seen; and as I searched the Red for him, I saw men across the river wiping their hands clean, and clapping each other on the back. Alfred appeared again, and lay a hand on my shoulder.

"C'est fini, mon gars."

"He was just there," I said. The bridges began to flicker into sight again, solidifying, and the towers across the river grew upwards over the crumbling stone walls. I turned to Alfred, but he too was gone, and I sat heavily on a grey, weathered log by the river and wept.

The rhythmic chopping returned, and I glanced at the helicopter that circled overhead. It hovered nearby, over the street up the embankment. I swung my legs over the log, and climbed up the bank, through a small bush, and out onto the street not far from Le Canot. My chest grew tight as I spied the old bar where Monique had once brought me to dance. Where I had puked on a woman not long after, and a bouncer had kicked me out, and I had lain atop a picnic table, out front, in the snow, for what felt like ages, waiting for Monique to notice and take me home. The bar had been shuttered not too long ago, slated for demolition, and I was happy to see it go. Now it was encircled by a chain linked fence, and festooned with garlands of barbwire, fortified with stacks of sandbags. It served as a military outpost. Soldiers stood on the roof, surveying the city through binoculars. Others manned the gate below, rifles slung over their shoulders. Men and women in brightly coloured vests circled the bar and shouted at the soldiers, "Army, go home!"

Then from behind me, I heard the jangle of steps, boots clattering on the cracked asphalts. I turned to see a group of them, rounding Dumoulin, onto Taché, walking, jogging, leap-frogging one another as they hurled themselves into the shadows, their orange-tipped rifles raised, almost ready to fire. Some knelt behind a utility box, and seemed to check the windows for gunmen, as their comrades pushed ahead. Then rumbling around the corner, behind them, came an armoured personnel carrier, sputtering diesel smoke and menace. Soldiers formed an escort around it, and marched warily toward the old bar. The helicopter circled overhead, its spotlight slicing through the night, sweeping the river, the bank, the street, and I stood, for a moment, in the blinding light of its sight. A few soldiers spotted me, instinctively raised their rifles towards me, and I stepped back, showing them my empty hands, and they seemed to realize I wasn't supposed to be there, and they shrugged, and hurried after the carrier.

"Fuck me," I croaked as the last of the soldiers vanished into the compound and the gates squealed shut. I turned away, toward the hospital, and I noticed a police cruiser and an officer leaning against the hood, his arms crossed. He stared at the bar, the soldiers on the roof, and he frowned, abruptly looked at me, and flinched.

"Hey, you," he hailed.

Reluctantly, I turned toward him. He raised a flashlight, pinning my silhouette against a placard that rose from the ground behind me and read: Site future du parc commémoratif Elzéar Goulet Commemorative Park.

"What are you doing there?" the officer called.

"Nothing," I said, and winced as the word left my lips. I could see the officer straighten, his flashlight sweeping around me, before keying in on my feet: wet, muddy, flecked with vomit.

"Come here. Let me see some I.D."

Trudging across the street, I pulled my wallet from my jeans, plucked my driver's out, and offered it to him. He took it from my hand and skewered it with his flashlight, then flicked the light up into my eyes.

"What are you doing here, Richard?"

"Ree-shar," I pronounced. "It's French."

The officer studied my face. "You're French?"

"That's right," I said. And Métis, I thought, but I held my tongue.

"I've seen you before, Richard."

"What?" I said. "Non, I don't think so."

The officer drummed my license against his flashlight. "What's that smell?" he asked.

I glanced around and shrugged. "The river?"

"Have you been drinking, Richard?"

"Oh, yeah. I had a couple at my girlfriend's. She told me about les soldats icitte. I wanted to have a look see—"

"Where is your girlfriend?"

I chucked my thumb over my shoulder. "At home, on Des Meurons. She's writing a paper for university."

"Didn't you see the road closed sign?"

I glanced up the street, then shook my head. "I walked along the river."

The officer stared, resting his eyes on my pale skin. After a short pause, he handed my license back. "Okay, Richard. The army asked us to keep folks away, so I'm going to ask you to keep moving."

Heart racing, I turned and headed south along Taché. An intolerable heat pinched my ears and the back of my neck, it suffused my pores and entered my blood—a great and heavy sense of shame—as though in the face of a test I had not seen coming, and that I did not understand, I had been found wanting. I clenched my jaw and slinked meekly down the street.

Dad was sitting outside Alfred's room when I stumbled out of the elevator. He glanced up at me, his eyes wet and red, and he seemed to stare at me without recognition. Cheeks drawn tight, he pursed his lips and nodded.

"Alfred y'é mort."

"I know," I said. Dad rose from his chair, and we threw our arms around each other. I had sensed it, on the riverbank, that Alfred had moved on. And while the words had struck me like a stone, I did not buckle, but held my dad steady as he shuddered. After a time, he pulled away and wiped his eyes, cleared his throat, and pointed to the door.

"Ça fait une demi-heure, là," he said, and he stared at the door.

"Where's Mom?"

Dad looked at me and frowned. He glanced around the hallway and nodded. "À poigné une ride avec Roger," he said.

"You waited for me?"

Dad frowned again and turned his red eyes toward me, and he shook his head. "Non," he said. "Chu resté parc'qu'on laisse pas qué'qu'un mourir tout seul."

Though I sensed an undercurrent of disappointment in his words, a subtle accusation of neglect, a question of where I had been, I saw also a profound relief in his eyes at my presence. I would tell him later about what I had seen, how Alfred had sat with me by the river, but for the moment, I let his words echo in my ears. We do not let someone die alone.

D'la ligne à Faucher à la Poche aux Lièvres

16.

The Resurrection
of Chains

THE HIGH-PITCHED WAIL OF A CIRCULAR SAW CHEWING
through lumber woke me from the dead-eyed sleep I'd finally found
earlier that morning. The sound ricocheted like a banshee wandering
through the woods. Its cries haunted my steps as I stumbled groggily
from the bedroom, and into the kitchen, where I saw through the window the wreckage outside.

There'd been a black bear in the yard overnight. It had torn open
the bin we kept by the road and strewn garbage across the driveway.
Bears were fattening up, devouring anything they could get their paws
on before the long winter descended.

"Ostie d'ours," Dad cursed the first time it happened, the first
time we saw trash chewed up, spat out, and scattered upon the road.
Monique had been the one to discover it; coming home late one evening, she'd nearly drove into the bear as it sat on the gravel and chewed
on a turkey carcass. This wasn't long after Thanksgiving. Monique
stopped and stared at the bear through the windshield; seated on its

rump, holding the carcass up to its maw, teeth crunching through turkey bone, the bear stared right back at Monique.

We'd had a dog once, Chains, who'd kept bears away for years. He barked at anything that moved in the bush, darting after squirrels and jackrabbits that ventured into the yard. He was a fine dog, but funny looking. See, Chains was a mutt. He had the head of a German Shepard, the fur of a Golden Labrador, and the legs of a Chow. He was beautiful at first sight, when laying in the grass, but when he stood, rising a mere handful of inches, he became clownish. Awkward. Disproportioned. He ambled easily enough, but never as quickly as you'd expect.

When I was younger, just starting high school, Chains and I used to explore the bush together. I would zip down the old cattle trails on a quad, whipping around bends and dodging overhanging branches, while Chains galloped alongside. What Chains lacked in speed, he made up in tenacity and endurance. When I would get too far ahead of him, I would stop and wait for him to catch up, listening to him plough through the underbrush like some fugitive pig.

Chains disappeared once. I had zipped far ahead of him before I realized it, then stopped and waited for him to catch up, but he never did. After a while, I shut off the engine and shouted his name. There was no reply. I whipped the quad around and roared back down the trail a ways, then shut the engine off again and shouted his name. I heard him bark somewhere in the trees; he barked and whined, and barked again, refusing my commands to come. Wondering what the hell was wrong, I hopped off the quad and headed toward him. The underbrush was thick, difficult to pass through. I kept getting turned around, ending up back at the quad. Eventually, I discovered a path, probably the one Chains had ploughed, and I followed it until I came upon a small clearing by a creek. Chains lay in the grass alongside a deer. Blood dripped from his lips, down his jowls, his neck. I circled the dead animal and noticed that it had no head; someone had killed and then decapitated it for a trophy, and left the body to rot. An animal had come along later, ripped open its belly, and gorged on the flesh. Chains had taken a turn, eating his fill. I grimaced at the wisps of red flesh caught in his teeth, and I glanced around, and wondered if the poacher was still near, even though I knew the kill was already a few days old.

"Come on," I said, inching toward the quad. But the dog refused to listen. "Chains," I said. "Come here."

He rose, ambled over a couple feet, then looked over at the carcass again, and sat down. He began to whine. Exasperated, I walked over and grabbed his collar, but a low rumble bubbled out from his throat and twisted his lips. I pulled my hand back and glared at the dog.

"Crisse de chien," I said. "Fuckin' reste icitte then."

He stayed out there in the bush for almost a week, guarding and gorging on that poached carcass. Dad tried to fetch him, but Chains snapped and growled, and Dad decided to leave him be. Chains came home eventually, dragging a gnawed haunch we took away from him and tossed in the garbage once he fell asleep.

But it was too late. He had developed a taste for meat.

Some weeks later Dad got a call from the neighbour down the road. The man ran a sheep farm, and he had spotted Chains chasing his sheep in the pasture. He'd warned the dog off with a gun blast, but he worried it would return and kill his livestock. Dad assured him Chains wouldn't be a problem; he would take care of it. And so, we tied him up.

Chains hated it. We provided him a 50-foot rope to allow him to roam a bit, but Chains kept circling the tree and his doghouse, wrapping himself up into a knot until he could no longer move, and he would begin to whine and howl until one of us would come outside and take him for a walk. After a while, we thought he would have forgotten about the taste of wild meat, and we began to untie him—he seemed so depressed, leashed to that tree—and he padded freely in the yard. One night someone forgot to tie him up again and he wandered away. A few days later, Dad got another phone call. Chains had gotten into the sheep pen.

"Yinqu'une chose à faire," Alfred said that Sunday, over dinner. "Faut y'planter une balle dans tête."

"Menoncle!" Monique gasped at the idea of shooting the dog. Mom gulped her wine. Dad stared at his food—roast beef growing cold on his plate.

Alfred snorted. "Un chien qui t'icoute pas sert à rien."

Dad drove to neighbour's farm, looped a rope around Chains' neck, and led to him to the truck. He brought him home and tied him up while he went inside to fetch his rifle.

"You're just going to shoot him?" Monique said. "Of course," she scoffed. "That's how they do things in the army, eh? Shoot first and—"

"Monique, arrête," said Mom.

Dad stood in the doorway, holding his rifle, and glared at Monique through wet, red eyes. "Quessé qu'tu veux qu'je fasse? Crisse de chien vient d'arracher la gorge d'un mouton!"

"Well, I don't know," said Monique. "Maybe, like, send him to a rescue or—"

"Voyons donc, Monique," said Mom. "He's a sheep-killer. Y va faire la même chose sur une ferme."

"But we can't just kill him!"

Dad shook his head. "Pas d'choix," he said.

I sat in the kitchen, at the dinner table, trembling as I listened to them talk about what to do with the dog. I listened to Monique plead for its life, but our parents swatted away every point Monique raised until it was clear that they would suffer no other option.

"Fine," Monique said, defeated. Then she glared at Dad. "But I want to watch."

"Non," Dad shook his head again. "No way."

"I want to watch," said Monique. She stomped over to the kitchen table and grabbed my hand. "We have to bear witness!"

"I don't want to watch," I said, and pulled my hand away.

Monique glared at me for a second before turning back toward our parents. They argued for some time, and then, recognizing that Monique would do whatever the hell she pleased, they gave in, and we tramped outside to say goodbye to the dog. We took turns hugging him, telling him he was such a good boy, until Dad grew impatient and told us to wrap it up. I retreated into the house with Mom, and we busied ourselves peeling potatoes while Dad and Monique took Chains into the back. I watched through the window as they disappeared around the woodshop. A short time later, I heard the gunshot echo through the trees.

Monique later told me how Chains had sat patiently where Dad had commanded him to, how he tilted his head with wonder when Dad raised the rifle and aimed it at him, and then how he whimpered when Dad pulled the trigger. She would recount this story to Alfred too, around the dinner table in Alfred's cabin, while I stewed in silence, ruminating over the moment earlier that day when I had broken a boy's nose. Monique held her fork like a small rifle before her face.

"Bang!" she said.

Alfred jumped in his chair and laughed.

Monique described how Chains lifted himself off the ground. How blood leaked from a small hole above his brow, how a string of red pearls curled down around his eye, and dripped from his snout. Chains stumbled backwards, startled, and then he steadied himself, growled, and barked at Dad, and lopped off into the forest as Dad and Monique watched in disbelief.

"The Resurrection of Chains!" Monique shouted.

"Ho-wa!" said Alfred. He'd heard the story before, but he liked to play along.

"Merci," I'd said that day when Dad shot Chains, and Monique told me afterwards how the dog had lived. It felt better to believe that he had survived the bullet and wandered off to live his life in the forest than died over some fucking sheep. Deep down, I believed Chains was dead, but the fantasy of that miracle dulled my grief. Monique met my lightning-quick acceptance of this fact with skepticism and scoffed.

"You can't believe everything you hear, Rich."

"But you just told me it happened!"

"Well, it did. But still." She frowned, then glared at me, and retreated into her bedroom.

Three days later a sound awoke me, and, in a haze, I jumped to the window and glanced outside. In the shade of Dad's truck, Chains lay panting. He looked up at the house and barked.

* * *

The saw spun up again and the sound of steel carving wood fractured the morning. I held a cup of tepid coffee in the kitchen, and watched through the window above the sink as Dad wrangled another warped 2x4 onto his sawhorses. Sawdust and chopped boards littered the driveway. He measured a length, marked his cutline, and then brought the saw up. Then Dad frowned and ran his thumb over the pencil mark. He stepped back, looked over the wood again, and shook his head. He put the saw down, pulled the measuring tape from his toolbelt and began to measure for a second time. Aluminum crackled as the measuring tape flopped off the 2x4. Dad whipped the tape straight, and the tape end wavered like a fishing rod as he tried to settle the tip back in place.

I wondered if he'd slept.

Slipping outside, I stepped partway down the stairs and sat overlooking the driveway.

Glancing at me, Dad nodded. "Matin."

"Where's mom?" I asked.

He looked up again and squinted. The sun was coming up over the house. "À messe," he said. "Pas sure quand le funeral director y'é s'posé d'arriver, so I figured, j'vas rester icitte."

I vaguely remembered Dad and I being whisked through a series of forms and phone calls last night, after Alfred passed. One had been to a funeral home, in the city. A funeral director had answered, and hastily arranged a meeting for this afternoon.

"Do you want help?"

He shook his head. "Ch'capable."

"Okay, watch your fingers, eh?"

Dad snorted.

I reached for my cigarettes, before I remembered I was out. I grimaced and leaned over the side of the steps, and spat. I took a sip of coffee and grimaced again. The coffee tasted sour; the machine hadn't been cleaned in some time. Mom drank tea, mostly, and Dad usually took his coffee in town, so no one used the machine much except me. After being reminded, so viscerally, of my own lack of care and attention, I tossed the coffee out. I looked up at Dad again, his pencil in hand once more. I cleared my throat.

"So, how big was it, you figure?"

He frowned. "What do you mean?"

"L'ours," I said, waving toward the shattered box at the end of the driveway.

Dad looked at the road. "Oh. That was me," he said. "J'ai foncé d'dans, c'matin."

"Fuck," I said.

"J'partais pour aller prendre un café, et pis—" he spat and turned to the sawhorses. "Bin, anyways. J'ai dit à ta mère que c'tait un ours." He grabbed the saw, and brought the teeth closer, right to the cutline, then he glanced up, and offered me a weak smile. He pressed the trigger and the blade spun up in his hand, then as he pushed the saw forward, sawdust erupted over his head.

* * *

Monique said the bear huffed when she pressed on the car horn. Grunting, it dropped the turkey carcass and rocked forward, off its haunches, onto its paws, and padded toward the car. Monique squeaked and locked the door. She slid down her seat, under the steering wheel, as the bear came near and ran its wet nose along the fender. She could hear it breathe: a hot, wet, mess of air that fogged the window. She peeked over the doorframe at the black mass of fur. The bear lifted its head—nostrils flaring—and glanced toward the treeline. Then over the rim of the steering wheel Monique saw it, a short, squat, majestic dog darting through the trees, like a bullet in molasses, straight for the car. Startled, the bear spun and scampered away. Nipping at the bear's heals, the dog chased the bear out of the yard and down the road. "It was Chains," Monique said the next morning, around the breakfast table. "Just like he fucking used to—"

"Hey, langue," Dad said, out of habit.

"Monique," said Mom, placing a hand on Monique's arm. "Chains y'é mort."

See, after Chains returned to us, he wasn't the same. Something had been lost in the act. Some part of him had been severed, sloughed off, left to wither in that spot where Dad had shot him with a rifle. Monique wondered, much later, when she'd moved out to the city and I'd gone and spent a weekend with her, whether the bullet had sliced through some part of the dog's head that held his memories, or perforated that part of him that contained his motor skills, and left him with only a vague notion of what he used to be. That third morning after Chains was shot, when he came back to us and barked at the house, he tried to rise, to meet me as I sprinted through the doorway, and down the steps toward Dad's truck, but he stumbled, bumping into the fender, tried to bite the front tire, and fell onto his side.

The bullet hole had healed up; at least, his skin and fur had knitted over the wound. You could feel a divot in the bone when you ran your thumb over his brow, the scarred flesh covering that gap in his skull. The bullet had left him half blind, deaf, and without a sense of balance. The eye beneath where the bullet had entered no longer worked—it wobbled around inside its socket for a time, before it grew cloudy, and crusted over. Chains had difficulty too keeping his tongue inside his mouth and bit it constantly when he ate.

Monique pushed herself between us, that morning that Chains returned, and she threw her arms around the dog. On the landing, Mom froze momentarily, and squeezed Dad's arm.

"Non, Émile," she said. "That's not right."

"Je te l'avait dit," said Dad. "Un ostie d'miracle!"

Mom wanted Dad to finish the job and put another bullet in the dog, but Dad refused. He believed it was meant to be—Chains was meant to live.

"La volonté de Dieu," he said. Mom frowned, bit her lip, and glanced nervously outside at where the dog sat, beneath an oak tree, staring back into the house.

"Ou un tour du diable," she muttered, but Dad ignored her. He phoned his brothers and sisters and boasted of his wondrous, miracle dog. The price he'd paid the man down the road for the dead sheep not worth a mention. By the window overlooking the doghouse, where Chains lay and stared unflinchingly back into the kitchen, Dad stood and described the miracle.

"C'est ça," he said into the phone. "Trois jours plus tard."

We didn't tie him up anymore. Chains could hardly cross the yard without falling over. It was pitiful, but in the joy of his survival we blinded ourselves to his struggles. Only a few weeks later, Chains wandered out onto the road into the path of an old Ford truck. Dad cursed when he got the man's repair bill in the mail. Enough for a flock of sheep.

It was as though Chains had planned it, Monique later said.

Hauling on a wet roach in the living room of Monique's grimy basement suite in Saint-Boniface, waiting for the acid we'd dropped earlier to take effect, I frowned, and wondered out loud. "Do you think he wanted to die?"

I passed the roach clip to the girl on my left, Monique's friend from the call centre, and turned back to find Monique staring up at the cloud overtop the coffee table. "I do," she said, but, she continued, "Chains had waited for a moment that would extract some modicum of revenge on the man who'd wounded him."

The girl on my left giggled. "What does modicum mean?"

Affecting Alfred's voice, I said, "Aen tchi peu."

I never believed Monique about the dog. And I struggled to reconcile how my joy at his return had grown out of his suffering. How Chains had briefly shattered that boundary between life and death and cast all that I thought I knew in doubt.

And as the acid took root in my mind and the walls curled darkly around me, I wondered if Chains still somehow patrolled that oak-topped gravel ridge, on the edge of the prairie, east of Winnipeg, his spirit chasing bears through the underbrush.

17.

Water Held Firm in a Bucket

THROUGHOUT THE DAY FOLKS CAME AROUND TO DELIVER condolences and platters of food. Sliced kubasa, cheese and crackers, and assortments of wild fruit gathered on the kitchen table as word of Alfred's passing spread around Ste. Geneviève, Ross, Richer, and down through Ste. Anne. At first Dad—all covered in sweat and sawdust—was unsure what to do when the neighbour up the road pulled into the driveway. Dad shook her hand and flinched when she gave him a big hug et une tourtière gelée. Menoncle Dave had come over on his quad and he sat in the shade in front of the house, sipping his flask as he watched Dad repair the garbage bin.

"Un ours?" he said. Dad shrugged.

Still more folks came and carried food like newborns out of their cars and trucks: a bag of perogies, a bowl of coleslaw, a meat platter, un panier d'galette chaude that we quickly ate with butter and saskatoon jam. Mike Lemoine and his wife Brittney. The old guy from the coffee shop with the John Deere hat. Annette Simard. Bernie Kowalchuk.

Diane Friesen. All people that had at one time known Alfred, and knew what he had meant to Dad. We invited them into the house for a cup of coffee; Monsieur et Madame Groscoeur accepted and stared pensively at the kitchen table while Dad fiddled with the coffee machine. Dave limped into the kitchen and sat with us. He poured whiskey into his coffee and grimaced over the taste.

"Y goutent drôle ton café."

"Tu devrais l'prendre avec d'la crème, à place," snapped Dad.

After they'd fixed their coffees with cream and sugar, les Groscoeurs told us how Alfred had once helped them in a pinch. How they'd never forgotten. When they built their house, the original cabinet maker had pocketed their money half-way through the job and taken off. They could not afford to hire someone to complete the work, and they languished in a half-finished house, until Alfred caught wind of it and offered to complete the work for a fraction of what it would normally cost. The Groscoeurs wept as they told the story. He had done such a fine job.

"Une vrai bonne job," repeated Madame Groscoeur.

"Y savait travailler avec du bois, boy," said Dave.

Une fois les Groscoeurs sont partis, I told Dad he ought to wash the machine before he offered anyone else coffee. Dave snickered, dumped his coffee in the sink, then poured whiskey neat into his coffee cup. Dad frowned at the machine. He reached into his back pocket and pulled out his wallet, then he plucked some cash from inside and gave it to me.

"Tiens," he said. "Vas nous ach'ter une vingt-quat'e."

Behind the wheel of the Buick, all alone, grief creeped into the passenger seat. I thought, briefly, as I wheeled out of the driveway, and I sped and pushed the engine up to a high-pitched growl, that I could somehow outrun that grief. It was sucked out through the window, but then it seemed to return, and reach out from the trees like shadows spilling across the road and grasping toward the Buick. I felt myself crack, eyes growing wet, and I stomped on the gas. I was water held firm in a bucket as long as the bucket kept spinning. Down the ridge, and onto the Dawson, the bucket spun.

* * *

"Richard," said Alfred. Through a dreamy blur, I felt his bony hands pressing down on my shoulder, shaking me. "Richard, réveille-toé mon homme." It was the morning after Alfred had taught me to shoot, after he offered me a beer, after he told me about Goulet. With difficulty, I cracked open my eyes, and saw him standing over my bed. His hair glowed: a halo in the early morning sun. Deer head over his shoulder. "Réveille-toé," he said again. "J'ai bésoin d'ton aide."

"What?" I said, groggily lifting myself up onto my elbows, and watching Alfred hurry to the doorway, where he sat on the small chair and pulled on a pair of rubber boots.

"Écoute," he said, lifting a hand to his ear before hurrying outside.

Grunting, I did what I was told. Unsure what to listen for, I heard little except the usual sounds: a soft wind rustling through the trees, the branches rubbing and knocking together, the birds chirping, and the sound of waves breaking. I frowned. The water seemed louder, as if it had risen dramatically overnight, leapfrogging from the bush line to the foot of the cabin.

"Fuck," I said, and swung my legs over the cot and dressed quickly. I chased Alfred out into the morning, the crisp air like thin ice breaking around me. Alfred called, and I followed his voice around the side of the cabin, toward the back yard. He stood ankle-deep in water, grabbing his forehead as he surveyed the yard. The woodshed we had built yesterday was underwater. The firepit a small island. Ice piled against the makeshift garage, blocking its doors.

"J'ai jamais vu ça," Alfred confessed as I splashed up and stood next to him in his old rubber boots. I glanced over, glimpsing for a moment in his weathered face an echo of that scene in the canoe when we had come across that chair in the tree, that ill-hidden and profound sense of helplessness, a flicker of resignation in his brow as his hair trembled in the soft wind and the surface of the water shimmered. Then a rumble emanated from inside him, growing loud in his belly before it burst from his throat, and he slapped his hands together. "Tabarnak! J'ai jamais vu ça," he laughed. "Y'a même pas d'rivière alentour d'icitte!"

* * *

The hotel sold beer on the side. In a small room, separated yet attached to the bar, you could order a case of beer, which the vendor would fetch from the cold room and deliver on a small steel counter. Beer posters lined the walls around the small window through which the beer was passed, where you'd slip the money over, or grab the debit machine to swipe your bank card. One door led outside, while another led into the bar, in the event of a sudden decision to drink at the bar instead. On the far wall, a corkboard perforated with rusty thumbtacks held an assortment of ads that folks had posted over the years: trucks and tractors and 26-foot fifth-wheels for cash, OBO; phone numbers on paper fringes dangled limply. On the other side of the bar, separated by another wall, though sharing a roof, was the Chinese restaurant. As far as I could remember, there'd been a Chinese restaurant there.

"What'll it be?" the vendor asked.

"Two-four of Blue," I said.

As the woman vanished around the corner, into the cold room, my eyes drifted over the corkboard, the assorted layers of paper tacked to the wall. Some had grown yellow and brittle. A simple touch could render them dust. As I looked over the board, I spotted Joe's ad—Honeyman Septic—and its fringe of phone numbers all torn off and taken, revealing beneath it a glimpse of something familiar. I lifted Joe's ad and saw that it had been tacked overtop of Dad's old wood-carving ads from when he ran night classes out of the school wood-shop. He had stopped doing it a few years ago after one of his students, an old man not much younger than he, had lost a thumb in a band-saw accident. I heard about the accident the next day, from Karine Belleheure, who had signed up for Dad's class after I told her about it. She and I used to work together at the powder coat plant in Steinbach. We would often speak French together to piss off the Mennonites. I must have been at Larry's, smoking pot in his basement, or over at Al Verrier's when it happened, so I wasn't there when Dad came home, his face haunted, and drained of blood. Karine said that the man who lost his thumb, Jerry, had been tracing a simple pattern out of a piece of basswood with the bandsaw, enough to give it a rough form that he could whittle with a knife, but as he pushed the basswood through, turning as he followed the outline, he lost track of his fingers, his thumb, and the position of the saw. Bandsaws whip around quick, fast enough that you can lose sight of the blade. Jerry pushed the basswood too far, and the blade sliced through his thumb, severed it below the knuckle, and spit the tip onto the floor. Jerry just stared at his bloodied stump, stunned, unable to comprehend what had happened. Someone screamed. Karine nearly fainted when she saw blood spurt out of the stump. Blood dripped and pooled over the floor, soaking the sawdust. Dad rushed over and killed the bandsaw, and Jerry wavered like a birch tree in a windstorm. Dad grabbed him by the elbow and led him over by the first aid kit, wrapped his bloodied stump in a bandage, then told him to sit still while he fetched his thumb. Afterwards, he drove Jerry to the hospital, which was only two-minutes away, and he stayed with him while Jerry worked through the shock and realization of what had happened. Dad called Jerry's wife and told her about the accident; she nearly blew out his eardrum yelling into the phone. I saw Dad after work, the next day, Karine's story fresh in my ears, and I stepped carefully around him as he sat quietly in the dark living room.

"Do you want light?" I asked. He had pinned his eyes to the dark television, as though watching a projection of his memories. "Papa?"

"Non, non," he said, and he shook his head. "I should have been watching closer." He muttered other words I could not hear, then turned toward the television. Mom sat in the kitchen. I could tell she was worried, but she told me to leave him be. He had to work through it himself.

A while later, Dad received a notice in the mail. He was being sued for negligence. Jerry had named him in a suit. For a time, Dad worried about losing the house. He grew thin, unable to eat much until he heard the suit wasn't going anywhere. Jerry had signed a waver; it was the only way that the school had allowed Dad to run a woodcarving class on its property. In the end, Dad was not legally responsible, but it took him a long time to recover, longer even than it took Jerry to heal after his thumb was reattached. He couldn't let go of the blame that he placed on himself. It weighed on him. An immense, but invisible bundle of furs.

Dad never taught again.

As I stared at the old poster on the corkboard, beneath Joe's ad, I wondered if Dad had finally forgiven himself, or if he had been daring himself that morning with the saw because he still carried that sense of guilt, and on some level, risking his own limbs had become some form of penance. A thumb for a thumb.

The bucket slowed and drops of water splashed darkly on the ground. I pressed on the gas, but the Buick coughed, backfired, and whined. Bottles rattled in the backseat. I pulled back, lifting my foot, and the car slowed; the blur of houses and trees on either side of the road came back into focus, solid and distinct. La Coulée. Lake Riviera. And with it, memories of yesterday. The search for Dad. Alfred's passing. And water spilled faster now, great waves falling out of an overturned bucket, suspended mid-air, at the peak of its arc. Grinding my teeth, I pressed on the gas until the Buick trembled beneath me, and my memories were drawn into that swirl of colours beyond the windows.

When I returned, I discovered Mom and Monique sitting on the deck, sharing a cigarette. They watched as I carried the two-four over and dropped it at their feet.

"Hi Rich," said Monique.

"Mon."

"C'est ton père qui t'a envoyé pour ça?" Mom asked.

"Yeah," I said. "I told him his coffee tasted like shit."

Mom grunted. "Y'avait yinque à laver la machine."

"That's what I told him." Pain flashed down my back, through my leg, and radiated into my toes—a tingling heat that left a strip of numbness from skin to bone—and I pressed my hands to my lower back, thrusting my belly out, and stretching to alleviate the sting. Monique eyed me and frowned.

"I heard a tree fell on you," she said.

"Oh," I glanced back toward the road. Like a compass finding north, I stared toward that spot in the bush. "Was just a brush," I said, and I pulled back my hair, to reveal the cut along my hairline. "See? Just a scratch."

Mom snorted. "That's not what you said yesterday."

Monique glanced over. "What's that?"

"What was it again?" Mom pointed her chin at me.

I stepped back from the deck and dropped a load of spit between my boots. "Deux pieds à gauche, pis—"

Monique laughed. "Of course."

Deux pieds à gauche. Over the years it had become a refrain of sorts, growing out of each retelling of Alfred's story, when he had fallen out of the tree. We'd begun to use it to make light of our own mishaps, to soften the sharp realization of our own mortality, a humorous recognition of danger avoided, or death kept at bay. Years ago, when Monique rolled her Chevy Nova on the highway a few miles east of Deacon's and narrowly missed wrapping the car around a lamppost, first thing she said when we met her at the hospital was "deux pieds à gauche."

Voices echoed from around the house, and I glanced back at the driveway, at the array of vehicles parked halfway into the bush to make room. I spotted an old Dodge Ram, and glared for a moment, peering at its side, examining it for colour and damage to its side mirror, then I caught a glimpse of Monique's Grand Caravan and I recognized the peel of laughter that echoed through the trees.

"You brought the kids?" I asked, and Monique nodded.

"They're out back with John," she said. "Dad's showing them his workshop."

"What are you doing over here?"

Mom pointed her chin toward the road. "Watching the driveway," she said. "Le funeral director y'é supposé d'arriver any minute."

"Oh," I said, and I brought my arm up over my head and arched backwards again. "Well, guess I'll go say hello."

Mom nodded, but Monique slapped her armrests and stood up.

"Christ sakes, Rich. Give me a fucking hug."

Reluctantly, I waited as Monique came down the steps and wrapped her arms around me, but as she squeezed me tight, and I buried my head into her shoulder, I felt a warmth seeping out of my eyes, dripping into a bucket, newly placed on the ground.

18.

Deux pieds à gauche

OVER THE YEARS SINCE SHE'D LEFT, MONIQUE AND I HAD mended the tear in our relationship caused by her sudden departure. Though I'd known it was coming—she had always promised to move out as soon as she could—I had been wholly unprepared for the depth of her absence. Not three days after her high school graduation, it was as though she had dropped off the face of the earth. She ceased to exist. She had packed her Chevy Nova to the brim, strapped a twin mattress to the roof, and blasted off down the highway. Months went by without even a word.

"For all we know, she's moved to Vancouver," Mom said.

"Voyons," said Dad. "Evelyne Groscoeur a dit her cousin saw Monique at the Safeway in Osborne last week."

"Might as well be Vancouver!" Mom said.

Monique's disappearance affected us all in ways we had not expected, but it hit Mom the hardest. As if a planet had vanished from our skies, our paths became unhinged as we adjusted to this new gravity. Dad and I began to walk on eggshells around Mom, careful to not upset her, or draw attention and invite her short-tempered, sharp-tongued, criticism. She had taken Monique's departure most person-ally. At the dinner table every evening, she complained about the lack of communication, the gall of her first-born, her one-and-only daugh-ter, to go so long without even a word, to put us through this torture.

"We've been disowned, Émile!" she shouted.

"Bin, voyons," Dad would say, and shake his head, and while Mom would spend her evenings puttering around the house, hovering near the telephone, yelling at me to get off the dial-up, in case Monique called, Dad would retreat outdoors, and spend ever more time in his workshop. Veering wildly off-course, we began to tear and claw into each other the way moons tug at the surface of planets.

"You're not going to leave us like that are you, Richard?" said Mom, another evening at the dinner table. "Sneaking away like a thief!"

Dad shook his head.

"Uh," I said.

"No, you're not like that wild one," Mom said to herself, nodding.

I glanced at Dad, and he shrugged, cleared his plate, and quietly slipped out of the house.

In the fall, after what Mom had called une éternité, Monique phoned and left her number on the answering machine. For a brief moment, Mom seemed buoyed, happy, and dinner passed without bit-terness, guilt, or lament. Then Mom tried calling, once every few days to keep tabs on Monique, like some reference point on a long journey, stars at sea, but more often than not, she would get the machine, and Mom's peace of mind began to erode before us once more. Monique had grown distant, obscured by clouds.

"She's avoiding us," Mom accused, one evening in late fall after she'd got the machine again. "I bet you she's screening her calls."

"She's a young woman living in the city," said Dad. "I'm sure she's just busy."

"It's not right," Mom insisted.

Dad shrugged and told her it was only a phase. Monique would call. He too had vanished for a time when he was young, he reminded her, when he'd joined the army, only to return years later. They had to let Monique live her life. Mom grunted, and it seemed as though the thought of years passing without a word from Monique caused her eyes to grow wide. She reached again for the phone.

As Monique's absence stretched from weeks to months, my parents eventually turned the full weight of their attention onto me. They watched me, closely. They kept tabs on my comings and goings, on my friends and acquaintances, and they policed my time as though jail wardens. I chaffed under their scrutiny, struggling to re-establish the same freedoms, that independence that I—and Monique—had enjoyed when Monique was still around. And I came to blame Monique for this unfair surveillance. I resented her. When she finally came to visit over the holidays—her Chevy Nova whipping into the driveway dragging a nebula of icy dust and snow behind her—I glared across the table, over our turkey dinner, as she described her life in the city. She had an apartment, a car, and friends we had never met. She was living with a woman—a roommate, she said. She also had a job in a call centre.

"Slinging dick pills to old men who can't get it up," she said.

"Monique," Mom gasped.

Dad coughed, spraying beer over the table.

Monique laughed and said it wasn't all bad. She sold all kinds of crap. Whatever shit you saw on T.V., in the middle of the night, that was her. Answering the phone. A million fucking ab machines. Blenders. Pillows. Dick pills.

"We have to upsell them too," she'd say. "Get them some lube and some desensitizing cream for their wives. Can you believe that? Like the sex is so bad they have to numb themselves to endure it! Can you pass the cranberries?"

"Ho-wa," said Alfred.

We chewed on our turkey as Monique talked. She told us about her decision to push her education back another year. She told us that she was thinking about travelling, maybe taking a trip to Thailand.

"To find myself," said Monique.

I rolled my eyes.

Monique would visit periodically over the next year, mostly over the holidays, or some random weekend whenever she needed to do laundry—"Someone busted up the machine in the building" she'd explain—or to ask Dad something about the family. He was always easier to pin down in person than on the phone. I figured she came by to see Mom's reaction to her changing appearance. She'd shaved off her already-short sheared purple hair. She perforated her nose and twin-studs now sprouted from each side of her nostrils.

Mom shook her head.

"T'as l'air comme un boeuf," said Dad.

Monique scoffed.

She pierced the skin beneath her bottom lip with another stud, drove a length of stainless steel through cartilage in her ear, and added a ring in the corner of her eyebrow. Ink pooled over her shoulder, then spilled like a sleeve down her arm. We came to expect some new modification each holiday, and my parents braced themselves to her ever-changing appearance.

"Franchement, Monique," said Mom, at Thanksgiving, when once again assembled over a turkey at the dinner table, Monique revealed her latest piercing, standing suddenly, and lifting her shirt over her belly to display a small ring nestled in her navel. "No one wants to see that."

"Shit, you should see where the next one is going," said Monique. She grinned and stuck her tongue out as Mom shifted uncomfortably in her chair.

"It's a lie, Rich," said Monique, as we shared a cigarette under the snow-drenched eaves the second Christmas after she had moved away. We huddled by the door, along the wall, out of the wind, which lashed the trees relentlessly with snow and ice. Our breathes mushroomed thick and white, turning to ice before it even parted our lips. Monique flicked the cigarette clumsily in her new, large, garbage mitts. She was all thumbs.

"What's that?" I managed to say through my chattering teeth.

"En français, ça s'fait pas mal, mal, it turns out."

She took another drag from the cigarette, then held the smoke out for me.

"No shit?" I said, and brought the cigarette up to my cold lips. I could hardly feel the butt against my skin.

"Yeah," said Monique. "Turns out, c'pas facile vivre en français en ville. You gotta be bilingue, t'sé." Monique nodded sagely and I grunted. I tried to drop a loogie between my Sorels but the spit evaporated before it hit the ground. "But I get an extra two bucks an hour at work for speaking French, you know."

"That's good."

Monique nodded and glanced out over the temporary tundra that was our driveway, at the dark sliver of road between the trees, a salt-sprinkle of stars above. We could just make out a hint of light from the town through the bare trees. I glanced at her out of the corner of my eyes, and I wanted to ask her all about living in the city. I'd seen her a handful of times in a year and a half, and she seemed so different now: older, wiser, and maybe a bit rougher around the edges than before. I wondered about my own future, whether or not I could make it in the city, and if I even wanted to try—Mom's words, "you won't leave us, right, Richard?" echoing in the back of my mind. But I couldn't bring myself to speak. It wasn't the cold that had frozen my tongue inside my mouth—though it certainly didn't help—but the fact that I couldn't bring myself to admit to her how just much I'd missed her. Despite everything, I had always looked up to her, and when she left, her sudden departure—like the shearing of a limb from the family tree—had wounded me. Over the months since she had moved away, I developed a scab over that part of myself that loved her, to protect myself from the void that she had created. I tried to avoid thinking about the city—too close to picking at the scab. Now that she was here, I didn't dare rip the scab off, afraid of what it might reveal, what it would mean when she once again left. And so, I said little, but I listened quietly as she filled that uncomfortable silence between us with the sound of her voice, as though she was at work and I was some stranger on the phone, calling to buy a blender in the middle of the night.

"Did you know," said Monique, "That a Métis civil war almost started here?"

"Sure," I lied.

Monique stared at me for a moment, then continued. "Back in '70, Riel was pissed with this Métis guy from around here, and he sent some soldiers to arrest him. But when they arrived, they found this guy holed up in his house with his brothers. I guess one of the brothers was a hot-head, so when he saw the soldiers outside his brother's house, he went out and tried to shoot one of them."

"No shit?"

"But his gun misfired. The soldier then tried to shoot the guy who almost shot him. Eye for an eye, eh?"

"Misère."

"Except *his* rifle misfired too! Can you imagine? Two misfires. What are the odds?"

"Crisse. Almost enough to make you believe in God, eh?"

Monique snorted. "I wouldn't go that far."

We smoked for a bit, and I smacked my lips, trying to worm some blood through the cold skin. "So, did that really happen here?"

Monique glanced toward the sliver of light knifing through the trees to the west and she nodded. "Fuckin' rights it did. Ste. Anne used to be a Métis town. Back avant qu'les Québécois et les Anglais sont venus icitte."

"Still some around," I said, thinking of Alfred.

"That's right. More than you'd think, too. Some don't like to admit it."

"That's changing," I said.

Monique nodded. "Some have forgotten too." She took the cigarette stub from my hand, trembling glove and all, and brought it up to her lips. The cherry tip had grown short, and was starting to singe her new mitts.

"You really give a shit about this stuff, eh?"

"Lotsa time to read and think, eh."

"In between talking to old men about their dicks?"

Monique sniffed. "That's right." She threw the cigarette butt into the snow. "I work nights, so. Anyways," she stared at the smoke and steam rising from the snow bank. "You ever wonder whose side our ancestors were on?"

"Does it matter?"

Later that winter, after I visited Monique in the city, Mom and Monique had a falling out.

Mom had had a tough time accepting Monique's growing who-gives-a-shit attitude, she'd grown up in an old-school home, avec des vrais catholiques—like fish on Fridays sort of thing—and she struggled to reconcile Monique's behaviour with her faith. After Monique got me drunk and high in the city one weekend, and then left me out on a snowbank for an hour while she danced inside Le Canot on Taché, Mom had enough, and quit talking to her for almost a year. I'd come home Sunday evening, still coasting on the acid I had dropped the night before with Monique and her girlfriend, and I sat on the couch and watched the TV pulsate. Mom looked at me and gasped. My face was red and raw, all wind-lashed, already starting to peel like an onion. She asked what happened, but I stared at her blankly as she spoke. Her lips curled and grew, sprouted wings, and spiralled around her head. Her arms flailed like hot spaghetti noodles, like some mannequin at a car dealership. She loomed over me, a giant, brushing the ceiling, her eyes becoming maws that yawned as she peered down at me, her millions of fingers crawling through my hair, clutching, grasping, pinching my head. Her voice sonic-boomed through the house.

"Oh lord, look at his eyes, Émile! He's high!"

Dad was a bird perched on her shoulder as she interrogated—inquisitioned!—me about what I had taken. Had I driven home like this? I must have. The Buick was parked outside. And Dad squawked, shook his beak, and flew off toward the workshop.

Then Mom was on the phone with Monique, yelling into the receiver.

"How could you let your brother drive like that? He's still in high school, Monique!"

I sank deeper into the couch, as if falling into a sarlacc pit between the cushions, where I could lay in its digestive track for a thousand years without confronting the horror unfolding in front of me as I listened to my mother and sister yell at each other. I could hear Monique's voice through the phone, hitting back at Mom's accusations. He seemed fine earlier, she said. He said he could drive. Mom grew exasperated. I cowered whenever she raked me with her eyes. Fresh worry lines seemed to etch themselves around her eyes, Red River gumbo in a drought, cracked and webbed, they grew deeper, darker, with each passing word. At her wits' end, Mom threw a Hail Mary, and begged Monique to come out next week and go to church with her to atone for her horrible lapse in judgement, but Monique laughed, her voice sharp and raw over the phone.

"I don't want your fucking religion."

At my high school graduation that spring, Monique and Mom managed to sit next to each other through the ceremony, the dinner, and the social without saying a word. Dad wasn't thrilled about her choice to let me drive home that weekend in February, but Monique had apologized to me. Even though Mom wanted penitence, contrition, and reparation, Dad wasn't about to break off communication with Monique over this mistake, and ultimately her choix d'religion. He tried over and again to get them to speak to each other, but they just grunted, and glared, and scoffed at his attempts, until Dad too grew quiet and eventually drifted toward the bar, where he planted himself in a circle of awkward men clutching red solo cups.

The party was held in the old Legion building behind the school. They'd kept us penned in like animals that year, figuring it was safest after what had happened at last year's grad party, at Rosanne LaRocque's place, when Joey Lafleur smacked his head on the lip of a swimming pool and almost drowned. We partied in the hall, the lights growing dimmer as the music grew louder; our feet darting like waterbugs, noisy shoes tearing band-aids off the floor.

I drifted between friends, hugging, and screaming. "Class of 2000 baby! Whoo!"

And always glancing back at Mom and Monique, still seated, like statues at a table along the wall, nibbling on pretzels scattered on Styrofoam plates. It was as though they were locked in a contest of wills—each trying to make a point the other refused to acknowledge. Their positions hardened, grew heavy, until the foundation between us all began to crack. In that crack a toxic seed took root and began to grow, driving a wedge between Mom and I, between Dad and Mom, and between Monique and the rest of us—until the edifice of our relationships began to crumble.

I'd wondered often in the years since, if this was the source of that unspoken tension, that force that seemed to repel us when we were all together, like distended echoes of that shattering, after-shocks that still rumbled occasionally beneath our feet, and reminded us of that time when we wanted nothing to do with each other.

Even after Mom and Monique had patched up their relationship—after the accident that nearly killed Monique the winter after my graduation—a few cracks remained, growing now and again under stress and pressure, to threaten their newborn intimacy. Dad and I would catch sight of it once in a while, in the way that they eyed each other across the table at family dinners, in the tone of their voices when they asked each other questions, and we would exchange a look, but sheathe our dull tongues.

Only a few years ago, shortly after Monique married John, and they had their first child, and they came over for an early Réveillon, the ground had seemed to tremble beneath us as she opened a Christmas gift from Mom, and looked into a jewelry box. She plucked a small, golden necklace, and held it in the air. She glared at the crucifix on the chain.

"Ça appartenait à ma mère," Mom said.

Monique breathed, and after a moment she placed the chain around her neck, and cinched it closed.

"Marsi," she said. "But I'm still not going to church."

The accident happened midwinter, when a blast of Gulf air rose and raced up through the Midwest, showered the prairie with ice and rain, and turned the highway into the world's longest skating rink. All it took was a small bump for the wheels to lift, to lose contact with the road, and then gravity took over. Monique panicked and slammed the breaks, but it was too late. Catching the shoulder, the car was pulled off the road and tumbled through the ditch.

Monique squinted at us through dark, swollen eyelids. Bandages wrapped tightly around her head. One leg hung mid-air. Machines beeped at her side. Dad stood frozen at the foot of her bed. I crumpled into a chair in the corner. Mom slowly approached her bedside and Monique slid her hand out from underneath the sheets—her fingers flicked blindly through the air until finally, Mom grabbed her hand and squeezed. Monique smiled weakly, and mumbled.

"Deux pieds à gauche."

19.

Le bison

"AFTER LEWIS THREW BOOGERS IN IS'BELLE'S HAIR, I told him don't do that!" said Danny, and he stood as straight and as tall as his three-foot frame would allow, fists on his hips, elbows out. "Or, I toll 'im, I'm gonna beam 'im up!"

"Beat him up," said Isabelle.

"No!" Danny shouted. "Beam!"

Isabelle scoffed. "Daddy! Danny is being silly!"

"Don't worry about it," said John.

We sat around the firepit in the back, next to Dad's woodshop, on small benches he had carved out of old pieces of timber. Dave sat atop his quad, staring into the oil drum at the centre of the circle. We'd replaced our old pit—a rough circle of stones—after flames leaped the sides some years ago and nearly set fire to the bush. Everyone had gone, except Monique's crew and Dave, who watched Dad build a small hut out of kindling in the pit.

"Ça va pas marcher," Dave said. "Tu d'vrais le placer comme une tipi."

"Crime, j'ché comment bâtir un feu."

"Hey," Danny whined suddenly, thrusting a finger at Dave. "That's not nice! I'm goin' to beam you up!" He began to march around the firepit like some toy soldier. Isabelle climbed onto a bench, grabbed her juice box, sipped, and glared at her younger brother.

Dave blinked and looked at the rest of us. "Quessé qu'i' dit?"

"He's going to beam you up," said Monique, glancing from an array of hotdogs buns on the picnic table before her. Ketchup dripped from the bottle in her hand. "You know, like in *Star Trek*?" She gestured with the bottle, as though trying to mime the act of disintegration. I shifted in my seat, away from her, as the bottle swept over my head. "John watches that with them."

Dave grunted and began to scratch his chin.

"Comme avec what's his name, là? Sprock?"

John coughed, and shook his head. "No, no. Not that one. That one's—not appropriate."

"Isn't that show kind of violent?" Mom asked.

"I'm more of a *Voyager* fan," said John. "Lots of kindness and teamwork."

Monique snorted. "You just like that girl's butt. What's her name again? Sixty-nine?"

"Seven of nine," John said, his cheeks on fire.

"I'm goin' to beam you up!" Danny shouted at the woods.

The funeral director had come and gone. Dad had gone inside to talk to him, with Mom and Monique. I'd stayed behind by the firepit with John and Dave and watched the kids. Danny and Isabelle chased each other through the yard, dashing along the edges where underbrush rose thick. John talked about *Battlestar Galactica* and his hope for the final season. He watched all those space shows. Dave drained his flask. Whenever he thought we weren't paying attention, he glanced up at the sky and frowned.

I hardly heard a word. My mind kept wandering toward the house, wondering what the director was asking. Despite my curiosity, I couldn't bring myself to go over. When I thought about it, my chest grew tight, as if my heart became tangled in chicken wire, constricted, unable to pump enough blood through my veins. My breath grew shallow, and I forced myself to stretch, arching back in my chair, arms above my head, and I yawned—I tried everything to keep that rising sense of dread and despair from settling. I trudged back and forth between Dad's woodshop, the beer fridge he kept tucked under a workbench, and the firepit that Danny and Isabelle kept poking with sticks.

"See that?" said Isabelle.

"Yeah!"

"That was a tree once," she said.

"Whoa," whispered Danny. "What happened?"

"Fire," said Isabelle. "Ate it up and pooped it out."

When I finally screwed up enough courage to head inside the house, I met Monique on the path to the house. She shoved a tray of food into my arms. "Dad says to grab some wood."

"What?"

"For the sausages."

I glanced at the tray of food in my arms: cheeses and crackers, chopped veggies and dip.

"Funeral director's gone," Monique said. "You can come out of your hole."

"I—," I could feel the blood draining from my cheeks.

Monique pursed her lips and as she studied my face, her eyes softened, and her fingers touched my elbow. "Sorry. Don't worry about it," she said.

Fire roared over the lip of the old oil drum.

"C't'assez d'bois, Émile," said Mom, frowning at the load of wood in Dad's arms.

Dropping the wood next to Dave's quad, Dad glanced at his brother and snorted. "See," he said. "Ch't'l'avais dit qu'ça poignerait."

We cooked sausages over the flames. Dad complained that the fire had not quieted down and formed a proper bed of embers, but Mom reminded him that his grandchildren were hungry. They stood on either side of him as he crouched by the drum and held a skewer over the pit. Fat dripped off the meat and sizzled in the fire.

"Ostie, ça sent bon," said Dave. "Du chevreuil?" Dad nodded.

Mom told us what the funeral director had said. The director wanted some photos for the service. A list of songs to play. Fiddle music was discussed. I stared intently at the browning sausages over the fire, trying not to dwell on Alfred, and the void that his passing had suddenly left, as Mom talked, and I grunted when Dad called me.

"Sound good, Rich?"

"What's that?" I said.

"J'ai dit, y faudra allez checker la cabine demain," said Dad. "Get that stuff. Close it up."

After we ate, Danny pulled a small plastic bison from his pocket and began to stampede along the armrest of his chair.

"Patch-e-coupe, patch-coupe," he said.

"Sounds like a horse," said Dad.

"No," said Danny. "It's a buffalo, silly!"

"Un bison," I said. Bee-zon.

"No," whined Danny. "A buf-fa-lo!"

"In French it's bison," said Isabelle. "I learned that in school."

"You're not in school!"

"Yes, I am. I'm in kindergarten!"

"That's right," said John. "And you're learning French!"

Isabelle nodded shyly. "Un petit peu."

"Show Memere, Pepere, and Uncle Rich what you've learned!"

"Hey, I can speak French too!" Danny shouted. "Un, deux, toi, cat—"

"And Opa taught me German, too," said Isabelle. "Ein, zwei, drei—"

John shrugged sheepishly and Dave laughed.

Staring at the fire, Dad began to talk. "Dans l'temps, y fallait cacher nos livres à l'école."

Isabelle and Danny looked over at him and frowned. "What?"

"Oh boy," said Monique. "Here we go."

Dave nodded atop his quad. "Oh yes. We had to hide our books," he said. "We weren't allowed to learn French in school."

Isabelle looked over to Monique. "Is that true?"

Monique sighed and nodded, gesturing toward Dad.

"Dans l'temps, le gouvarnament wanted everyone to learn and speak English. They'd send someone to check our classes, to look at our books and make sure they were all in English."

Isabelle's eyes grew wide.

"We had to learn French in secret. And whenever les inspecteurs showed up, les soeurs courraient alentour pour collecter nos livres, then they'd hide those French books in the vents."

"Your sisters!?"

"Huh? Non, non. Les soeurs—ah, the nuns," said Dad.

"Oh," said Danny, and he glanced at his mother, as though wondering what a nun was.

"They'd run around like chickens with their heads cut off, checking our desks in case we forgot anything."

"Dad," said Monique. "Don't scare them."

"Bin, it's true."

Isabelle nodded solemnly while Danny picked his nose and stampeded his plastic bison.

I'd heard these stories for years, how, as children, Dad and his siblings had to learn French in secret. How every now and again a school inspector—seemed that it was always an Englishman—would come to look through the classrooms and glare at the children, berate the nuns, and ensure that no one was learning anything other than English. I had heard these stories enough times that I could have recounted them as though I had been there. Leaning back in my chair, looking through the shrivelled leaves above, at the sky, the odd ember carried up by the current, I sifted through the accumulated details: the sound of the inspectors' footsteps, the creak in the floorboards, the stern look etched on his face, the way his pencil scratched the paper on his clipboard, and the sound of his voice as he looked down at Dad, and said, "Tell me, son, what have you learned today?"

Dad's young voice trembled.

"Cow shit," he said, "makes good fertilizer."

"I see," said the inspector, and he glanced at the nun whose face turned the colour of the flag in the corner. The red ensign. The inspector gestured toward the hallway. The nun followed reluctantly.

"You could hear him through the walls," Dad recounted once. "Yelling. Telling her we'd amount to nothing unless we washed our mouths. I could tell she had taken it to heart when she came back inside. Her eyes red and cheeks wet. She went straight to her desk, grabbed a ruler, and marched up to me, then, forgetting that the inspector was still in the hallway, she said, 'tes mains,' and I held out my hands, and she smacked that ruler down on me." Dad would then show us some nick in his fingers. "Right here," he'd say. It was always a different scar, and sometimes a different finger or even on the other hand, but it didn't matter, the sight of his hand was enough to draw out the horror of the act—as a boy he had been punished for embarrassing a nun because he could hardly speak English.

The French lessons continued, every morning before class officially started, and through the day they learned enough English to fool the inspector.

Listening to Dad deliver yet another version of this story to Isabelle and Danny, I thought of Alfred, and how the evening after he'd wondered what in the hell they were teaching in school nowadays, I had asked him about what he had learned in school. And I repeated to him what Dad had told us, about learning French in secret, and Alfred snorted and shook his head.

"On faisaient la même chose," he said, but then he frowned. "Mais les soeurs 'taient pas des saintes." He sucked on his pipe for a while, the play of light on the water casting odd shapes across his stony face. The day after our fireside talk, we stood on the small makeshift dike we'd put together that morning when the water rose up from the treeline toward his cabin. You could hear water seeping through the dike, and it was only a matter of time before it gave way. Alfred grunted and stared at the woods. "Sure," he said. "Y-nous ont appris à parler l'Français, mais y-nous ont arraché la langue itou." They ripped out their tongues. He looked at me and said. "Les soeurs y v'nait presqu'toutes du Québec, hein. N'connaissaient pas li Michif,

et nous disait tous qu'on parlait mal, et pis nous ont lavés la bouche."
Alfred tapped his pipe, ash fluttered into the floodwater below. I
tried to imagine the scene: a flock of exasperated nuns scrubbing the
Michif from Alfred's mouth with soap. Elbows firing like pistons.

"Le pe-tit chat," he said. "Pas l'tchi shaa."

Le bi-son. Pas li bufloo.

"Rich," said Monique. "Rich. We're leaving."

I rubbed the memories from my eyes, then glanced around the
fire. Embers glowed in the pit. Someone had taken away the food
from the picnic table. Dave was gone—I missed the sound of his quad.
Isabelle was running down the path toward the driveway, and John
was jogging after her. Monique stood at the edge of the firepit, coax-
ing Danny away from the hot drum.

"But I wanna throw more wood in there," he whined. Monique
shook her head, and she crouched down next to him, placed her
hands on his little shoulders and looked him in the eyes.

"But it's time to go, my little man. C'est presque l'temps pour dodo."

"Fine," said Danny, pouting.

"Grosse babine!" I said and he looked over at me and frowned.

"Hey!" he shouted. "Menoncle Rich, your eyes are all wet."

"Are they?" I reached up to wipe my eyes and discovered tears
leaking down the sides of my face. "Look at that," I mumbled.

Monique stood and looked at me with concern. "Are you okay?"

I nodded. "Yeah," I said. "Was just thinking about—" I cleared my
throat and shook my head. "I'll be fine."

Danny glanced back and forth between us. "Is Menoncle Rich
okay?"

Monique nodded and rubbed her hand on his head. "He's okay.
Just a little sad, I think."

"Oh," said Danny. He took his mother's hand, and as they began to
turn toward the path leading to the house, Danny glanced back at me
again. "Menoncle," he said. He pulled his hand from his Monique's,
stepped toward me, and offered me his other hand. "Here," he said,
and he dropped a toy in my palm.

I held it up against the dim light of the embers and saw it was his plastic bison. I shook my head. "I can't take this, it's your bison."

"You can have it for now," Danny said. "To make you happy."

"That's very nice, Danny. C'est très gentil," said Monique. She crouched down again to his level, and wrapped her arms around him. "Uncle Rich will give it back to you la prochaine fois, okay? Now it's time to go."

"Okay," said Danny, yawning as Monique lifted him up and positioned him on her hip.

I stood and gave Monique a quick hug, and tried to sneak the plastic bison into her hand, but she smiled, softly, with weariness, and shook her head. "Next time," she mouthed the words soundlessly. I saw that Danny was already asleep on her shoulder.

We walked toward the house, around to the front, where John was buckling Isabelle into her booster. Monique placed Danny gently into his car seat, then secured the harnesses, and John hopped into the driver's seat and started the engine. I stood off to the side, watching as Monique climbed into the van, and I closed my fist around the small toy bison in my hand and watched as the van pulled out onto the road.

20.
Y'en a d'l'eau dans swomp

GRAND FORKS WAS UNDER WATER AND THE CITY WAS ON fire. All day images had flashed and replayed on the small television that hung in the corner of the Esso: flames sprouting like weeds from big, old brick buildings up to their hips in a soup of debris and brown river water. Out front, firefighters floated pumper trucks on barges down the street to shoot water onto the flames but as the newscaster repeated, incredulously, they had run out of water. The hydrants were underwater, the pumping houses were flooded. Firefighters watched as flames spread like prairie fire through the attics, leaping from one building to the next, until the whole block was alight.

Alfred had gone into the station to pay for a jerry can of gasoline to fuel the small pump that Dad was bringing out. I sat in the truck, guarding the handful of sandbags we'd been able to scrounge up around town. I doubted it would be enough, but Alfred had a plan. After a while, I wondered what was taking Alfred so long, and I glanced into the gas station, and noticed he had stopped amid a small crowd gathered near the counter: a half dozen men and women, who'd left their cars and trucks parked around the gas pumps, drawn like moths to the television. Curious, I went inside. On the TV, I saw the national guard drop water from the air. Plane after plane swept over the city as if it was some patch of burning bush and dropped small lakes onto the flames.

We stood in the hushed and crowded solitude of our own shock, watching unfold on TV the horror just a few hours up the valley. Though there were no rivers here along the edge of the valley—just a few creeks and a checkerboard of scrub bush and ranch land, a few farms, swamp, fens, bogs and gravel pits—the waters rising in the valley below, that sea spreading to the south of us, and moving northward, crowded out all other thoughts. It was all that the TV and the radio talked about. Everyone knew someone fighting to save their house. The army had been called in and there was talk of more evacuations; mountains of sandbags were filled, thrown, and stacked in bulbous, and towering walls that snaked along the Red. The floodway was full. Even Chrétien showed up. He tossed a sandbag before he flew back to Ottawa and called an election.

"Ça va t-êt' la panique," said Alfred, later in the truck, as we raced back to his cabin, and listened to folk spin nightmares on the radio. I ground my teeth as the voices grew shrill, and the grim and dire images they painted—a slow-rising, lethargic tsunami swelling over the border—drilled into my nerves. Glancing nervously at Alfred, I took comfort in the soft, weathered lines etched into his face, the easy manner he held his head and stared at the road as horrors from the radio washed gently over him like rainwater. He shook his head, then nodded, and muscle began to jump at the back of his jaw. "Ça va t-êt' la panique," he said again.

We laid a layer of poly around the back of the cabin, and tossed a line of sandbags onto the plastic to weigh it down. Alfred had called in a favour and someone delivered deux verges de sable. Dad arrived with the pump and we set about installing plywood sheets in front of the bags, and wrapping the poly overtop. The job was quick, rough, and ugly, and it wouldn't hold a river, but a half dozen inches of swollen swamp water was a different animal. There was no current to contend with: just the tapered edges of a swamp and the gentle sway of its windswept waves.

After we'd thrown together the makeshift wall, and I backfilled the plywood with the last of the sandbags, Dad set up the pump. Some water had already gotten into Alfred's shed, against the back of the cabin, behind the plywood and the sandbags, and we needed to pump it out. Dad showed Alfred how to work the pump, adjust the intake, and position the outflow. The air filled with exhaust, and the pump motor whined like a dirt bike. I watched, and listened, as they talked about when to run it, and how often to check the shed and the ground out front.

"À chaque couple d'heures, au moins," said Dad.

"Ma t-êt' deboute toute la nuite," said Alfred.

Dad grunted. "I can stick around, si tu veux."

Alfred shook his head. "Non, non. Moé pis Richard on d'vrait t-êt' capab'." He glanced at me, and I nodded. Dad studied me for a second, as though assessing the accumulated layers of dirt, mud, sand and sweat caked on my pants, shirt, hands, and boots as evidence of my ability to take on this responsibility.

"Okay," he said. "Bin, I suppose. Since you're still suspended."

"Tabarouette, c'est broche à foin," said Alfred, after Dad left, and we stood staring at the makeshift barrier we'd erected to hold back the small lake that had formed in his back yard. Poly flapped in the breeze and small waves broke against the sandbags. "Mais, ça d'vrait tenir."

"Think the new woodshed will be okay?"

Yesterday's work sat in a half foot of water.

Alfred shrugged. "We'll see," he said.

Then Alfred taught me what Dad had just taught him about the water pump: how to start it, and run it, and ensure it didn't suck straight air and burn out the motor. I nodded, knowing that this meant that I'd be out here, alone, later. I could tell Alfred was tired by the way he leaned his elbows heavily onto his knees as he pointed to the water pump, then slowly straightened out and pointed vaguely into the shed, telling me where he kept the jerry cans. We ran the pump for a bit, enough to drain the small shed, then turned it off.

Inside, we heated the oven and threw some chicken on a baking pan. Alfred sat down in his recliner and fell asleep. I sat at the kitchen table and waited. Running my fingers on the table, tracing the scratches and dents on the surface, I wondered at the time I'd been here—it had been days already—and how it had begun to feel like home.

Though I'd grown weary of the long, quiet nights, the pervasive silence that allowed the world to bleed through the walls—crickets, owls, and small snorting rodents running through the yard. Until the water came. Now as I waited for the chicken to bake, I heard nothing except for the water swirling around the trees, and lapping through the underbrush, and breaking against the barrier.

I turned the radio on, and flipped through the stations, searching for one that didn't put me on edge: I would listen to a song, something fast and heavy that pulled me from our present, but then the song would end abruptly, and the jockey would start yammering on about the flood. News reports kept interrupting the tunes: thousands of folks in Winnipeg were told to evacuate, like the thousands in the towns and the villages strung like pearls along the Red who had already left for high ground. Emerson, Morris, and St. Adolphe, St. Jean Baptiste, and others, had turned into small sunken islands, belly buttons, below the resting level of this giant, growing, sea. The arena in Ste. Anne had become home to hundreds of folks from Roseau River First Nation, Dad had told us this morning. They had been packed in there like sardines with hardly enough food or water or blankets. My fingers froze over the dial as I listened to reports of the army helicoptering out over the water to pluck people off the roof of their swamped homes.

I flinched as the telephone rang. Alfred stirred in his chair, but kept snoring. I answered it reluctantly.

"Richard?" I was surprised to hear Dad's voice. He had called to warn us. "La ligne à Faucher est fermé. Water jumped it just north of the highway, eh. Y'avait un truck dans ditch là, avec l'eau jusqu'au miroir. Had to circle back through Ste. Geneviève and take the number 12. You guys okay there?"

"Uh, yeah," I said, glancing as Alfred grunted and opened his eyes. He pulled himself out of his chair, and then cracked open the oven to look inside. Heat blasted out. He flicked the oven off. "Yeah, we're okay. Just having supper," I said.

"Okay, bin. Call if you need help," Dad said.

"Okay."

Alfred pulled the baking sheet from the oven, stabbed the chicken with a fork, grimaced a moment, and then chuckled. "On a brûlé la poule. Aussi bin d'manger nos bottes en rubber."

Sometime after midnight, the wind picked up and lifted water through the trees, hurling drops the size of sparrows against the cabin. Half asleep, I followed Alfred outside, into the rain, then stood in a puddle behind the wall of plywood, polyethylene, and bags of sand, and stared at the recent snow melt rising around my boots.

Alfred cursed under his breath as he yanked on the rope to pull start the pump motor. The wind raked us with a wet gust and Alfred yelped as a sheet of plywood suddenly see-sawed over the sandbags next to him. Water rushed in underneath, swamping his feet and the small pump.

I grabbed the plywood sheet, lifting it up, pushing aside torn poly, and wedged the sheet back into place. The pump motor coughed and whined as Alfred yanked on the rope again—his elbow shooting out behind him, the rope tight in his hand. I shifted some bags around, stacking them up high against the back of the plywood sheet, and hoping it would hold, but the wind kept pressing them back, and I watched as a whole row of plywood began to waver. The pump motor whined once again, sputtering, and spluttering, and Alfred stood back and glared at it.

"À floodé," he said.

"Too much gas?"

"Non," he shook his head. "Ya d'l'eau dans l'moteur. Faut attendre qu'ça sèche."

"Shit."

We looked out into the yard at the body of water that had risen silently through the trees, only to burst like thunder against the cabin. Water churned, swirling around the woodshed we'd built yesterday; and the old woodshed was being sucked back into the bush by the waves. Water swelled against the firepit where we had sat last night, splashing over the rocks, and pouring into the pit. It spread relentlessly, claiming everything.

Alfred grabbed my elbow.

"Mon homme," he said. "Écoute. Y faut serrer la pompe."

Together we lifted the pump out of the water and brought it into the shed, and we placed it on a small bench where it could dry. Then, we began to scrounge through the shed and around the cabin for lengths of 2x4s to nail against the plywood sheets. Alfred wanted to nail one end to a stake, driven into the ground, behind the wall, but as we drove stakes into the ground, the earth began to gurgle and burp, and water oozed out from the wound, eroding the dirt around the stake, and undercutting the brace. After a few minutes of fruitless labour, like bailing swamp water in a rainstorm, driving stakes into a mud pit only to watch the stakes slowly topple, I shook my head, and turned to Alfred.

"It's not working."

Alfred grunted, wiping rainwater, and sweat from his brow, leaving a trail of dirt across his forehead. "Okay," he said. "Y faut sauver mes affaires."

"What stuff?" I said.

"D'dans cabine, là. Pas mal sûre qu'on va en avwayr d'l'eau à swayr."

Water curled around my boots as I sat on the floor of the kitchen, and my legs drooped into the crawlspace.

"It's wet," I said, and Alfred nodded. He carried a candle, which he'd sparked with his lighter, and placed it gingerly on the table, away from the stack of boxes we had brought from beneath his bed. A small fire crackled in the wood stove along the wall, and orange light flared atop the linoleum. We had prepared for the worst—a foot of water in the cabin. We had lifted the couch onto some wood blocks like an old car with no wheels, and then rolled the throw rugs and tossed them onto the couch. We pulled the bottom drawers out from Alfred's dresser and cleaned out the bottom of his closets, tossing everything we could onto the bed and the kitchen counter in case water began to seep through the floor hatch in the kitchen. Then Alfred had me look into the crawlspace, and when I saw water curling around my boots, Alfred went over to the electric box and cut the power, plunging us into darkness. We sat around the kitchen table. Firelight filled the room as we caught our breath. On the coffee table in the living room, we'd placed the old chest that Alfred kept in his bedroom. It was heavier than I'd suspected, filled with old photo albums, papers, and furs. A ratty hat with a racoon tail, a pair of mukluks. There was an old piece of hide, in the shape of a flat octopus, covered in brightly beaded flowers. I glanced at it briefly as Alfred tossed some of it onto his bed to lighten the load. Then Alfred showed me the attic hatch in the closet, and he had me climb onto a chair to stuff a couple boxes up there too since the kitchen counters were overburdened, bristling with drawerfuls of assorted things, and piles of clothing, shoeboxes of cassette tapes, and books that teetered over the edge.

After everything had been secured, Alfred placed a kettle on the woodstove, and fetched a couple mugs from the cabinets. We sat and waited for our tea.

"Faudra checker la pompe, après," he said, and yawned.

"Okay," I said, and closed my eyes, resting my lids for a moment. The kettle howled atop the wood stove like some neighbour's dog down the mile road. Flinching as something struck my foot, I blinked. Alfred stood before me, his outstretched hand offering me a mug of steaming tea.

"Tu cognes des clous," he said.

"Sorry," I yawned, and taking the mug from his hand, I tried not to nod off.

"C'pas grave," he shrugged. "Deux minutes," he said. "And we'll check that pump."

I nodded, and sipped at the tea. Alfred settled onto his chair, groaning as he stretched his legs out—I could tell his back was hurting—and he sipped noisily on his tea as though the sound had become a necessary part of our vigil. Dropping my eyes, I stared at the sheen of firelight that skipped along the boxes on the table. Out from a box, and through the distended accumulation of dust and the pale turn of time, a woman gazed at me. Sporting a big hat and an old-timey dress that ballooned over her lower half, the woman sat in a parlour of sorts. Potted plant in the corner. A rug on the wall. She forced a smile, for the camera, that did not touch her eyes. Faded and lost edges, the photograph rested atop a small pile of black and whites. Curious, I reached into the box, plucked the photograph from the stack, and held it up in the firelight. On the back, a word and a date, barely legible: Saint-Adolphe, 1909.

"Menoncle," I said, lifting the photograph for him to see. He took it from my hands and peered at the woman. "C'est qui?" I asked.

He sipped his tea and smiled.

"Ma mère."

21.

La chicoque de Ste. Geneviève

THE MORNING AFTER THE FUNERAL DIRECTOR'S VISIT, we drove out to Alfred's cabin to fetch some things for the service, find Alfred's will, and lock up the cabin so that critters—squirrels, mice, racoons—didn't nest over winter and wreck the place. Alfred had made Dad executor of his will, but we had little idea what was in it. Alfred had gone on for years now about his final wishes, the funeral service, and how he wanted to be cremated with his favorite camo-coloured ballcap, but in terms of possessions, he had never mentioned his plans. Mom didn't think there was much to consider. Alfred had never been a rich man. He had mostly scraped by on the odd job most of his life, living on that small patch of bush south of Ste. Geneviève; but there was the question of land. No one knew how much land he had or what was to become of it.

"Peut-être qu'y t'la laisser, sa terre, Émile," said Mom.

Dad shook his head. He gripped the steering wheel, and edged the truck out of the yard, onto the road. Wind knocked the branches together, and dry, shrivelled leaves fell softly with the snow overtop the gravel. I stretched in the seat next to Dad—Mom sat on the pullout seat behind me—and groaned as pain flashed down my leg. I'd taken a pill before we left home, but it hadn't kicked in yet. I tried to ignore the discomfort, and wondered who Alfred would pass his land to. I turned to Dad.

"Who else then?" I said.

"I don't know," he said. "But ça sert à rien à s'imaginer."

"Well, that's sad," said Mom. "I like to hope."

The truck juddered toward the highway. Rain and low temperatures had caused water to freeze overnight, bursting open the gravel and etching the season onto the land so that we felt it through our bones and teeth as the truck rattled over the pockmarked road. The rain had turned to snow, a dusting of flurries, before it tapered off. It had been an otherwise warm, dry November, but the unseasonable warmth was receding now, and that familiar cold returning. Dad swerved around holes covered in a skin of ice and filled with some unknown depth of water while Mom complained of being tossed like a rag doll in the back seat.

Near the highway, a big, bright golden bee hovered over a ditch full of water. Large hose held tight in its tiny arms. From a certain angle, it had always looked like the bee was jerking off. The phone number was half submerged in shimmering fluid, twinned in the ditch water.

"That reminds me," said Mom, "Joe called last night."

"What?" I said, twisting to glance back at my mother. "Why didn't you tell me?"

"I'm telling you now," she said.

Dad grunted. "You were asleep."

"Oh."

"He asked if you'd be able to run a couple jobs this week. He's swamped," said Mom.

Dad grunted. "C't'un peu mal élevé, non? Demander à un temps comme ça."

"It doesn't hurt to ask, Émile," Mom scoffed.

Hair rising on my neck, I could sense Mom skewering Dad with her eyes.

Fighting the swift chill that shot along my skin, I stuffed my hands into my coat pockets, and felt a hard, plastic object brush my knuckles. Big head. I traced its shape with the tip of my fingers, and turned it over with my thumb. Spindly legs. I pulled the small object from my pocket and stared at the small horns protruding from the sides of its head. The moulded coat of thick fur and its thin legs gave it an uneven look, as though it ought not to have existed. Imagine a million of these things stampeding around, as though on matchsticks. How people used to hunt these things, on horseback, no less, with muskets and lead balls stuffed in their cheeks like squirrels with nuts, was beyond me.

"Well," I said, as some vague notion of the future—a pack of cigarettes, and a side mirror for the Buick, maybe even something for Becky—began to take shape in my mind. Though I had not thought of Becky much since the night Alfred passed, she had begun intruding again, the idea of us together in the city demanding consideration. I knew we were on a knife edge. "The money would be nice." I stuffed the plastic bison back into my coat. "And the distraction."

Dad grunted once more and glanced at me out of the corner of his eye. I could tell that he had something to say, but he swallowed his words and laid his foot heavily on the gas. The truck surged ahead, north across the highway, and back onto the gravel. Clouds of dust rose up behind us, pulled from the earth by the fury of our passing.

Alfred's cabin had changed some over the years, mostly growing old like its owner—time etched in the wear. I'd hardly noticed the crooked eavestroughs or the sagging roof when I had swung by earlier this fall to clear the yard of leaves and branches. Alfred had sat quietly on a bench, wrapped in a woolen blanket, and watched me work. Afterwards, he invited me inside for a cup of Red Rose, but I told him that I had to run. Joe was waiting to teach me how to work the vacuum truck and clean out a septic tank. And so, I shook Alfred's bony hand, and left him in the yard as I hopped into the Buick and drove away.

Now, as we exited Dad's truck, the full weight of the cabin's deterioration struck me: the broken shutters, the rotten, porous window frames and sills, the wind-scoured walls peeling like sun-burnt skin, the missing shingles, the web of cracks through the foundation.

"Crisse," said Dad as we walked up to the cabin. "Paramedics forgot to shut the door."

Inside, the cabin was a mess. Flies buzzed over a bowl of cold soup thickened with time. Dirty dishes on the counter. The phone receiver hung from the wall, the earpiece lying crookedly on the floor. Boot prints covered the linoleum, in a circle, around where Alfred had waited on all fours. Paw prints snaked through the cabin as though some rodents had come in during the night in search of food or shelter. Something had knocked the saucepan off the stovetop and tasted the soup splashed on the ground. The lightbulb above the table crackled, bathing a mound of dead flies in hot light.

Then we noticed the papers scattered through the living room. Boxes overturned, emptied onto the old sofa. Books strewn haphazardly before bare shelves. Cassette tapes tossed along the baseboards. Drawers and cupboards opened—their contents dumped on the floor. I surveyed the chaos in quiet confusion. "What happened? Did Alfred do this?"

Dad shook his head. "I don't know."

"Voyons donc, ça fait pas d'sens," said Mom.

We talked ourselves out of calling the police after we searched through Alfred's tossed belongings. Even the old heirloom he had once showed me, and which he kept in the large trunk in his bedroom, remained, though it now lay crumpled on the floor, its beads strewn, seeded into the carpet.

"Ça doit être des gamins," said Dad. He lifted the old fire bag from the floor and beads dribbled through his fingers like sand in an hourglass. He scratched his head, and tried to make sense of the ransack. "Mais y'ont rien pris."

There didn't seem to be anything missing.

We plucked the beads out of the carpet, and dropped them in a small jar we fetched from the kitchen, then Dad placed the jar and the heirloom back into the chest, allowing his fingers to gently caress the old leather and velvet, the shorn, faded flowers, before he withdrew.

We set about cleaning the cabin, placing things back where they'd always been. I washed the floor and started the dishes while Mom and Dad began to look through Alfred's papers. They set aside his photo albums as they reshelved the books: histories, biographies, old encyclopedias. Stacks of papers.

"Tabarnak," said Dad. "Regard ça." He waved some brittle old sheet at Mom. "Fucking forty-year-old church hymns. Quessé qu'il fait avec ça?"

"He was a pack-rat, Émile," said Mom.

I watched my parents work, glance at every sheet or paper before stuffing it into a box. Alfred had accumulated even more boxes since the time I had helped pile them atop the counter. Water had come up so fast, filling the crawlspace, that we feared it would seep through the floor, gush in through the hatch, and spread about the cabin.

Fetching the bowl of cold soup from the table, I paused as I saw myself sitting there with Alfred over a decade ago. He told me, in the dead of night as water crashed outdoors against the bags of sand and plywood sheets, how he had ended up here, shoved to the gravel-laced brim of the prairie. Alfred told me how his mother had been raised in the valley below, already in retreat. Her folks had left behind the river lot on the Assiniboine—that place stained now with the name of an old general—and sought shelter amid the trickle of French Catholics settling along the Red. Cognant des clous at the kitchen table, Alfred kept sleep at bay with the sound of his voice. And later, as we stood wearily upon the makeshift dike, small pump motoring behind us, he explained that they'd washed up here like driftwood. Uprooted. Tossed aside. Bleached through that killing sun. His grandmother had heard the cannons. Though I heard only every other word and was left with a vague and hazy impression of this line of grandmothers, and I wondered which cannons, I also glimpsed at how the stories had become shrouded. How, perhaps through the act of holding on to them so tightly, the stories had fractured, were passed down in bits and pieces, wrapped in whispers, like seedlings swathed in le grand silence. Scattered. Forgotten. Then, painstakingly reassembled like a puzzle without a reference. Over the years, Alfred had gathered the pieces and reshaped them into a story.

"Dans l'temps—" his voice faded.

A glimmer on the table caught my eye. Lifting the corner of a dishtowel, I discovered a bright, silver flask. It seemed familiar, if out of place, much the like the one I'd picked out of the grass at J.P.'s. I'd never known Alfred to keep a flask, let alone some bright, gaudy thing. But, as I grabbed and placed the flask on the counter next to the sink, I conceded that my visits had dwindled of late. In the end, I wondered how well I knew Alfred. The last time here, I hadn't set foot in the cabin.

I finished up in the kitchen, draped the dishrag over the faucet, and looked over at my parents—they were still seated on the couch, slowly thumbing through the photo albums—and I asked if they'd found what they were looking for, if they'd found the will.

Dad shrugged, and Mom shook her head. "Non," she said. "Va donc checker la chambre à coucher. I bet it's in there."

Though I suspected she'd urged me there because of their own reluctance to trespass into Alfred's private space, or because of their inability to tear themselves away from the photos and the memories they brought up, I let them be, and I ventured into Alfred's bedroom.

Drawers hung limply from the dresser. Clothes lay piled on the floor. The room smelled of sweat and something else, something faint—some familiar stench that hovered at the edge of my awareness like shadows in a shallow creek. Bitter dust drifted in the wake of my movement and settled atop the picture frames on the wall. Stoic, sun-stained faces stared out through time: Mémère and Pépère. Alfred's parents in front of un gros chêne. Others I did not recognize, their names buried in a bank of memory. Catching my reflection in the mirror, over the small desk, I stepped aside so as not to dwell on the bags beneath my eyes, and I spotted a small cross, its twin in the glass. The cross hung from the tip of un chapelet strung over the corner of the frame. I had never noticed it before, never seen Alfred with it, but from the greasy shine of the beads, I could tell it had passed repeatedly through someone's fingers. Next to the mirror and the desk, sat the gun safe where Alfred kept la *grande* carabine, and his shotgun. The safe was locked, although someone had at one time chipped the paint trying to pry the safe open. Finally, I peered into the old chest along the wall. Reaching inside, I pushed aside some of the objects, picture frames with black and whites, mukluks, gloves, and old clothes, as I searched for the bundle of papers. Beads rattled inside the small jar. I stepped backwards and bumped into the bed, causing the headboard to bounce against the far wall. Something chittered in the closet, and I glanced over my shoulder as the closet door began to rattle against the doorframe. Claws scratched at the wall.

"Hey," I shouted. "There's something in here."

"What is it? Did you find the will?" Dad called.

"No. There's something alive."

"Quessé qu'tu veux dire, something's alive?"

The closet door clapped against the frame.

"There's something alive in the closet!" I shouted.

"Bin, va checker," said Dad, appearing in the doorway. "Maybe a mouse."

"That's no mouse," I grumbled.

"Vas-y," he said, nodding toward the closet.

Grunting, I approached the closet slowly. The floor creaked underfoot. The closet door grew still, before it burst loudly against the frame again, as though the animal inside sensed my approach. Dad blinked, and glanced back into the living room. He called mom to come and see.

"Fuck," I said. "Here goes." I grabbed the doorknob and yanked open the closet.

Dad yelped. He recoiled and tripped backwards as a big, black, snow-striped beast burst from the closet and dashed beneath the bed. It paced there in circles; chittered and hissed angrily. Pancaked to the wall, I watched as the animal finally darted from underneath the bed, through the bedroom door into the living room. Dad yelped again, and dropped his eyes into the crook of his elbow, as the beast clambered overtop. Heading over to see what the hubbub was all about, Mom yelled as the beast leaped over Dad, and she flung herself over the sofa. I peeked into the living room, and saw la chicoque scamper beneath the dining table where it paused, and still chittering, spun around, searching for an exit.

"Émile!" yelled Mom. "Fais quètchose!"

La chicoque turned and pinned Mom with a look. It charged forward again, but stopped at the edge of the kitchen, where lino-leum turned to carpet, and smacked its lips. Dad scrambled backward, bumping into the wall. Mom peeked over the sofa.

"Richard!" she yelled. "Poigne une couverte!"

The skunk stomped its feet and hissed.

"Dépêche! Avant qu'a spray!"

Without thinking, I yanked the comforter off Alfred's bed, sending boxes of clothes and things crashing to the floor, then stretching the comforter like a sail between my hands, I hurried out of the bedroom. Mom yelled again, panicked, and flung her finger toward the stomping beast in the kitchen, and I ran toward the thing. Peeking over the sheet, trying not to trip on its edges, I saw la chicoque freeze and stare at the moving wall. As I stepped closer though, the skunk began to squeal. Its tail snapping upwards, the beast aimed its rear-end at me as I hurled the comforter over it. Under cover, la chicoque hissed and growled, clawing at the comforter, but draped in the warm and heavy blanket, and unable to move or spray us, it began to settle. Dad appeared at my side—fingers interlaced atop his head—and we stared at the chittering bundle on the floor. Mom crept quietly around the blanket and opened the front door. Dad gestured to the living room, and I grabbed a box and passed it to him, and he placed it carefully over the bulge in the blanket. The skunk grumbled, and the box quivered.

"Let's drag it outside," said Dad.

Each lifting a corner, Mom and I gently pulled the comforter toward the door. Dad held the box down over the skunk, herding it so that it didn't dart out from under the blanket and back into the cabin. We squeezed onto the gravel and dropped the corners, yanked the box off to allow the beast to worm its way out from the blanket, and we hurried back into the cabin. We watched through the window as the animal wound its way free and scampered into the forest. Pent-up air burst from our chests.

Mom sat heavily at the kitchen table.

"J'ai jamais vu ça," she said.

"Tabarouette," said Dad. He suddenly folded in half and slapped his knee. I reached for him, thinking he had broken down and began to weep, but as I placed my hand on his shoulder, and I felt the elated tremors of his body, I realized he trembled with the force of laughter. Mom began to shudder in delight at the table. And as I watched them, I felt a barbed knot in my chest unravel. Laughter spilled from my throat.

After la chicoque had gone, and we had drenched ourselves in laughter, and grown silent again with the dull echo of our voices faded in the walls, we turned once more to Alfred's things. I ventured into the bedroom and peeking into the closet, I discovered a flannel jacket crumpled in the corner. Wrinkling my nose, I lifted it off the floor, and recognized the broad collar, the faded stains, and the galaxy of burns down the front, small holes singed through careless, accumulated flurries of cigarette embers. It was J.P. Gauthier's. The jacket stank of animal musk, like a skunk had slept on it. For a moment, I thought J.P. had transmuted into that skunk and locked himself into the closet. I imagined him scurrying like the weasel he was through the forest, trying to find his way home to the farm. Then, as the fog of this dream parted, I realized J.P. had been the one to tear through Alfred's things. He had likely run into the skunk in the bedroom and, in a panic, had tossed his jacket at the animal, then locked it in the closet. He must have left his flask on the table as he fled. I wondered briefly what he had been after, but then remembered him at the party last Friday.

"Pigs!" he had shouted. "Pigs!"

He planned to raise pigs and build an empire. The problem was he didn't have the cash. He had finally gotten his hands on the farm only to discover a mound of debt and some worthless cows. He had masked his terrible disappointment with an extravagant, barn-shaking party, only to reveal afterwards his own bitter pettiness. My shoulder still pulsed with the bruise-echo of the fist-blows he'd meted out two mornings ago; my fingers still burned, stung from the force that tore the flask away from me. In the dim light of Alfred's bedroom, I saw how J.P. Gauthier had sniffed an opportunity with Alfred's stroke. How in his hunger, he attempted to fuel his ambition with Alfred's meager wealth. He had been after the will. Maybe even Alfred's land. And failing that, I supposed, the old guns.

"Fucking J.P.," I shouted through the door to my parents. As they came into the bedroom and stared in wonder at the flannel jacket, noses wrinkling instinctively, I glanced once more into the closet and noticed the attic hatch in the ceiling. Clambering atop a box, I reached and wedged the hatch open. It creaked, hinges stiff with rust, and clattered on the crossbeams.

"Enfant d'chienne," I heard Dad mutter below as I poked my head into the attic.

Dust swirled through the air, and I waited for my eyes to adjust to the darkness.

"Si c'était pas parenté—"

"Bin, so what si c'est parenté?" Mom said.

Peering through the softening cloud of dust, I spotted a lockbox, tucked between a pair of crossbeams. Stretching across the ceiling, I felt the wood creak under my weight.

"Fait 'tention, là," called Dad.

I dragged the box across the beam, then hauled it down, and passed it to Dad. After we'd placed it on the kitchen table, Dad slapped me on the shoulder while Mom fiddled with the lock.

"Do you have the key?" asked Mom.

"Must be in the bunch," Dad said, and from his pocket he pulled a keychain that bristled with a half-dozen old keys. After he tried a few, each one grinding into the lock like some rusted-out engine trying to spin, the lockbox clicked. Crowding together as Dad lifted the lid, we looked in the box. Dad plucked out a bundle of old letters, set them aside, then peered inside once more.

"Here we go," he said.

He held the will in his hand. Unfolded it slowly. Began to read.

"Quessé qu'ça dit?" asked Mom.

Dad grunted.

"Bin?"

"Ostie," he said.

"What is it?"

"Ah bin, sacrament."

"What?" I said again.

"I knew it," he said. "I fucking knew it." And he slumped into a chair and began to laugh. We glared at him as he laughed and wiped tears from his eyes. Then Dad looked up at us, and he shook his head, and he pointed his chin toward Alfred's bedroom. "Le vieux pet savait garder un secret."

Mom swiped the paper from his hand. She read quickly, her eyes growing narrow as they darted over the words. She came to the bottom and frowned, turned the page over and looked at the empty, blank side, then back again. She held it out for Dad to take. "What is this?"

"God damn it! What is it?" I shouted.

Dad leaned back in his chair, fingers laced over his head again, and he looked out through the window at the woods. "Bin," he said. "Y m'a presque tout laissé, but Alfred has no land."

22.

Et pis y'avait
vendu la terre

AND SO, IT CAME OUT. NOT THE WHOLE TRUTH OF IT,
but enough to glimpse at the sordid mess of how it happened. How
Pépère had lost his land because Alfred had sold it from under him,
and how le vieux Gauthier had been at the centre of it all.

We crowded around the table and poured over the bundle of letters—there was a slew of correspondence between Alfred and Mémère
explaining what had happened. Alfred had written near the whole of
it down, in broken French and half English, recounting details of the
events—how he had lost his brother's land, their fallout, and his self-
imposed penance—over, and over, as though trying to understand the
whole of it himself. Like a confession. He begged Mémère for forgive-
ness, and she, in her strong, nun-taught hand, wrote of how it was not
her place to forgive him. His brother, Alexandre, was dead, and their
reconciliation would be possible only dans le prochain monde.

The words dropped in like keystones amid the honeycombed
stories Dad possessed; the fragmented bits of history he had carried

without understanding, the hints of an old fight that no one talked about, coming into focus.

See, Pépère had been a carpenter too. It was a useful skill that his father had taught him, and which he passed along to his children. During the Great Depression he'd somehow found a job with the Greater Winnipeg Water District Railway—there'd been a rail stop nearby, at one time, over in Ross—and so Pépère had scrapped and saved and eventually bought a small plot of land near Ste. Geneviève for him and Mémère and their kids to live on. Enough land to grow some things and support a cow for milk. There'd been a ton of rabbits and hares around 'la poche aux lièvres' back then, and some of the older boys—Dad's older brothers—would snare them by the dozens whenever the pantry grew empty. I'd seen old photos of Dad as a boy, rabbits strung through his belt by their heels, ears brushing the gravel. He'd hoofed it back and forth, hauling the rabbits and hares between the house and the snares while his older brothers and sisters reset the wires. They had hunted deer with a bow or a rifle depending on the time of year, and grew potatoes and other things that sprouted thinly in the gravel-laden soil. Dad told us these things in parts over the years, often when we visited the old plot to pick chokecherries and saskatoons for wine and jam. The land where Dad's old house once stood had been chewed up and spat out by a gravel company—now riddled with yawning pits, mounds of waste-rock and a mop of weeds, it was mostly abandoned, roved by dirt-bikers, and settled only by coyotes.

Before the war, Pépère and Alfred worked together at the GWWDR. Then something—Dad knew only the broad strokes and Alfred had only once mentioned it in passing—happened. Some words were exchanged, some of the other workers said something against the Métis, or maybe it was the French, and, still young, Alfred spoke back. There was a scuffle. He broke an Orangeman's nose. Afterwards, both he and Pépère lost their jobs.

Out of work, they considered moving and maybe following relatives west like others had done years earlier. But the stories their relatives had sent back—how they'd ended up in logging camps or shovelling gravel or coal or shit for pennies—kept them from that road. When the war broke out, Pépère was glad for the work. He joined the army for the income.

While Pépère was curled up in some fox hole in Europe and German bullets screamed over his head, le vieux Gauthier approached Alfred with a proposal. There was a piece of land half-way between Ste. Anne and Richer that he had his eye on, but, said Gauthier, he needed help to purchase it. He needed some collateral, he said. Alfred didn't know him very well; his older sister, Marguerite, had married him only a few years before, and they had moved around looking for work, only to come back when the war broke out. Now a widow was selling some land and Gauthier wanted to try his hand at ranching. Since Pépère was away and Mémère had her hands full avec les gamins, Gauthier came to see Alfred, and showed him the papers. All he needed was a signature, he said. Alfred listened to Gauthier explain it—how the bank needed to make sure Gauthier could afford the land. Alfred looked over the papers, but did not understand them. Always butting heads with the nuns, Alfred had dropped out of school early, and had never learned to fully read in French, let alone in English. Words such as *transaction* and *in lieu* swept by him like a cold breeze that he hardly registered.

"Just an X will do," said Gauthier, in French. "Drette là."

Alfred signed.

A few years after the war ended and Pépère returned home, secreting scars from bullets that had burst inches from his face in a concrete bunker, men from the gravel company appeared to survey the property. Sleeves rolled-up over their arms, ties drooped, hats pushed back on their heads, they stood in the late morning sun and wondered at the house sitting on the land they had planned to overturn. On the hood of their car, they'd spread out a map. They stabbed their fingers on the hood then pointed at the house. From the yard, by the cow pen, where they were fixing a busted fence board, Alfred and Pépère watched the men fold up their map. Then, when the men began to hike toward the house, Pépère clutched his hammer and went to meet them halfway.

"C'est assez loin ici," he said. "Quessé qu'vous voulez?"

The men stopped and glanced at each other. Mémère came outside, planted herself on the porch with Matante Yolande perched on her hip, Dad clutching her leg, plucking at her apron.

"Qu'est-ce qui se passe?" she shouted.

"What d'you want?" Pépère repeated.

Pépère had picked up a bundle of language during the war, if not a smooth tongue. The men glanced at one another once again. Flies whirled around their ears and locust hummed in the grass.

* * *

"Enfant d'chienne," whispered Dad. "It's all here." Leaning back in his chair, he glanced through the window where Alfred had once shot a deer, at the poplars and the birch, and the oaks and beyond at the swamp, toward the gravel pits where they'd once lived.

I spread the bundle of letters out across the table, and Mom began to move them around in some sort of order, tracing the back and forth between Alfred and Mémère. We had wondered at their relationship— Dad had told of their estrangement right after his parents moved the family to town, how Alfred stayed in the bush—how it grew worse after Pépère's passing—and was not welcome for a time, but then how Alfred and Mémère eventually made up and, for a few years, he became a fixture again at holidays. Then something must have been said because, in the final years before Mémère passed, they drifted apart again. We'd never know the whole of it, but Dad once let slip after a couple beers how Alfred loved Mémère more than he should. We knew that they'd occasionally written to each other—some of Dad's brothers had hauled letters back and forth—but we had never imagined such lengthy correspondence. Dozens of letters across nearly two decades. The last one dated only a few years before Mémère died. Staring at the letters, I thought perhaps they held some key to the causes of their fallouts.

Dad rose and began to search the cupboards, muttering about un p'tit coup—pour calmer les nerfs. Mom read over a letter and grunted.

"Listen to this," she said, and as she began to read the letter aloud, a vision washed over me.

* * *

Pépère fought a while for his land. After the gravel men showed up the first time, he went with Alfred to talk to le vieux Gauthier who professed to not know a thing about it, then admitted that Alfred had signed some paperwork that the bank had drawn up for him, since Alfred was a better reader than him. Alfred scoffed, but le vieux just shrugged and said what was done was done. Their sister, Marguerite, listened to them bicker around the kitchen table for a while, then she grew sick at the talk and the less than subtle insinuations about her husband. She had no idea how her husband had obtained the land, but shook her head and refused to accept the implication of some wrongdoing, and so when Pépère pressed them all for some details of just what in the hell had happened, while he had been away fighting for their crisse de liberté, Marguerite stood and put an end to it. Non. She would not listen to their accusations, et pis sans preuve itou. Then she politely asked her brothers to leave.

Pépère went to the bank and asked them about the land and the gravel company. Before he went, he pulled out his old war uniform, and even polished his shoes, because he had learned that this was sometimes the only way for him to get through the door. The bank manager politely listened, then complimented him on his French. He had been born in Manitoba, but his parents were from Belgium, and he thanked Pépère for his help liberating his country. Then, he said that, regarding the land, there was nothing to be done, unless, of course, Pépère was accusing Alfred of fraud, and of forgery, in which case this would become a criminal matter.

"Djis-quoè?" Pépère blurted.

"Est-ce que j'appelle la police?" the man asked, his hand hovering over the telephone on his desk while Pépère sat across from him, aghast, his mind racing through the horrors he almost unleashed: thoughts of his younger brother being dragged away screaming in chains, never to be seen again.

"Non, non," said Pépère, his stomach suddenly roiling as if Germans were charging his foxhole, "Ça doit êt'e aen nashpatistamihk," he said, his cheeks flushing as the manager blinked. "La koonfuzyoon," he said. The managed blinked again. "Un malentendu," Pépère clarified.

"Ah, bien sure," the manager nodded and rose. Pépère jumped to his feet and his fingers twitched as if wanting to salute the man behind the desk, or knock his lights out, but instead, he shook the manager's hand when the man offered it, and then left.

"Y voulait l'fendre en deux, comme y'avait fait aux Allemands," Alfred wrote to Mémère. "Mais y savait qu'ça servirait à rien."

Eventually, Pépère went straight to the gravel company, the men who now owned the land, again in his uniform, freshly laundered and pressed, his shoes polished to the colour of a midwinter sky on a moonless night, medals pinned across his left breast. Their offices were in the city, so Pépère took his horse to Winnipeg. Alfred followed close behind on his small mare. Mémère stood on the porch with Dad—only a toddler then—banging a wooden spoon on an old pot at her feet, watching them ride away. Some of the older boys—Frank, Roger—had asked to accompany them, but Pépère said that it was best that he and Alfred do this alone.

They were gone for three days. When they returned, Pépère collapsed from exhaustion and had to be dragged to his bed where he slept through the afternoon, the night, and well into the following morning.

He'd talked for two days straight, Alfred said. And he recounted the story.

The gravel men who'd initially come out to survey the property had spotted them on the street outside of their small office, and reluctantly brought them inside to meet with their bosses. The gravel men listened politely, their eyes drifting over the medals pinned to Pépère's chest, and though they scoffed, and they shook their heads whenever he pressed for compensation, they continued to listen, and Alfred saw how, in the flick of their eyes and in their curious patience, a calculus emerged over the question of dispossessing a war hero. Although the question of who had signed the paperwork came up, it was dropped early on after the realization that any scrutiny might tie the land up in red tape for years, and worse, they might lose the land, and so gradually, as the sun began to dip over the city and moonlight washed over the room, an agreement began to emerge, and they agreed to continue in the morning. At sunrise, they were back—hammering away at it. Pépère spoke of the land, how it represented life for him and his family, how without it they would be destitute, and Alfred spoke of how they'd hunted for their meat, taking deer and hares, and birds, and how those skills with a rifle had served Pépère well in the war. He pointed to his brother's chest, and the medals that glowed under the electric light. He spoke of Pépère's sacrifices. The gravel men glanced at the scars riddled across Pépère's face, the bullet fragments and bits of concrete gouged into his cheeks.

"Deux pieds à gauche," Alfred waxed.

The gravel men wavered, gave ground, and eventually an agreement was struck. Pépère would be allowed to lease the land from them as the land around him was broken open for gravel extraction. The gravel company would then chip in for the cost of moving the house within a few miles—Ste. Anne, Richer, or Ste. Geneviève. Ten years would be sufficient time to allow Pépère to raise the funds to purchase some new plot of land. Greatly impressed with Alfred's account of his brother's war stories, the gravel company even offered them a free load of gravel.

The entire sordid story oozed out of the letters, that correspondence between Alfred and Mémère. Years after Pépère died, struck down by a heart attack only a short while after they had finally moved to Ste. Anne, Mémère wrote to Alfred, asking him what had happened between the two of them, why their relationship had become so volatile in the last years of Pépère's life. At first Alfred had reluctantly explained how Pépère had never fully forgiven him his mistake, but then he began to unburden himself. Even as Alfred had vowed to never let it happen again, and he taught himself to read and write, and he stuck by Pépère as best he could to help him out of the mess that he had created, Pépère began to occasionally lash out at him. At first it was only a word here or there, but it grew, usually after a few drinks, into petty acts of spite, when Pépère would suddenly open the door and throw his brother's coat into the mud or, after a few more drinks, he would try to provoke Alfred into a fight. Pépère even threw a punch once, after Alfred said something about his drinking, but Alfred stepped aside, and he watched his brother trip and tumble to the floor.

Then, about a year before they lost the land for good and moved to town, and though he would later protest that he had become confused in the woods, that the light had knifed through the tops of the branches and the falling snow in such a particular way as he'd held his rifle and watched for deer, Pépère had suddenly believed himself back in the war. All in a moment, when he spotted a man up in the trees, caught like a German paratrooper, he panicked, and reflexively lifted his rifle, and with cold, mechanical efficiency, he took aim and fired.

Alfred hurled himself from the tree as the rifle cracked.

Torn from his delusion, Pépère saw his brother motionless beneath the tree, and a torrent of shame flooded inside, and sent him running through the bush.

Some hours later, Alfred awoke; a thin layer of snow had accumulated around him, and he shivered in the cold autumn dark. He ground his teeth, rolled onto his stomach, nearly passed out as pain cascaded down his back and his leg, but he began to crawl toward the house. He sang, Alfred said, he sang as though his life depended on it, and through the cold and snow and dark of the evening fall he wound his way home. Finally, in the early morning as blood spilled across the eastern sky, Alfred pulled himself through the treeline, and at the edge of Pépère's yard, he cried out for help.

"J'avais peur qu'y m'tue," Alfred confessed shakily in writing. "Mais y'était mon frère, et j'cré qu'i n'm'avait jamais voulu le mal, qu'y'était juste malade."

Mom finished reading the letter then folded it up and placed it back in the box. Dad stood by the sink, leaning against the counter, a half-emptied bottle of brandy in his hand. He uncorked the top and took a swig.

The memory of each time Alfred had told that story swirled through my mind. I looked at the table under which Monique and I had crawled as kids, chasing Alfred around the cabin, and I imagined how he must have tried so often to tell us what had really happened, but that each time, as he approached the truth of it, the story must have grown too real, too close, raw, and he would veer away from the awful truth and turn it into something silly. Something to make us laugh.

And as I searched through the parts of story scattered amid my memories, I wondered then if in every telling Alfred had seeded some bits of truth, as though he'd hoped that one day, out of the seeds, something good might grow.

Au bord des bois

23.

Things Best Left Where They Fell

WHEN WE FIRST MOVED TO THAT PIECE OF LAND ON the gravel ridge east of town, Alfred told us a story about a man who had disappeared into the brush not far from where our new house sat. It had been about midway through a long and cold winter, and the man had run out of food, and his wife had pleaded with him to find something for their children to eat. So, the man had asked his neighbours, but they had not a thing to share, and with sparkling French from across the ocean, they berated him for not better preparing for the harsh winter. The man tried to see their point of view. Perhaps he ought to have better saved his money and his own food the year before when he had helped these very men after they'd settled nearby and struggled through a similarly long and cold winter, but he had learned in his youth that neighbours help each other, and he had not been prepared for the sudden reversal of that old tradition.

Desperate, the man hitched his meager horse and decided to ask the priest for help, but as he rode through town, and he saw men and women looking at him with disdain and contempt, he sensed that his pleas would come to nothing. The butcher who'd once laughed in his face when he asked for un paquet d'li jeur—because he didn't know the *proper* word for liver—snorted as he went by. The postman's wife wrinkled her nose. Nuns scowled. Finally, as he sat across from le gros prêtre and he listened to the fat cleric speak, the man knew that it was useless. They had been absent from church too long, the priest said, and all the help he could give had been given. The man nodded and kept quiet, and did not mention the bags of potatoes and flour that he had seen piled in the hallway as the priest led him into the office.

When he returned home, his wife met him at the door and stared at his empty hands. She then told him the neighbours had stopped by and offered to help, to give them a few dollars for a portion of their land, enough to get through the winter. The man rubbed his hide-covered foot in the snow; he kicked at the hard crust. He could not understand how they had had nothing to give him earlier when he asked for help, but now suddenly they had enough to buy land. Though his wife asked him to speak again with the men down the road, the man decided that he would give them nothing and he would accept nothing.

He would try his luck in the forest.

Early the next morning, with a bow slung over his shoulder, the man set out into the bush. He had learned to rely on the bow again since the arrival of these men, so as not to alert them, to give away his hunting ground. But these men had grown suspicious of his absences, and so when they came by the day after he had asked them for help, to again offer some pittance for his land, and saw that he was not there, they forced his wife to tell them where he had gone.

The man's wife shivered in the doorway and rubbed her arm as she watched the men go. With rifles slung over their shoulders, they disappeared into the treeline. The woman hurriedly bundled up her children, saddled the horse, and brought the children to her sister's house. Then, returning home, she grabbed her husband's rifle, hopped back onto the horse, and drove after the men into the forest. Through the late-winter-snow, she rode after them. She followed the ragged tracks, the broken twigs over the shattered skin of ice. She eased her horse along and listened for sounds of men—the trudge of their feet and the cracking of snow and ice, the snapping of wood, the occasional word or wisp caught in the wind. Though she rode for what seemed like hours, the sun, towering far above the trees, had stopped moving.

Then a gunshot ricocheted through the woods.

"Bang!" Alfred shouted and clapped his hands together. I jumped, nearly falling from the front steps where we sat listening.

Monique frowned.

"Then what?" she said.

Alfred cleared his throat and, casting his eyes to the treeline, said that the woman looked through the trees, edging her horse deeper and deeper into the bush, but the tracks she followed seemed to veer left and right and looped around again, crossing over each other. Then she heard another shot—much closer—and someone cried out. The woman aimed her horse towards the sound and, as she pushed ahead, the trees gave way to a wide, snow-lashed clearing.

"Une forêt d'vieilles quenouilles," said Alfred.

Wind-sheared and shredded cattails swayed over ice-topped snowbanks and tufts of tall, brown grass. The horse snorted, unsure of its footing, reluctant to venture further. The woman peered into the bog at the scattered clumps of stunted trees and uneven ground. She recognized this place—she had picked medicines here before—and knew that it spread out in a labyrinth of cattails and willows with dips of deep water and soft earth that could swallow a horse whole in the spring.

In the distance, she saw a figure in the snow, and without heed she kicked the horse into a run. As she approached, the colour of the snow turned pink with a trail of hot blood melt, and the figure became clearer, the details of the man's jacket visible, discarded rifle dropped in the snow. Clutching the shaft of an arrow buried in his stomach, the man lay back, resting his head against an old tree log.

"Putain," he growled as the woman and the horse walked up to him. "Où qu'yé moon maarii?"

Groaning, the man waved his hand toward the bog. The woman nodded, turned her horse, and urged it on. The man blinked, and he cried out, begging for help, but the woman just kept on without looking back. She had spotted another trail in the snow, it wound through a winter-shorn copse, down over the water, where men had crashed through the ice, clambered ashore, and kept running. She skirted the open water, guiding her horse around to the other side, where she saw a trickle of red upon the ground—like a drizzle of fat—leading toward a copse of willows. Over a small rise, she saw her husband on his knees. The other neighbour stood over him and waved his rifle, pointing it occasionally at her husband.

Snapped in half, her husband's bow lay at his side.

Without hesitation, the woman swung her husband's rifle from her shoulder, lifted the sights up to her eyes, and aimed it at the broad side of the Frenchman. She fired. The neighbour staggered. He glanced over at the woman on the horse, his eyes the colour of ice. He took a step forward, and as he began to raise his rifle, he collapsed dead in the snow.

"And then what?" Monique demanded, her voice a husk.

"Yeah," I squeaked.

"Bin," Alfred shrugged. He pulled out his pipe and a pouch of tobacco from his pocket, slowly filled his pipe and brought it up to his lips.

"Menoncle!" we whined.

"So," he continued. The man and woman left the bodies in the bog and trekked out of the woods. They knew it was only a matter of time before someone would ask about the neighbours, and so they packed their things, fetched their children, and fled north. Once the Frenchmen were missed, a search began, but by then fresh layers of snow had fallen, melted, turned to ice, and covered the tracks and the blood, and when spring came for real and the snows melted for the last time and the water rose high, as it always does, the dead men sank deep, swallowed whole by the bog. Their flesh rotted, fell off the bone, and their bones nestled into pits of mud where they still lay.

Alfred was going on about how, in the dead of winter, at night, just as the wind howled a certain way through the frozen trees, you could hear the dead men wail—putain, putain—as their spirits blindly wandered the bog where they died, when Dad stepped outside, listened to the story for a moment, and then cleared his throat.

"Crisse, Menoncle. Don't give them any ideas," said Dad.

Alfred sucked on his pipe and winked.

After Alfred left, Monique scoffed. There was no truth to his story she told me, but when I turned to go inside, she stayed on the steps and stared doubtfully at the trees. See, Monique had had trouble accepting the move. She hated the idea of leaving town, and at first, she had refused to accept it. Our parents had tried talking to her about it, but she shut herself up in her bedroom and ignored them. Dad tried to get her to come with us to check out the new place, the forest, the house, but Monique ignored him.

The day of the move she again locked herself up in her bedroom, curled up in the corner amid towers of boxes, the bedframe propped up against the wall, and cried. As Dad called from the hallway, asking her to unlock the door so that he could bring the boxes and her things out to the moving van, Monique refused to listen.

"Non!" she shouted. "Just leave me behind!"

"Voyons donc, là," Dad muttered. "Ouvre la porte, Monique."

Dad rattled the door handle and asked her again to unlock the door, but Monique refused. In the doorway to my soon-to-be-ex-bedroom, clutching a last box of toys and books, I stood and wondered why Monique could not accept this change. Mom and Dad had taken me out to the property before they'd even started building, when it was nothing but a patch of trees, gravel, and cattle trails chock-full of old, desiccated cow patties disintegrating in the knee-high grass. Though I would miss the river behind the old house, the idea of exploring the new woods was tantalizing. Our parents brought me out again, and again, as the house was built, but Monique refused to come, refused to see the possibilities. She tried desperately to sabotage the plan. She yanked the FOR SALE sign out of the yard, chucking it into the river; refused to clean up after herself whenever a showing was arranged; and even punched a hole in the wall, but after a hard talking-to from Dad, she tearfully apologized, and helped him patch it up. The day of the move, her desperation spiked, and she staged a sit-in in her bedroom, refusing to come out and watched in horror as Dad patiently removed the door from its frame and opened her room up to the world.

Chains took to the woods quicker than Monique did. He had always loved the bush, and he darted through the trees whenever we'd brought him out to the gravel pits between Ross and Richer. He tore up and down the mounds of overburden as we picked chokecherries and cooked hotdogs over a small fire. Now he had started to venture deeper and deeper into this new patch of bush, returning reluctantly and ever later, as Monique remained pinned to the steps and called after him to come back. About a month after we moved in, Alfred's story fresh in the backs of our minds, Chains came out of the bush carrying a large white stick and dropped it at Monique's feet. I was close by, helping Mom with the new garden, pulling weeds and pic-pics from a raised soil bed, when Monique lifted the stick from the ground and screamed.

"Bone!"

Mom went and checked, and she turned the bone over in her hands, wiping mud and dirt off with her gardening gloves. There were lots of old trails in the woods behind the house.

"Une patte de vache, probably," Mom said.

Monique glanced from the treeline to Mom.

"C'pas humain?" said Monique.

"Non ma chère," Mom laughed, and she tossed the bone back to the dog.

All summer Chains dragged bones out from the bush, dropped them at Monique's feet, and Monique would chuck them back into the woods. Thinking it was a game, Chains would happily retrieve them. She tried to ignore them, these bones pilling up at her feet, tossing them away without a second glance, but each bone seemed to chip away at her resolve. Alfred's story had taken root in the back of her mind, and it bloomed in her imagination. Finally, one morning after dreams of Frenchmen swallowed in mud, clawing at roots and wisps of grass as they sank ever deeper in blood and muck, Monique deter-mined to put the myth to rest. Knocking on my door as the sun peeked through the blinds, she convinced me of the urgency of her quest.

"What if they're reviving, Rich?"

Being all of ten years old, the thought of zombie Frenchmen ris-ing out from the swamp beyond our back yard filled me with dread. Placing her hands on my shoulders, and pinning me with a steady, serious look, Monique said, "Y faut aller checker."

"Okay," I gulped.

Why Monique needed my help, I wasn't sure. Though even back then, I suspected it was because I had taken to the bush sooner than her, and begun venturing out with Chains, exploring the old trails while Monique sat in the house reading and dreaming of all the hor-rible things that might exist in the world.

Our parents watched bemused over their coffee and newspaper at the kitchen table as we filled our backpacks with things we thought we'd need: granola bars and Ziploc bags filled with peanuts for the journey; a Swiss army knife; a compass; waterproof matches; a flash-light and a few glowsticks in case we lost the flashlight; lighter fluid to torch the old bones; and bottles of water and old rags to wash or bandage the wounds we might suffer in battle against the undead.

"Vous allez ou là?" Mom finally asked, frowning over the lip of her coffee cup.

Monique explained that long ago a man had disappeared into the brush not very far from where our new house sat—Dad snorted and waved away the rest of the story.

"Perdez-vous pas, là, hein?"

So, with walking sticks—quarterstaffs, said Monique—of polished diamond willows that Dad occasionally carved to sell to tourists along the highway, and Chains by our side, we started out. We followed the old cattle trails for a bit, and then the sun, as best as we could, through the underbrush and canopy overhead. Monique kept glancing at me, checking if I knew the way, and with all my unearned confidence, I boasted that we'd hit the swamp in no-time.

Instead, we went around in circles. We came upon the same gnarled stump three times, and Monique stopped and glared at the old thing. Our shoes, socks, and pants had soaked up the morning dew and clung uncomfortably to our legs. Clouds of horseflies and mosquitoes began to gather thick and dark, billowing around us. Chains growled as flies landed on his snout, and he snapped at the probing swarms, whining whenever a bug bite into him. With our hands smacking skin like drums, we ran, crashing through the underbrush. Finally, as we came upon a swathe of grass snaking across the forest, a clearing opened up. A small creek babbled at the centre. Wind beat the bugs back into the bush behind us, and we pushed ahead, through the willows, and stood at the edge of the creek and peeked at the low water. Dry stones protruded the slow current, and Monique stepped gingerly onto one.

"It's safe," she said.

"Une grenouille!" I said, and bent to pick up a small frog that hopped from stone to stone, but Monique grabbed my arm and dragged me across the creek.

"There's no time pour ça," she said. "Let's have a snack, then keep going."

The sun spilled hot light upon the ground, and we retreated into the shade to eat and rest. On a felled tree, we sat and rifled through our packs. Monique pulled out a granola bar, tore off the wrapping, and offered it to me. By our feet, Chains began to growl. He stiffened—his neck aimed at some spot in the woods, his tail pinned straight back. Monique glanced at her compass and chewed on her granola bar as she studied the small, twirling arrow. Chains took a few steps forward, his nose tracking some beast as it moved toward the creek.

"This here says north is par là," said Monique tossing her hand back over her shoulder, toward the highway, and I blinked, glancing back and forth between Monique and Chains.

"Monique," I said. "J'pense que—"

"Wait," said Monique frowning as the arrow wavered again in her compass. "No, north is là-bas. So, I guess la swomp is that way?"

Chains barked, and Monique finally glanced up. I peeked over my shoulder, hoping that whatever it was, wasn't a bear—Dad had warned us not long after we moved to watch for bears. He said they would come around, especially in the fall, to feed on the acorns and the berries that dotted the ridge, and I'd built up the idea into a sort of terrible and fantastic encounter that would shape my being. But as we peered through the underbrush, and held our breath, we spotted a doe jumping over the felled trees that littered the woods, her white tail like an arrow to the sky.

After our lunch, we set out along the creek. Monique figured it was swamp-fed, and so it would lead us to our destination. We trekked for a while, and I grew tired, and began to whine, asking Monique to turn around and go home, but she shook her head and insisted we continued. The sun began to track west, sinking slowly like a hot air balloon. Monique urged me onward, but I could tell she'd also grown tired. Her forehead peppered in sweat, her cheeks the colour of low fire. Chains wandered in and out of the trees, his nose drawing him further away. We came to a bend in the creek where it curled upon itself like cursive writing on the ground, and Monique pushed forward through the veil of willows along the thin bank, and stumbled into the cold water below. I laughed and hooted, tears springing from my eyes at the sight of her arms flailing, only to grow worried as the echo of my laughter faded, and I stood alone in the hot afternoon sun and the ceaseless chirping of crickets and grasshoppers.

"Monique?" I said as my voice broke.

I pressed ahead, eyes on the ground as I wedged open the wall of willows, and then I saw Monique sitting in the water to her hips, eyes pinned to some shape half-buried in the creek-bank up-current. I saw the skull afterwards, as Monique slowly reached out with her walking stick and brushed a tuft of grass from the bone. The empty sockets where eyes had once rested gazed at us. The shattered snout had been worn smooth by the gentle passing of the water.

Some violence had been visited upon the old cow, although when, or why, eluded us. As I stood overlooking Monique and the old cow, and imagined how it might feel to discover those old Frenchmen's bones in the swamp, I groped naïvely towards that which would take me years to grasp: that some things were perhaps best left where they fell.

24.

À côté du junk yard

WE WERE ON OUR WAY TO CARLSON'S PLACE, OUT BY Dufresne, the first time Becky mentioned living together. She dropped it in real casual between some gripe over work—something about bartenders not sharing their tips—and how she'd picked up an application to go back to school.

"Wouldn't it be great if we had a place together?" she said. We stared out the windshield at the flat road. Loose gravel pinged underneath the Buick, and we rattled over the washboard as the road veered alongside the rail tracks. It seemed as though she expected me to say something, but I clenched my jaw and pretended to concentrate on the slow bend. Becky finally continued. "Anyways. It would be cheaper than living on my own. You know how much school costs?"

"Arm and a leg," I said.

Becky snorted. "'Bout that."

Then Becky glanced down at her jeans and swore, and she began to fuss over some spot above her knee, rubbing at a fleck of polish or mascara. I looked over and studied her, and in the amber glow of a late-autumn sun, as the hot light swirled through the Buick, I thought about how things were fine the way they were, what it would mean to change that and whether it would be worth the risk to disrupt what we had already created between us. As Becky rubbed at her jeans, and peeled that small, nearly invisible speck from her clothes, I thought it best to let things be, so I turned quietly to the road, and cast my eyes into the distance to watch for Carlson's junkyard.

Across the canola fields, cars crawled along the highway like insects on a tabletop. Al Verrier and I sat on the hood of the Buick and blew smoke up into the air. We shared a joint in the quiet and the dark beneath Carlson's two-and-a-half stories of weathered siding and cracked windows, and watched the cars move. Firelight and fiddle music spilled from behind the house, and voices howling with laughter shattered the night. Verrier sucked the joint down into a roach and flicked the red nub to the gravel.

"You hear from Larry at all?" he asked.

I shook my head, and he nodded. We stared westward, off toward the city and beyond, at the thousand dark miles of prairie between here and the mountains.

"Fucking guy."

Larry Lechene had left over a year ago after he'd served some time for killing the woman that he loved in a rollover accident. He had mixed beer and oxy, then fell asleep at the wheel and woke up in the hospital to the news that he had orphaned her little boy. He wasn't ever the same after that. Though he came back for a time after his stint in jail, it was clear there was no room for him around here anymore. He decided to head west to find his dad. I'd driven him to the bus station by the thrift store, and watched him climb onto that Greyhound bus without looking back.

I'd been standing around the bonfire behind Carlson's earlier, half-listening to Becky yell with Roxanne Groscoeur about what to expect from university, when I spotted Verrier sitting on a stack of wooden pallets Carlson planned to burn. Men and women laughed and shouted, their voices coming on and breaking in waves as they swayed, while others around the fire hummed and casually strummed guitars. One woman took out a fiddle and tuned it up. Someone blew into a harmonica, and another began to sing a song about a hole in a bucket. Despite all the music and joy and laughter around us, Verrier sat there, looking pensive, so I walked over and asked if he wanted to share a joint. He peered up at me and shrugged.

Verrier and I still ran in the same circles, mostly, but I'd started spending more and more time with Becky. Verrier had lost his driver's license, after being caught over the limit at a check stop, and was stuck at home most time, and we had drifted apart. We had been insepar-able for a couple years after I had met him and Larry while they were cooking honey oil over in Marchand but, once Larry left, I came to realize that he had been the glue that'd kept us together. Verrier lived only a few miles down the road from me, but seeing as he was a couple years older and he and his folks had lost their French somewhere along the way and he went to the English school, I had never really known him and, after Larry left, we'd found ourselves on different paths again. Leaning back against the Buick, watching stars pierce the night sky, and letting our minds sail through the hazy clouds of our high, I asked what he made of it.

"Nothing," he grunted. "Just the way it goes."

I glanced over, but he just stared up at the stars.

"That's doesn't seem right to me," I said.

"Man, why do you have to question shit like that?" Verrier sighed. "Can't you just look at the fucking stars?"

"Sure," I said, but when I leaned back on the hood, and stared up at the pinpricks of light above, all I could think about was the curl of the fiddle and driving rhythm of the guitars coming from around the back of Carlson's. Firelight spilled across the sky masking the stars, drawing my eyes down to the sea of junk: the old trucks and cars and tractors and things that folk tossed away and that Carlson gathered, chopped into pieces, and sold back to them. My leg began to twitch as though my bones were a tuning fork. I looked over at Verrier. "Let's head back," I said.

"You go," he said.

"Come on man, let's grab a beer and go see what's going on," I said, and I grabbed at his arm to pull him along with me, but then Verrier snapped.

"Fucking Christ, just leave me alone dude." In a spike of anger, he flung his fist at me, and brushed my chin. Blinking, I stepped back, rubbing the spot where his knuckles had grazed me. Verrier slipped off the hood, shook his head, and began to walk toward the road.

"Dude, where're you going?"

"Home," he shouted over his shoulder.

"You live in Richer!"

"Just fuck off," he shouted, and he turned down the gravel road toward Ste. Anne. I stood there, without another word, and watched him go until he shrank to nothing.

Chin throbbing, I wandered through the crowd behind Carlson's, searching for Becky. I sucked down a bottle of beer someone handed me and then tossed it toward the rail tracks.

"Fucking save that shit for the train," someone yelled.

The music kept getting faster, louder, as everyone tipped their elbows back, and their feet flashed in bursts of colour in the dirt and they tore up the lawn and lifted clouds of black dust and coughed over fat, pregnant joints that sprouted from our hands, and I searched for Becky, trailing her laughter through the crowd, pressing through folks squeezed in between Carlson's house and the rail tracks, when a train horn suddenly blasted over the music. Folks began to howl like dogs. The train horn blasted once more, closer, louder, and we drifted toward the fenced-off ditch next to the tracks and we watched as the train bore down on us, its diesel engine chugging, its wheels clattering over the rails. Folks cocked their elbows, drawing cans and bottles behind their heads, and when the train appeared, someone tossed their can at the side of a passing grain car. The can exploded into a cloud of foam and mist. Then like hailstones bottles sailed by the dozen over our heads and burst against the train cars, showering the tracks in shattered glass and beer, and folks howled again as the train horn blasted, and it pulled quickly away as though we had driven it off. We laughed and shouted in the rumbling echo of its passing, until we could hear nothing but our own sad voices filling the haunted emptiness of that faded sound on the horizon. Eventually our voices grew hoarse, quiet, cut out. In the wake of that train, we stood empty-handed, surrounded by scattered wreckage.

25.

Swallows Nest

STEAM WHISPERED FROM THE HOLE IN THE GROUND and waste rattled through the steel-ribbed hose in my arms, swirling on toward the vacuum truck behind us. Watching as I manoeuvred the hose mouth along the bottom of his septic tank, an old man mined his nostril with a thumb.

"Been sayin' we might need a new tank," he said, glanced at his thumbnail, and then he flicked something away. "Sprung a leak last year and had to patch it up, eh."

I nodded, half-listening, when the hose began to shudder. I held it tightly, but it bucked, juddering violently, then popped out from my hands. The hose landed with a thud and quivered on the ground. Inside the tank, the nozzle-intake snapped and rattled against the sidewalls.

"Whoa-boy," said the old man while he rooted around the other nostril.

Carefully, I pinned it with my foot, then grabbed hold of the hose, and lifted it up, out of the tank. The pump motor whined behind us like a vacuum cleaner chewing carpet and the hose bucked again. As I drew the nozzle-intake out, I saw the problem. Wedged at the end of the hose was a shorn, shit-sopped chicken wing, trembling under the suction. The pump motor revved up again—the pitch spiked—and the hose juddered as the wing shifted and some of the bones broke apart, were then drawn into the hose-mouth, and rattled up toward the tank. The motor seemed to cough and bark in quick, successive bursts, as though choking on the carcass, and then suddenly, before it could burn itself out, the emergency cut-off kicked in, and the motor ceased.

The old man peeked into his tank.

"Good enough," he said.

In the quiet, fading echo of that pump motor, and as snow floated around us, the chicken wing drooped from the hose-intake and in the cold breeze fluttered.

After returning yesterday from Alfred's cabin, I had called Joe to ask about the job, and he offered me a half day of work, which had turned into a full day as he kept calling on the old bag phone inside the truck and adding stops. I was glad, at first—thankful for both the couple of bucks it would give me and the distraction from Alfred's upcoming funeral, which wasn't for a few days yet as folks drove in from across the country—but as I swung the truck down another gravel road, lined with bare aspen and birch, and I squinted at the postal boxes and the property numbers searching for the next place to empty of waste, I began to think Joe was just trying to keep me busy. The sharp pain that had slowly needled down my back and into my leg over the past week seemed to throb with every bounce as I whipped over the late fall washboard on the roads. The small plastic bison that Danny had lent me rattled on the dashboard; it had tipped over, not long after I had set it there, and now lay like some felled beast of old, as it waited for les femmes to slice it into pieces. The cookfires warming.

I was rounding a corner, off a mile-road near Blumenort, when I recalled Larry Lechene's stories about working at the poultry-rendering plant along the highway there, and how he used to clean the killing floors, pushing blood and guts and bones with a high-powered spray nozzle into little trenches that would drain into a furnace hot as hellfire, and I wondered what he would have thought about the chicken wing I'd plucked from that pool of shit this morning. Laugh, probably, and make some terrible joke about slow cooking.

The antique bag phone squawked beside me atop the centre console.

Glancing at the side-mirrors, checking for traffic, I pulled over, and grabbed the phone.

"Got another job for you," said Joe. He rattled off a name and an address—some house trailer near Paradise Village—and I scratched the details down on a pad of yellow legal paper.

"They got septic tanks in Paradise?" I laughed.

Joe snorted. "Too small for a sewer system," he said. I rolled my eyes. Joe didn't have much of a sense of humour, I thought. "Listen," he continued. "How's the tank? Think you have room for another one after that before you hit the lagoon?"

"Maybe, I don't know. Depends on the job, I guess. One of your hoses is clogged up with chicken bones."

"Fuck," said Joe, and through the quiet buzz in my ear, I pictured him pinching the bridge of his nose. "Didn't I tell you to watch out for those?"

"No," I said. "What the hell's up with that?"

The way the receiver scratched, I figured Joe shrugged. "Guy chucks his sick birds in there so that he doesn't have to report them to the health inspector—but don't repeat that."

In these few, short weeks I had been working for Joe, I'd clogged his hoses a few times with the discarded ruins of people's lives. I'd seen some of the oddities that people flushed away, and glimpsed at the dark, underside of their existence, the hints of their stories: the party bags of used-condoms, the decapitated heads of Barbie dolls dangling by their long, once-yellow hair at the lip of the hose mouth, old dentures snapping under pressure, teeth rattling like gravel up the hose. Cellphones were more common now, as they shrunk, slipping from peoples' hands into the toilet. Joe said the Lord had risen once from a tank when he pulled a rosary from the muck. The chain of beads had curled around the hose mouth in the current, and the figure of Christ vibrated against the steel. And as he drew the hose out, and saw in the midday sun a radiant halo exuding from the tarnished, precious, gold, he had been so affected by the scene, at once taken aback and inspired, that he came to see it as a sign from God.

"Was a sign, clear as day," he said, and shot a stream of spit out from between his teeth onto the gravel behind the septic truck. "He told me then and there, I was on the right path. That I was doing the Lord's work."

Joe retrieved the rosary and hosed it off. He carried it around his pocket for a month or so, attributing its influence over the growth of his business. He eventually polished it, and then hung it from the rear-view of his truck as a reminder of the blessing that he had received, that his enterprise operated under the grace of God.

I put the phone down, then pulled a roadmap from the glove box, and spread it out over the steering wheel. I traced my finger along the map, the paper crinkling as I circled closer and closer to home, and I realized the next job was a stone's throw from Gauthier's farm.

A lump dropped from my throat and slammed into my stomach like some space rock. My stomach twisted. The map crumpled as my fists curled and the scene from Alfred's cabin burst to mind. The flask on the table. La chicoque. The Gauthiers. Le vieux and how he had screwed over Alfred. J.P. and his skunk-stenched jacket, which we had burned out of pragmatism and spite in the firepit behind the cabin.

As I spun the truck back into gear, and tore down the gravel road toward that place not far from J.P.'s, toward that next job, I resisted the gut-clamping urge to wheel the truck over to the farm and dump a load of shit on J.P.'s front lawn.

All through the job next door, I thought about it, envisioning piss and shit sloshing over the frost-tipped grass, soaking through the front steps to the porch, seeping into the ground, and staining the earth with the stench of his betrayal.

Half-listening to the homeowner prattle on about how cold it was outside—wasn't even that cold, took minutes before you felt a tingle in your fingers—I wondered what J.P. would say if he found his yard buried in crap.

"So, how many do you think?" said the homeowner.

I blinked. "Sorry?"

He pointed to the septic tank.

"Bales," he said. "For the winter. How many?"

The man paid cash. I stuffed it in my jeans, thanked him for his business, and with a curt goodbye, climbed into the truck, and spun the engine up once more. I rolled out of the driveway, determined now to see J.P., and the truck sped up slowly, stalled by the sloshing pool on the back axles. Gravel showered the undercarriage. Great waves of dust burped up behind me as I floored the gas pedal and the truck groaned down the mile road. I was determined to do it, to empty that tank on his house. Soon the farm appeared through a windbreak, and the truck careened into the driveway. I mashed the brakes, but the weight of the sewage pushed us along; the truck wobbled as the waste sloshed. Then the truck teetered, its wheels lifting off the ground on the one side, and in an instant, my vision crystalized, sharpened into focus, and I sucked my breath deep and quick, glimpsing at the reality of that thirty-thousand-pound vacuum truck overturning, its tank cracking open like an egg, sewage spreading like lumpy oil over the gravel and the thin brown lawn. And in that moment I prayed to whoever, whatever would listen, to spare Joe's truck. I could not imagine having to explain this to him. I wondered if God heard, because then, like a pendulum, the sewage sloshed again, and the wheels slammed to the ground.

The truck rocked back and forth as the momentum slowly diminished, but the wheels remained glued to the gravel. A pent-up gulp full of air burst from my lungs. The truck creaked and groaned beneath me, the oil and gas in the lines draining away, the engine block crackling as heat diffused.

Knuckles white on the steering wheel, I anchored my eyes to that ragged horizon I had awoken to only a few days ago, that rough edge of the bush held back by the cattle, and my heart settled. I stopped trembling and my breath grew steady. As I turned to the yard, I saw etched in the dry grass the marks of that rowdy celebration, the footprints, the tire tracks, and the dips in the earth where the flatbed trailer sat and the band had played, lines in the ground where wires had run from the house, and the dark, soot-singed rings around the firepit. That spot where I had pissed lentement along the fence and watched the cattle scatter. Despite all the visits, all the time we had spent here as kids when Dad still visited le vieux, as I surveyed the land through the dust-coated windshield, I felt as though something had changed, that somehow, amid the current of my life, the sense of this place in my mind had shifted, a boat caught on shoals lifted by the high tide, and that the bristling veil of resentment that had built up through the years had, like rusted steel on a seabed, begun to dissolve. Climbing down from the truck, and wandering around the tank, I thought of how I had briefly planned to dump that full load onto J.P.'s lawn, and I shook my head and smiled at the idea of his coming home to a pile of shit on his stoop.

What a sight it might have been.

Water seeped from the back of the tank and I tightened the outflow valve. Then glancing at the house, I lumbered up the front steps, onto the porch overlooking the pasture, and I knocked on the door. I wanted to tell J.P. about Alfred's cabin. Tell him we'd burned his jacket. But there was no answer. After a moment, I took a step back, glanced at the driveway, and I saw that J.P.'s truck was nowhere around. Disappointed, I sat on the small bench under the window and decided to wait for him. I dug a cigarette from my pocket—I had swiped it that morning from Joe—and smoked it slowly. Through a thin dust of falling snow, I watched in the distance as cattle moved unhurriedly over the rocky fields.

Wind curled around the house and raked the porch. Chimes jangled overhead. I tipped my head against the windowsill, and spotted a string of small nests wedged into the corners between the soffits and the walls. Crisse d'hirondelle. Dad would have lost it over their mess. It had been more than a month since the swallows left for winter, and I wondered why J.P. hadn't yet cleared their nests. Dad hated these birds. The way they nested against houses, sheds, and barns, packing mud and shit and straw together to hold their eggs up in the air, it could stain the paint, and etch wood and siding. It could ruin a decent wall.

Dad had always taken it personally, as though the birds had it out for him. When we were younger, and lived along the river on the edge of town, Dad had bought Monique a BB gun, and told her to keep the birds away. There'd been a gulp of swallows living under the bridge over the Seine, on the old number 12, not too far from our old place, until a flock of pigeons had pushed them out. Searching for places to nest, les hirondelles began to scout the new houses sprouting in the nearby hayfields. That summer, only a few years before we moved out to the bush, the swallows lined up on the hydro wires running between our house and the river, resting there as they surveyed the land. Dad stood on the deck and glared at them; struck by visions of nests flaring like chicken pox along the side of the house, he ordered Monique to shoot those birds. Reluctantly, Monique listened, and from her perch on the deck behind the house, she fired BBs at the swallows; every once in a while, she actually hit one, and in a moment of panic, as the bird toppled from the wire and fell fluttering to the earth, she would cry for help. I would run into the yard with a baseball bat to end that stunned bird's suffering.

It was strange how, back then, what had felt like the right thing to do—hell the shit we had done to the gophers too, flooding their burrows with a garden hose as we lurked nearby with sticks and baseball bats to hit them as they fled—filled me now with shame and regret. Even Dad had changed. Years ago, he would've drowned that chicoque in Alfred's cabin without a second thought. When we'd first moved to that spot on the gravel ridge, Dad would trap small animals—pests mostly—that wandered into the yard, then drive over to the gravel pits and drown them in the slews. But somewhere along the way, things had changed. He could no longer bring himself to kill these small animals. Chains had been the final straw, I think. We had all changed after his brief resurrection.

Nowadays, whatever Dad trapped, he drove over toward Richer, and released.

I brought the cigarette to my lips and sucked it down to the filter, then as I flicked the butt onto the gravel, I figured waiting for J.P. to show up wasn't worth my time. Standing, I stretched and groaned; a hot knife zinged alongside my leg. Mom's advice to go get checked out swirled in my mind. Every tank that I did, my back seemed to get worse. The sun had dropped low already, and I had a job to do, but as I imagined rolling up to yet another tank, and that hot knife digging deeper as I lifted yet another concrete lid, twisting painfully as I dragged those hoses around yet another house, I knew I couldn't bear it.

Aiming the truck north, I drove toward town. Sewage sloshed loudly in the tank behind my ears, and I cranked the radio up to mask the sound. Turning westward onto Dawson Road, I began to smile. The realization I'd had at the farm seemed to lift me up, weightless and high, as though on a cloud. Zipping by the turnoff toward Paradise, pass La Coulée, and out through the ragged border between the tapered edge of the Shield and the prairie, I felt all the built-up knots in my chest, that chicken-wire of doubt that had long constricted my heart and clouded my vision of the future, begin to unravel. The bag phone squawked, but I tossed it aside, and as I careened toward town, I laughed.

Perched on a rock overlooking the lagoon, I sipped a can of Blue. Sewage gushed from the tail end of the truck. Dipping into the horizon, the sun washed red over the pools, and in the mix of rising steam, and flurries, and swirling expanse of human waste, the light danced upon the surface and caromed off in scattered bursts of colour. For a brief, bloated moment, I smiled at the notion that the whole town might have shot rainbows from their asses—though I never imagined rainbows smelled like shit—but as I drained my beer, tossed the empty aside, and pulled another from the plastic ring at my feet, I began to shudder. Tears welled in my eyes as fire seared down my thigh and calf and into my toes, and seemed to burn the nerves out. I tried to wriggle my toes, but was unable to sense them in my boot. As far and high as I had soared, I felt myself crashing back down to earth. The rundown bits of my body screamed, dragging me down from the elation. I stretched backwards on that rock, pressing that cold can into my lower spine for relief. I finally heard what my body was telling me: enough.

After this last load was emptied, I would tell Joe that I was done.

The fire cooled some, and feeling slowly returned to my toes. Cracking open the beer, I took a swig and tried to imagine what might come next. The emptiness weighed on me. The cold sense of unknowing, uncertainty, lifted goosebumps from my skin. Though I knew little of what might come next, or what I might do, I took comfort in the idea of who might be there. Becky's words on the rooftop in Saint-Boniface came to mind, how she had wanted more. I felt ashamed by my meager response and the silence I had let build up between us in the days since. Draining my beer, I imagined Becky nose-deep in a textbook, busy, getting on with things, and I envied her. Thinking of Alfred, and the truth of why he had stayed out there, in the bush, even as he'd grown to love that land, and the guilt and the obligation that he must have felt, that had kept him there, seemed so foreign to me. There was nothing like that keeping me here—not with Alfred gone. The sun hovered on the horizon and the light dimmed red on the lagoon. In between that growing dark, and the throbbing pain in my back and leg, rising in waves beneath the surface, I allowed myself to imagine a future with Becky. A vision of us together in the city—gorgeous against the backdrop—took root. Dropping the can next to the rock, I slowly stood, and stretched my arms wide overhead, and decided.

Feet hanging half-way out of the truck, I located the bag phone on the floormat, checked the battery, and saw that it had enough juice. So, I slipped out of the cab, and trekked back to the rock, sat, and dialed Becky's number. And as the sun dipped below the horizon, and its last light flared and burst gold upon the fields of sewage before me, the phone rang, and rang, and clicked, and Becky's voice cracked static in my ear.

26.

Le tour du monde

THE WALLS MOVED LIKE BEDSHEETS AND THE DARK SUN rained shadows on Monique's living room. Shadows oozed from the ceiling, pooled in the corners, grew, and shrunk, and grew again with the flow of the lava lamp in the bookshelf. The girl on my left jabbed me with her elbow and pointed to the dim-red roach drooping between my fingers.

After talking about our dead dog for a while, the conversation had looped around, circled back and, somewhere in between deciding to go dancing at Le Canot and Monique's sudden rant about language rights, including a vivid description of when some offices in Saint-Boniface were firebombed, and how the director of some francophone organization, along with his family, had been threatened with death for daring to advocate for the tongue, I began to drift in and out of my thoughts, sinking deeper into the couch, watching the walls come alive. We were in it now.

"Les murs sont mûrs," I whispered.

The girl on my left frowned. "What's he saying?"

Monique waved her cigarette through the air. "The walls are ripe."

The girl cocked an eyebrow. "What's that supposed to mean?"

Once we finished our cigarettes, we headed outside into the cold. Monique insisted that we walk even after I offered to drive. I'd recently inherited Dad's old Buick and wanted to show it off—I'd gotten my parents permission to visit Monique in the city on the weekend, as long as I kept up my grades—but Monique took one look inside, wrinkled her nose, pointed to the garbage strewn on the seats, and said forget about it. The girl who'd sat on my left—Krystal with a K, I think her name was—laughed and stomped her feet to keep warm while Monique and I argued.

"Not going to argue all night," Monique declared. "Y fait frette!" She blew white air out of her mouth, and we watched it drift upward and dissipate into the dry—her eyelashes turned to frost, and she tugged a scarf up over her mouth. My cheeks started to burn, and I had lost feeling in my toes. "Fucking come on," said Monique.

Krystal jumped to her side; they linked arms and marched off together in lock-step down the street. Stuffing my hands, mitts and all, into my coat pockets, I followed close behind, urging my legs onward. The cold pressed down heavily on us. It clawed and scratched and curled in like smoke through your zipper, gnawed at your skin. Movement seemed to help a bit; like a skittish cat, the cold would dart away, then wait for some lull to leap back onto us. We hurried as though trying to outrun a pesky cat. Snow squeaked like Styrofoam beneath our boots, crunched as we dashed across Provencher, up Des Meurons, where rail tracks swept along the brush. Turning, we trekked down Dumoulin—it wasn't as windy as on the boulevard—and on toward the Red.

Monique and Krystal huddled together for warmth, arms wrapped around each others' waists, heads pressed close. I would have hugged a bear for its heat, I thought, as I chased after them, shivering, wriggling toes in my boots to keep some warmth in my feet.

Somewhere, a train squealed over the rails. The sound of its wheels clattering and slicing along the cold steel ricocheted through the frost and air, and carried over distances unheard in the heat of another season. Sound carries far in the cold, moving easily over still, groaning, expanses of ice and snow. Pillars of light rose over our heads, like columns holding the shattered buckshot dome of stars above. Pinpricks. Where scatter shot pierced the deep. This sort of cold could kill you in no time; but could kill you slow too. Nibble your toes, blue, black. Necrotized. Eat away at your fingers, your nose, ears, freeze your eyes in your sockets until you can't see, can't move. Wait for your eyes to thaw before you can blink. The stars above laughed. Fuck man. As-tu déjà vu les étoiles au Manitoba? Au milieu d'un champ, au milieu d'l'hiver, au milieu d'la nuit, au milieu du pays, when the auroras drift like bedsheets stretched taught in the wind, the colours of knuckle-blows in the dark, les bruises après une puck dans face, fuck, me. Monique? I traced the outline of my boots against the pinprick of stars above. Someone shouted. At me? Get up, crisse. Come on. Get going. Out of the snow. Just another block and we'll soon be warm.

Monique slipped the bouncer a ten to ignore my presence as we squeezed by him at the top of the stairwell and into the bar. The room was warm, humid; breath and sweat of men and women on the dance floor washed over us like a chinook, fogged our eyes as our lashes thawed and dripped with melt. Everything was the colour of blood.

We circled the room lazily, pushing through folks unable to hear us over the noise, and found a bench along the wall, on the far side from the door, where I sat, alone, while Monique and Krystal with a K went and shouted drink orders at the bartender. They returned with bottles of Standard and stood before me and sipped their beer as they scanned the room. Music caromed off the walls and throttled our ears. I sank deeper into the bench, into the warm, downy folds of my winter jacket. Shapes drifted monstrously over the dance floor—dewy limbs and naked flesh, swinging hair, contorted bodies writhing to the noise. I found it hard to look anyone in the eyes; mine kept slipping off their faces. Fish through my fingers.

"Fuckin' take it," said Monique, pressing a bottle of Standard into my hand. "Not going to hold it for you all night."

Blinking, I glanced at the bottle in my hand, the yawning, vibrating bottle of brown glass, and I brought it tentatively up to the cusp of my lips, resting the cold glass against my lower, and I thought, now that's a strange feeling, the bottle was warm, and my lips were cold, and usually it was the other way around—and I saw Krystal with a K grin, and lean into Monique, as if leaping into her skin, whisper-yelling something in her ear. Monique glanced at her and smiled, and then suddenly Krystal with a K pulled Monique out onto the dance floor. I sat clutching my lukewarm bottle of Standard. I unzipped my jacket, bottle like a hot potato, tossed right to left, and I pulled my arms through the armholes, and tried to ignore the puddles of melted light on the floor.

Sipping my beer, unable to remember how to swallow, I doused the front of my shirt.

"Tabarnak," I shouted. A few people glanced my way—a Black man laughed and said something to me in some sort of French I had never heard before and I grinned stupidly, teeth too big for my mouth. "T'un accident," I said.

"Ah oui, ah oui," said the man. "T'en fais pas monsieur." He slapped me on the shoulder, and then drifted away, swallowed up by the dance floor.

I tipped the bottle back again, carefully, but still the beer came out too fast, and I coughed and spluttered, and cursed, finally squeezed my eyes shut.

"You okay?" Monique asked, and I opened my eyes to see her rooting through her purse. "Ah, here we go." She pulled a small vial out, unscrewed the cap, and emptied a couple pills into her hand. Krystal materialized next to her, hand rubbing Monique's lower back.

Frowning. I tried to understand what was happening, but Monique just looked down on me. "You want one?"

"Ah. What is it?" I slurred.

"E."

"Is that a good idea?"

Monique rolled her eyes. "It's called candy flipping, Rich. Fais pas la vieille mémère, là."

Stapled to the bench, I watched Monique and K-Krystal float away. They seemed in their own world—slipping through people as though they were phantoms—eyes only for each other as they danced and jumped and laughed, arms melded, heads pressed together, they lived in the hot breath of brushed lips. Music throttled my eardrums again, and the dim, pulsing lights caused me to look away, shut my eyes.

"Ah mais, regarde Jeannette. Un beau mec seul."

A hand slipped around my shoulder, and I peeled my lids open and glanced at the man on my right. He had pushed my jacket aside and squeezed in next to me. His eyes were the colour of a deep, dry well.

"'ello," he said. "May I, ah," his lips pressed thin, vanished, for a moment, "sit 'ere?"

"Sit where you like," I said, and as I waved toward the other side of the bench, a woman stood before me, hips swaying to the beat of the noise off the walls, black-rimmed eyes studying me. Un sourire de loup on her face—wisps of red flesh caught in giant yellow fangs, like Chains gorging himself on the deer—and she brought her glass up and sipped on a small red straw.

"Ah bin," said the man. "Est-ce que j'entends un petit accent français?"

"I guess so, oui."

"Jeannette!" the man exclaimed, glancing up to the woman, "Un petit lapin!"

The woman—Jeannette—flashed her teeth again. Eyes frozen, I stared at the woman as she stepped closer, hips still swaying back and forth, lips wrapped delicately around that little red straw, and she stood between my legs and leaned forward until I could feel her breath in my ear.

"Petit lapin, aimerais-tu me baiser?"

* * *

When I was seven or eight years old, Alfred tried to teach me how to make a rabbit snare. Dad and I had popped by for a visit and we sat around the kitchen table for a while, where Alfred was fixing some snares, twisting thin wire around these small, gnarled twigs. He planned to set a few snares in the bush behind the cabin. He mentioned that a tree had partly fallen over a trail out back and Dad offered to cut it down—it would only take a minute or two with the chainsaw.

"Sure," Alfred had said, and so while Dad went and started up the chainsaw—it growled to life, and barked and sputtered a ways as Dad headed off—Alfred saw that my eyes had turned to the snares on the table. He held one out for me to see, and I passed my hand through the loop of wire, and he pulled the wire tight around my wrist. The wire bit into my skin. I yelped, tried to pull away, but the wire kept my hand, and arm, strung out over the table.

"Watch-là," Alfred said. "Fais 'ttention." He loosened the wire, and I drew my hand back. "Tu vois?" he said, tracing the contour of the wire with his finger. "Une fois qu'li lièvre passe à travers, le fil lui serre autour du cou."

"Ça leur fait mal?"

Alfred grunted. He lifted himself from his chair and turned toward the countertop, where his tea kettle was cooling. "Pas pour longtemps," he said.

I nodded, trying to understand what this meant. I imagined Alfred patrolling the woods behind the cabin, watching for rabbits caught in snares, bending gently over the small, chittering beasts to loosen the wires from around their necks, to set them free. I couldn't figure out why he would set them—the snares—in the first place.

As Alfred poured himself another mug of tea, overfilled his spoon with sugar, and stirred it together, I grabbed one of the snares off the table—it was just a piece of wire, wrapped around an old stick—and I tried to imagine myself stepping through it, like a rabbit, and so I slipped the wire over my head; it caught momentarily on the bridge of my nose, but I yanked it down like an old sweater, loosening the wire, until it slipped and dangled from my neck like a rosary. The wire was cool, sharp, uncomfortable, and I tried to pull it away, pull it off, but it slipped tighter, and bit into my neck the way that it had on my wrist. In a panic, I tried to yank it off, but it only grew tighter, squeaking, I tried to yell—owie!—but the words were trapped in my throat, lodged with my breath beneath the wire. Spots of black snow danced before my eyes.

And then Dad was there, with Alfred, their rough fingers stinking of gasoline prying the snare wire loose from around my neck, and I coughed, I cried, and Dad wrapped me in his arms. Alfred held the old snare in his gnarled hand, the wire trembling, rattling against the table, and he dropped his eyes onto the floor and apologized.

* * *

The woman sank into my lap, "Petit lapin," she laughed, and booped me on the nose with her finger. Instinctively, I slipped an arm around her waist to keep her from falling backwards; as she felt my hand on her hip, she wriggled further into me. "Oh mais, tes mains sont gelées!" she said. "Tiens, laisse-moi les réchauffer." She pulled my free hand down between her thighs.

"Regards!" she said to the man. "J'ai attrapé un petit lapin!"

"Ah ouais, ou c'est-tu le petit lapin qui t'a poignée?"

They laughed, and I grinned stupidly, wondering what was so funny. Every second word seemed drowned out by the churning soundscape around us, my heart beating loud like some cop at the door. Bang. Bang. Bang.

"Petit lapin, as-tu une baguette dans les culottes?"

Her hot breath coiled around my lips and burst down my throat. Yellow-glint eyes in the red-dark glow of the club—her mate growled next to us as he licked his chops and pawed at my side—and the wolf on my lap whimpered as though she'd tasted blood on my lips. She began to claw at me, fingers curling around my belt, tugging at my jeans. La chasse au gibier!

"Quoi?"

"Me baiser," said the woman.

"J'comprends pas," I admitted. I don't understand.

"Non mais, tu es français?"

"Non, yeah." I said, tongue flopping like jackfish on aluminium. "Chu Métisse," I added, and blinked, confused by my candour.

"Ah bon," the she-wolf said. "C'est vrai?"

"Tout le monde est métis pour deux semaines, là," said the wolf-man. "Hého!"

"Je n'ai jamais baisé un sauvage," the she-wolf purred.

She nuzzled her snout along my neck, my jaw. Her hot breath spilling down my shirt. My guts began to roil. Caught between desire and revulsion.

"On rentre ensemble?"

"Viens, petit lapin," the she-wolf purred. "J'aimerais bien goûter ta bite."

"Ah oui, ah oui. J'aimerais voir ça."

"Qu'en pense-tu?" her hand drifted, her fingers curling around mon tchi' boute dure, and I groaned. I could feel myself pulsing in her hand. They grinned, teeth clattering, their wet breath soaking my neck. As they drew near, their hot, hungry tongues constricting like a noose around my neck, the blood-blur of the lights throbbing on the dance floor, and reptilian shadows roving the walls, heat bubbled up from my gut, through my chest, and I belched.

The woman flinched. Her grin vanished in an instant as realization flickered in her eyes. And as she began to lean backwards, pulling away from me, the heat thundered out of my chest, and doused the front of her dress in hot beer and foam.

"Mon putain de sauvage!" The woman howled.

She leaped from my lap and glared at her dress. Sopped in beer and vomit. Sticky like viscera. The man recoiled, and lifting his feet from the floor, cowered in the corner.

Words spilled like water, dribbles of foam from my tongue, and before I could apologize, I was lifted into the air by oak-tree-arms, like a child carried over snow, the blood-sopped floor a puddle of light my toes dragged through, and then these two oak-grown men hauled me down the stairwell, through the door, pis i' m'ont garoché dans neige.

"Fucking little shit," said one, and he pushed me away from the door with his foot, while the other one chucked my jacket into the snowbank. "Go home."

The cold jolted me awake—enough so that that swirling blur of colours solidified around me long enough so that I could crawl over and slip into my jacket. Rooting through the pockets, I struck fur; I yanked out mes mitaines et ma tuque, tugged them over my hands, my head. Then, à quatre pattes on the boot-packed snow beneath me, under the speckled towers across the river, I crawled over to a nearby picnic bench, domed with powder, pulled myself up onto the table, and rolled onto that soft, cold pillow. I lay there, my feet dangling over the edge, and peered into the crisp, buckshot sky, and watched the stars burn.

I began to sing.

27.

Le vieux Coup d'Coude

WHEN DAD WAS 17 YEARS OLD, HE NEARLY KILLED A MAN. It happened the summer after he'd run that boy into the boards headfirst, knocking him out cold during a hockey match, and Dad had walked away from the game. It had scared him bad, the thought that he'd killed someone, but it turned out that boy had suffered only a sprained neck, and a goose egg on the noggin, and once the bruise faded he was fine. Still, Dad kept his head low that winter, afraid of that heat inside his chest that occasionally came out through his fists, that turned his tongue to acid, that drenched him in cold sweat. Folks learned to leave him be—he had been through enough: the grotto, his father's passing, the thing with the boy at the hockey game. But then one Sunday that spring, as ice vanished in the arena and meltwater spread across the land, old Coup d'Coude again accosted him in the communion line, and asked Dad if he had ever considered playing baseball.

"We could sure use a slugger," Coup d'Coude said. "Un vrai frappeur."

Dad held his empty hands out, in supplication, and Coup d'Coude plucked a host from the chalice and placed it gingerly in Dad's palm.

"Think about it, eh," he said, then blinked. "Oh, ah, le corps du Christ."

"Amen."

Week later and Dad was standing in right field, dodging puddles and catching flyballs. Coup d'Coude stood at the plate and smacked hardballs into the sky. Dad ran them down easily and tossed them back with force. The balls would sail over the infield, basemen cursing as they hopped and tried to snatch balls from the air. See, Dad couldn't throw straight. He could run and hit and catch without equal, send balls screaming over the outfield fence, but hit a baseman with a throw from the wall? Impossible.

Old Coup d'Coude smacked a couple more balls into the field and scratched his head as Dad tossed the balls wildly back toward home plate. One sailed over the backstop.

"Sacrament," the old priest muttered.

"Y sait pas garocher drette," Dave told Mémère.

"Jeter," said Yolande. "Y sait pas jeter."

"Okay là," complained Dad.

Mémère pursed her lips and laid a worried look on Dad.

He would later confess, as we sat around the kitchen table and pried stories from his grip so that Monique could get her Métis card and go back to school, that he knew that that thing with the boy at the rink still haunted his mother. Mémère had heard the story recounted throughout the winter and she feared what he might again do when pushed. She had warned him when he came back from the first ball practice, to take care, and to keep his temper in check.

"'Fais pas le sauvage,' she told me."

Monique blinked and I stared at the cup of tea between my hands as though I had never seen such a thing. Dad cleared the lump in his throat.

"Étais inquiète," he said. Twisted with worry.

Yet Dad 'tait presque un homme then and Mémère couldn't keep him off the team, and so Dad kept playing. And it turned out that Dad learned to throw straight enough and developed into a hell of a ballplayer.

"J'frappais des homeruns presque chaque pitch," said Dad.

"Quit honkin' your own horn," said Mom over her tea.

"Tooting," corrected Monique.

Mom rolled her eyes.

"Right clear over la fence," said Dad. And he waved his arm over the kitchen table as though pointing to some ball sailing bird-like through the blue.

* * *

"Le vieux Coup d'Coude 'tait content," said Alfred, and he bent gingerly over the firepit behind his cabin and built a small tent of kindling. "Content d'avoir trouvé un vrai joueur."

I dropped a load of firewood next to the pit, and frowned.

"Dad was a ballplayer?"

Alfred peered up at me. "Un des meilleurs."

We stank of sweat and gunsmoke, and sawdust peppered our hair, and we sat on wobbly chairs around the pit as flames caught on the scrunched-up newspaper beneath the kindling tent, and fire smoke twirled upward. Water sloshed along the treeline.

Alfred spoke up again, "'Tait juste avant qu'i' joins l'armée. Before he shipped out."

"Mais ça c't'une aut' histwayr," I said and snorted.

Alfred glanced at me and grunted, then he lifted himself slowly from the chair. "'Tends 'citte," he said, and he went down the yard, and around the cabin, and I heard the door open and close, and I thought for a moment that I'd said something I shouldn't have. That I had somehow offended him. Then I heard his voice again as he reappeared around the corner holding a couple bottles of OV and pointing to the fire.

"Garoches-y une buche dessus."

After I tossed a log on the fire, Alfred handed me a bottle and I stared at the beer, at the cold, dew-drenched neck, at the drops of moisture condensing, leaking down the sides, dripping off the bottom. I'd tasted a beer before along the Seine, and so I bit my tongue when Alfred said I was finally old enough.

"C'est l'temps," he said. "Pour la vérité."

Truth was Old Coup d'Coude had glimpsed at the heat inside Dad and decided to mould that fire and wield it against les Mennonites. Alfred said le vieux Duhamel had grown ever more bitter with his old foes. Hockey fights—those perennial bench-clearing brawls between the teams in Ste. Anne and Steinbach—spilled regularly into the communities and infected other sports and events. Fistfights would break out at wedding socials or outside of Fritz's bar.

Most of the hockey team played baseball too, in the summers, and they brought that same glove-dropping spirit to the ball diamond. Coup d'Coude would happily exchange his skates and stick for a mitt and bat.

* * *

Monique scribbled distractedly in her notepad at the kitchen table as Dad went on.

"Y voulait vraiment battre les Mennonites," said Dad. "À n'importe quoi."

"'T'un drôle de prêtre s'y'savait pas pardonner," said Mom.

Monique glanced at her out of the corner of her eyes, and her lips twitched, but she kept her sharp tongue sheathed.

"C'tout qu'il voulait dans vie," said Dad.

* * *

Pitching another log onto the fire, Alfred described how in an old, converted passenger van, with wooden benches running the walls and leather straps dangling from the roof, and with le vieux Coup d'Coude at the wheel, the team plied the gravel roads between towns: from Anola to La Broquerie, Ross to Richer, and Lorette to Steinbach, the team travelled. Spilling out of the van into the late spring sun, they warmed up on the side of the field and eyed their competition across the ball diamond. Sometimes, when playing Richer or Ste. Geneviève, they would spot a cousin or three across the way and shout friendly insults over the diamond. Sometimes they would congregate at the plate to compare stories of their season on the road, share tales of hard-fought games won on the last pitch or lost on the last at-bat when some player would boast of their exploits or lament their errors. But other times, when facing Blumenort or Steinbach, they would keep their distance and glare across the infield at their foes.

Old Coup d'Coude would reluctantly, and stiffly, shake the opposing coach's hand. One quick and curt pump. And he would spin, and march back toward the dugout, where he'd stuff a handful of sunflower seeds into his mouth, and then with his cheeks bulging like a squirrel's, he would position himself along the baseline and mumble-shout the batting order. Sunflower shells machine-gunned from his lips. Clerical collar glowing in the hot sun.

Dad would usually bat fourth in the order.

Clean-up hitter.

"Un vrai bon frappeur," Alfred waxed. "Mais," he continued, Dad became a target due to it. Opposing teams began to clue in and by the third or fourth time they'd see him warming up on the sidelines, swinging his bat softly to loosen his muscles, priming his hips, shoulders, and arms to knock that rubber-cored bundle of cowhide into next week, they'd adjust their tactics. Fielders shifted deeper to patrol the fence line or, if Dad were really on, the pitchers would toss balls wide to make Dad walk the bases.

One game, against Steinbach, Dad grew fed up when, right off the first pitch he faced, he saw the ball sail wide of the strike zone. He recognized the pitcher—it was the man whose arm he had broken in the late fall with a slash behind the net, and the pitcher recognized Dad too. He glared at Dad over the tip of his glove, and shook off the catcher's signs flickering in his crotch. The catcher stood and turned to the umpire, the umpire lifted his hands, and the catcher ran up to the mound to speak with the pitcher. A stream of hot spit squirted through the pitcher's teeth, he glared at Dad, who was swinging his bat again to keep muscles loose, and the pitcher nodded. He chucked the ball wide.

But when Dad stepped up to the plate, he chased the pitch outside the zone, and smacked a double into left field. The pitcher glowered as Dad rounded first, and jogged to second.

Another stream of spit arched over the mound and a cloud of dust mushroomed upward as the pitcher smacked his glove in frustration. He turned toward the plate, and while Dad stole third, the pitcher struck out the next two to end the inning.

"La game 'tait tight," said Alfred. "Les Mennonites 'taient des bons frappeurs itou. Y'ont loadé les bases, et tout d'un coup, bang! Une flyball que t'on père attrape et jette à Homeplate."

* * *

"One of their guys decides to steal home and bulldozes our catcher at the plate there, eh," said Dad. His eyes seemed to track some dust mote drifting over the table. Monique scribbled on her napkin, her notepad full. Mom refilled her cup of tea.

Coup d'Coude marched out of the dugout and rained spittle in the umpire's face, his arms gesticulating as though delivering a sermon, but he was then told to sit the hell down.

"Ah bin, so when it was finally my turn to go back up to bat, c'tait tight. I mean, pas juste le score, hein. Mais l'atmosphère."

* * *

"J'lui avais dit, à ton père, après l'affaire avec le gars, de pas faire de mal, mais défends-toé, hein," said Alfred as the fire grew larger in the pit, the wood crackling in the heat, the sound of water breaking faint through the woods behind us. "Mais dans game là, le feu lui avait pris."

When Dad stepped up to the plate again, in the bottom of the seventh, and he waved his bat menacingly through the strike zone, and figuring that the pitcher would chuck that ball wide once more, he prepared to reach out as he had done previously, and was unprepared for a sudden lick of chin music. Glaring over the tip of his glove, the pitcher planned a different strategy. And instead of throwing wide, as the catcher frantically—fingers flickering in the seat of his crotch—implored that he do, the pitcher lifted up his foot, and glancing back at the man on second, stood momentarily silhouetted like a flamingo against the prairie sky, before he drove his foot onto the mound, whipped his arm round like a windmill, and drove that ball right at Dad's head.

* * *

"L'enfant chienne voulait me tuer," Dad snapped and slapped the table, jolting our cups.

"Émile!" Mom said.

Monique glanced up from her napkin, her genealogical documents forgotten at her elbow.

"Bin," said Dad, frowning at the tea that has splashed over the lip of his cup. "It's true."

Dad described how he flung himself backwards, the fastball glancing off his helmet and rattling the backstop. He lay there for a moment, staring at the clouds, before voices burst angrily around him. Le vieux Coup d'Coude spat fire from the on deck circle and John Deere, up next in the batting order, along with others, held back the priest from again accosting the umpire. Dad sat up, and he looked out over the infield at the Mennonite grinning silly on the mound in a half-crouch with his hands on his knees.

* * *

"Pis y'a explodé," said Alfred.

Dad popped up onto his feet and, before anyone could intercept him, charged the mound. The pitcher hurled his glove at Dad to slow him down, but Dad batted the glove away and leaped toward the pitcher, tackling him to the ground. The pitcher tried to throw Dad off, tried to protect himself, but Dad cracked him across the jaw, and the pitcher dropped limply to the ground, arms falling like stones, legs flattening out over the mound. Dad cracked him again, and again, across the face, busting open the man's lips, breaking the man's nose, and tearing open the man's face until blood poured like rainwater and soaked into the dry, dusty ground.

"Émile," croaked le vieux Coup d'Coude, caught between his own desire to see Dad beat the Mennonite bloody, and his duties as a priestly coach to act responsibly. "C't'assez!"

Then someone tackled Dad. The dugouts cleared. And the boys and men hurled knuckles and leather gloves at each other over the coaches and the umpires as they tried to pry them apart. Someone caught Dad on the nose, and blood poured down the front of his uniform. John Deere threw himself at a heavy-looking blonde boy in red just before the blonde boy could hit Dad with a bat. Parents scrambled from the bleachers, sprinting around the backstop, and chain-link fence, and tried pulling kids from the pile of knuckles and fists overtop the blood-soaked mound.

Face flushed red and sweating, the umpire threatened all manner of toothless measures.

Then they heard the sirens whooping down the road, growing louder, nearer, and they saw the lights spinning atop the roofs, as ambulances and polices cruisers burst through the gate down by the foul post, and poured over the field toward the diamond.

"J'pense que toutes les misères d'sa vie sont sorties d'un coup," said Alfred.

* * *

"J'étais vide," said Dad.

He hardly felt the pinch around his wrists as the handcuffs snapped shut, and he suddenly found himself seated in the back of a police cruiser, and watched through the window as le vieux Coup d'Coude pleaded with the police officer. Then Coup d'Coude flinched as the officer in turn upbraided the old priest. Down along the dugouts, the teams sat on their hands while more police scratched down their names onto small notepads. Paramedics lifted the pitcher onto a gurney and wheeled him toward the ambulance. Dad hardly noticed when the officer climbed into the cruiser and looked back through the wire-cage and spoke to him. He hardly felt the cruiser move as the old priest and the boys on his team shrunk in the window. He hardly heard the thick-barred door in the concrete cell slam close before him.

"They threw you in jail?" said Monique. She glanced up from her napkin, pen trembling between her fingers now.

Mom lowered her eyes onto the table and sighed.

Monique glanced over at us, at Mom and me, as we sat quietly and listened to Dad speak. His words washed over me, mixing with those Alfred had spoken when we sat around the firepit.

* * *

"On est allé le voir, à station d'police, là," said Alfred. He paused to toss another log on the small fire. The sky slowly turned orange overhead, shots, and streaks of red, and purple in the east through the tips of the budding trees.

I tried to imagine Alfred standing there, before the steel slit door, with Mémère. Eyes red with fear, and sadness, and shame at the sight of Dad curled up on a small, hard bed.

Dad glanced up. Spotted Alfred. Nodded. "J'mé défendu," he said.

Alfred's cheeks drained white, and Mémère glanced at him and frowned.

"Comme tu m'as dit," said Dad.

Mémère gripped Alfred's arm, and her wet eyes hovered over his face, brows flickering with the thought of that conversation, then growing hard with the realization of what happened.

Mémère wept.

"Ché pas si a ma jamais pardonné," Alfred confessed. "Mais y'avait pas d'choix. Même avec quoé qu'y'ont faite à mon frère, à son père, j'lui ai dit, à ton père à toé, anyways, qu'y'avait pas d'choix. C'tait ça: la prison ou l'armée."

* * *

"So," Dad sighed and sipped his tea. "I joined up."

* * *

So, Dad left. And for nearly a decade, through basic in Québec, then through all the years deployed in Europe, Dad dreamt of the day he might return.

28.

L'histoire des histoires

DAD SAT IN THE DIM LIGHT OF THE KITCHEN, A HALF-finished tumbler of whiskey at his elbow. He looked up from the old photos spread out on the table before him. "You're still up?"

"I could ask you the same," I said as I limped across the kitchen, opened the fridge, and grabbed a bottle of water. I leaned against the counter and cracked the bottle open. Wind gusted outside battering the windows with a thin rain and pellets of ice. The sky was dark, menacing. In the hallway, I could see a flicker of light, hear a whisper of sound. Mom was up, watching TV in the bedroom. I turned to Dad and saw that he had almost emptied Alfred's albums on the table— black and white photos, postcards, some polaroids, and overexposed colour pictures. The funeral was prepared—some of the photos had been scanned and loaded into a slideshow they'd show in the hall after the ceremony tomorrow. Photos of the holidays when Alfred was sur-rounded by nieces and nephews. Mémère during one of the good times.

In the end, Alfred had scant few photos of himself. He seemed to have spent his life capturing others' moments from behind the camera.

Dad shrugged and plucked a photo from the table, angling it toward me. It was old, and blurry, but I could make out Alfred as a young man, a boy really, surrounded by his brothers and sisters—most were long-dead by now, though, earlier today, Dad had let drop that there was still a great-aunt living in Vancouver. They had lost touch and hadn't seen her in decades. She was too frail to travel, but he had spoken to her over the phone this afternoon.

Then Dad picked another photo and showed it to me. I stepped forward and grabbed it, bringing it closer to my eyes. Straining to see it in the dim light. It was of him, as a young man standing in his army camos next to the little cabin in Ste. Geneviève. The trees and grasses were green, full of life. Dad stood awkwardly, at attention. He bore a big grin that didn't quite seem to touch his eyes.

"How old are you there?" I asked.

Dad frowned, searching his memories. "Early twenties," he said. "I had some leave, and I came home to visit. I thought that Alfred would be at the house in Ste. Anne avec tout le monde, t'sé, but maman hadn't let him through the door since I'd left."

"So, you went to the cabin."

"That's right."

"Who took the photo?"

"Alfred."

Wind gusted again, raking through the tops of the trees around the house, shearing them of their last few leaves, and peppering the roof. My eyes were drawn to a small bundle of older photos, and I slipped into a chair next to Dad. Atop the small pile was the old photo I had asked Alfred about: the photograph of his mother in the parlour. The memory of that long night, almost a decade ago, when Alfred had kept us awake with the sound of his voice, filled my mind.

"Ta grandmère," I said, plucking the photo from the pile, showing it to Dad.

"I think so," he said.

"No, it is," and I flipped the photo over to look at the date and the place scrawled on the back. Saint-Adolphe, 1909. "Rosalie." I said.

"That's right," Dad nodded.

"You never met her, eh?"

"Non, est morte avant qu'chu née."

The smell of burnt chicken wafted through the air, and torchlight flickered against the dark walls of Alfred's kitchen—memories of the drone of his voice as he spoke so vivid. At the table with Dad, I stared at the old photo, and remembered how Alfred had seemed to empty himself of stories that night.

"The photo was taken in Saint-Adolphe, hein." I said. "Alfred said a photographer from Winnipeg—Saint-Boniface, I guess—vraiment, went around to the small towns, and would set up a studio in the back of the general stores to take people's photos, those who couldn't travel to Winnipeg. Says Saint-Adolphe on the back here, eh." I showed Dad the back and he grunted.

I flipped the photo back over, and stared at Rosalie's face. Tried to peer into her eyes through the blur of time. Wisps of black hair leaking from under the big hat. Cheekbones visible above her round cheeks. A big cross hung down the front of her dress. "Alfred y'a dit she moved there young, hein, pour aller au couvent, but elle a quand même grandi en ville. Somewhere near Wolseley j'pense; but west, passed Omand's Creek. Y vivaient à Saint-Charles." I stared at my great-grandmother's face, and saw Dad in the shape of her mouth, Monique in her shoulders—in the strength of their posture. "Apparemment la famille tried to stick it out en ville, at first, à place d'déménager après '70. Mais sa toute tourner Anglais alentour d'eux, and they got harassed, eh, spit on, threatened. Got worse, après '85. Quelqu'un a garoché du sang d'cochon sur leur porte. Her brother was beaten in the street. Alfred learned that, eh. Said someone had found the story in an old newspaper, and passed a photocopy along to him. It's probably still in his papers," I said, waving toward the cabin, somewhere north of us. I could feel his words on my lips—describing the scene the way that he imagined it happened. Building it up from the fragments, the rumours, and the whispers that he had heard, gathered, confirmed, and fused together into a story. Two angry young English men—probably Canadians— recently arrived, had cornered his mother's brother, Alfred's uncle, in an alley off Portage, and beat him for his money and his moccasins.

"Left him for dead in the snow."

I paused and sipped my water, still staring at the photo; memories of the sounds of waves crashing at the door mingled with those of the wind gusts outside the house. The smell of Dad's half-finished rye whiskey like the stink of gasoline from the pump and the generator.

"But he crawled home, eh. Alfred thought he'd probably sang the whole way too," I said, and I shook my head. "But that doesn't make sense to me. If they beat him, they probably broke his jaw. You can't sing with a broken jaw, can you? Anyway, I guess it scared la famille plenty, and they had enough of the city. So, son déménager à Saint-Adolphe. I guess y'avaient déjà d'la parenté alentour d'là. Après une couple d'année au couvent, sa mère s'est mariée à un Canadien. Un bon catholique, Alfred said. They had some kids—Alfred, Pépère, and the others—but then she caught the flu. Pis est morte assez jeune." I cleared my throat, Alfred words evaporating off my lips. "Anyways, that's all I remember right now." And I laid the photo down on the table and leaned back in my chair.

Dad didn't move. I glanced at him, and saw that he was trembling. His eyes glistened. I swallowed hard, wondering if I had fucked up, and said something I shouldn't have, something that had come to amplify his grief, but then he looked at me, and it seemed that he saw me now in a way that he had never seen before, and he smiled.

"Merci."

29.

On parlent pas mal des morts

ALFRED'S FUNERAL WAS HELD AT THE SAINTE ANNE Roman Catholic Church. Mourners drove in from Ste. Geneviève, Ross, and Richer, some came from as far away as Saskatoon, Thunder Bay, and Calgary, to kiss and hug and comfort each other, to mourn, to celebrate, to laugh.

"Ah bin! Sacrament!"

Voices rang through the bright, cavernous church. Echoes pooled overhead, in the crown of the steep-pitched ceiling. Cream-coloured walls glowed like the afterlife.

"Ça fait un bout!"

Folks lined up for a last look at Alfred who lay quietly in a plain brown coffin before the altar. Mounds of flowers towered over the coffin and a wreath in the shape of an infinity symbol stood off to the side, next to a blurry, blown-up photo of Alfred bleeding a deer in the small shed behind his cabin. We'd talked about which photo to use—there weren't many it turned out—and finally settled on one which seemed to capture Alfred at his best, with joy in his eyes. One which he wasn't sporting his usual sunglasses. In the coffin, he wore his camo-coloured ballcap and his sunglasses. People approached the body, and quietly chuckled.

There hadn't been much in the will in terms of the funeral service itself, but Alfred had made his final wishes clear to Dad over the years. He had been adamant about having his ashes scattered in the bush behind the cabin, and he wanted to wear his ballcap and glasses right up to the end. The rest was up to Dad.

Menoncle Roger cackled when he saw Alfred. He turned to his brother, Menoncle Frank, and drove his elbow into his ribs. "Regards ça!"

"Tabarnak. Chu pas aveugle," said Frank, and he blinked and bit his tongue, and glanced around sheepishly for the priest.

Folks kept coming up to Dad to shake his hand—John Deere and his wife Lucerne, the old farmer with the camo-coloured ball cap who got ribbed by his wife for looking like the dead man in the coffin, and New Holland with his wife Beatrice. They recounted stories about Alfred, and slapped their knees, and laughed, until the line up to speak to Dad grew longer than to view Alfred. Folks squeezed by to shake my hand, and give Mom a quick hug, and smile and wave at Monique's kids. Annette Simard. Bernie Kowalchuk. Diane Friesen. The priest—a young man I did not recognize—circled nervously and he cleared his throat like an idling tractor as he tried to usher folks into the pews. I wondered briefly what had happened to the old priest who conducted Mémère's funeral. The pew rattled beneath me, bumping against the back of my knees, and pain fired down my back, and I shifted my weight around until it eased, and then I glanced back ready to glare, when I spotted Danny pouting and kicking the back of my pew.

"Hey, mon homme," I said. Remembering the small plastic bison nestled in my pocket, which I had carried for days, and drawn comfort from the gentle act that had first brought it into my possession, I prepared to return it. I had made sure to slip it into my pocket this morning. But as I grabbed it, and ran my thumb over the soft, rounded edges of its small horns, over the rough-ridged mound of plastic fur around its head,

I was struck by the sudden reluctance to part with it. Like in a custom ring, my thumb seemed to fit perfectly between the tips of the horns.

Danny stared at me, peering over the handrail. Isabelle shifted at his side and frowned. I took the plastic bison out and placed its hooves on the handrail.

"Patch-é-coupe," I said, winking, and stampeded that plastic beast down the rail. Danny laughed, and Isabelle rolled her eyes. Monique glanced over, turning away from the woman with whom she was speaking, and frowned as she saw the bison.

"Geez, Rich. Couldn't you have waited until after the service?"

The priest cleared his throat again.

"On va commencer, on va commencer."

People began to settle into their seats, and I looked out over all the men and women who had come, spotting familiar faces in the sea of mourners: Uncle Joe and Matante Jo. Monsieur et Madame Groscoeurs. Céline Petitcoeur. Al Verrier's dad, towering over others at the back. I was struck by the sight. Mémère's funeral, half-a-decade ago, had been larger, they'd had to open the balconies above to accommodate the crowds, her hundreds of descendants, but it had also been a somber scene, filled with a burbling sob, fluttering tissues sopped with tears and snot. But today, that somber mood seemed buoyed by joyous reminiscences—people kept smiling, and laughing quietly—and though the balconies remained closed, the church seemed full to bursting.

"Eyes front, Pichenotte!" shouted J.P. Gauthier.

The service puttered along through verse and prayer. A small grey-haired band played hymns in the corner using a six-string guitar, an electric base, and a pared-down drum kit; they crooned enthusiastically. Hallelujah! We whipped through a couple readings—the readers strode confidently toward the pulpit, manhandled the microphone down or up, and then zipped through some gospel according to so and so. I began to tune them out after the first one, listening instead to Danny and Isabelle hum some children's show theme song in the pew behind me. It sounded familiar, if distant, tickling some memory half-buried in the rubble of intervening years. *Sesame Street*, perhaps.

Then the young priest threw an *Our Father* into the mix for the hell of it. With his palms raised like a pauper with a beer-tab in front of the altar, he began in French. *Notre Père qu'yé au ciel…* a few folks boomed along confidently, but most mumbled, hummed, or emphasized a few recollected words… donnez-nous du *pain*, c'jour 'citte… et pis, délivrez-nous du *mal*. *Amène*, a few of Dad's brothers mispronounced, and snickered.

That was Alfred's old joke.

Whenever the priest was slow in handing over that holy cracker, you said amène!

Give it, quick!

After the old standard, the young priest stepped anxiously toward the pulpit. He adjusted the microphone stand, and filled the church with the sound of his wide-sleeved robe rubbing the foamy socked-tipped microphone. He cleared his throat again, an idling tractor low on fuel, and began his brief eulogy.

"I never met Alfred," he said, shifting gears. "Je ne le l'ai pas connu, but from what some have told me, il était très pieux."

A few uncles snickered again, and the matantes drove sharp elbows into their ribs; behind us, somewhere, Dave blurted, "Ah bin, tu racontes dés histwayr, hein, Émile?"

The priest blinked as the crowd tittered and he shuffled through his notes. He glanced up again, downshifted, and began anew. He recounted some of what Dad had told him at the house the day before last: how although he had spent nearly his entire life on that small patch of bush near Ste. Geneviève, Alfred had possessed a worldly spirit, filled with wonder and wisdom—the words he used were mondain, merveille, and sagesse—and the pews groaned under the weight of folks shifting cheeks on the hard wood and glancing at each other in puzzlement.

"Hein? Y'tait quoi?" le vieux Gauthier half shouted to his son.

"Orgueilleux! Y'tait orgueilleux d'appartenir à cette—"

"Quessé qu'tu lui as raconté, Émile?"

"Patch-é-coupe," Danny said, and hooves rattling, the plastic bison hurtled along the pew.

"You have to be quiet," Isabelle whispered.

"Shh! Shh! Shh!"

The young priest wiped sweat from his brow, mumbled some platitudes about piety, and then cleared his throat. "J'vais passer la parole, à—" he glanced at his notes, the papers shuffling loudly under the microphone as the pews groaned again, and he looked up, frowned, and peered into the crowd at the gaping jaws, the growing yawns—"à Fred, oui. Oui."

He retreated quickly, sat, sunk, and shrunk into the jumbo-sized chair next to the altar.

Matante Fred—Frédérique La Montagne—waltzed up to the pulpit, red file folder tucked under her arm, peered over the lectern, and nearly tore the microphone stand from its mooring as she wrenched it down toward her lips.

Dad's youngest sister, Matante Fred had married a Frenchman, un La Montagne, moved to Regina, and worked her way up in the education system there until she was in charge of more than half of the schools in the city. The incongruity between her appearance and her name—her short, diminutive, four-foot-odd frame and her married name—usually lasted only until the first words burst from her mouth and buried listeners in the avalanche of her personality.

Matante Fred had Alfred pegged: "Un vieux pet avec un coeur d'or," she described him. Peeking over the lip of the pulpit, she gathered all of the loose threads that we had carried with us into the pews and, before our eyes, wove together the story of Alfred's life. While she did not shy away from the darker bits, she framed them against the glow of his character and his deeds—his unending good humour while convalescing in the house after he'd fallen from the tree, or his frequent, unsuccessful attempts to learn the fiddle.

"Comme y tuait un chat à chaque fois," she said.

The crowd tittered over the image.

Then Fred turned serious, and spoke of Alfred's devotion: what he would do for family.

"Quand Papa est parti en guerre, c'était Alfred qu'yé rester avec maman et avec nous," she said. "Well," she paused, rocking back and forth on her toes, "Pas moi, je n'étais pas encore née," she laughed. "I wasn't born then, but j'ai toujours entendu dire comment Alfred y'était là, qui prenait soin d'la ferme, la vache à lait, pis les poules maigres, and hey boy, he took real good care of that farm, eh, et pis comment y'allait chasser du chevreuil—avec Roger—"

"Pis moé itou," grumbled Frank, and the crowed tittered again.

"Et Frank itou," laughed Fred. "Et c'est d'eux que j'ai entendu c't'histoire—that I heard this story—d'Alfred et les Allemands."

It was an old story. A silly story. A story told and retold over coffee and tea and beer and whiskey. During the war, while Pépère was in Europe, Alfred had quietly taken over the meager farm. If you could call a pair of old milk cows, a dozen chickens, and vegetable patch a farm. He taught Frank and Roger and the others how to hunt deer and hare—they even shot a moose once, when it ventured out from the Shield—and he picked up the odd job woodworking to supplement their income and help Mémère. At night, with his big, flat feet up on a small stool, he would look out over the dark, rock-studded field, the ghost of fence, the wall of stocky bush beyond the yard, and the perforated sky above, machine-gunned starlight bleeding onto the earth.

He cursed his feet.

"Patch-é-coupe!" Danny said. The toy bison stampeded behind me again, plastic hooves clattering along the pew.

"Shh, shh!" Isabelle shushed.

Curled over a small radio in the kitchen, Fred continued, Mémère and Alfred would listen for hours to reports from the front, until Mémère could no longer take it, and she finally banished the radio from the house.

One day as he worked in the small vegetable patch, Alfred heard a rumble in the distance; he looked to the horizon and at the colour of the sky over the crown of oak and ash and birch, the spears of evergreens thrusting into the blue, and he frowned over the absent thunderheads he had expected, the dark, bulbous clouds brewing storms over the Red River Valley below. The rumble grew louder, like a cloud of mosquitoes, or a squadron of wasps, billowing close. Then, over the horizon like migrating geese, a wedge of airplanes appeared—bombers, fighters, the details were lost—and Alfred stood transfixed for a moment. But as an endless series of them poured over the horizon, growing closer and larger, buzzing the treetops, Alfred acted. He dropped his hoe in the vegetable patch and sprinted toward the house.

"Les Allemands! Les Allemands!"

Alfred grabbed his rifle and scrambled out into the yard, away from the house. He aimed his rifle up at the sky, at the fleet of floating crosses above, and he fired, and fired, and fired. The planes buzzed in formation, and if the pilots noticed the panicked man below, who stood there in the hot sun and poured lead into the sky after them, no one would ever know. The planes neither veered nor banked away, but flew on, straight. But, in his mind, as the planes retreated eastward, over the horizon, Alfred believed he had succeeded in fending off "les Allemands!"

He told everyone about it. Only later did he learn about the allied airbase in Portage, the Empire-wide mission to train tens of thousands of pilots, and the realization dawned on him that he had probably shot up some Englishmen instead of Germans.

"Wasn't the worst thing in the world," said Matante Fred.

The crowd tittered again, some wiped tears of laughter from their eyes.

Despite his mistake, Fred continued, and above all the noise and the comedy, and there had no doubt been some merciless ribbing, what the act had revealed, at its heart, was Alfred's boundless devotion. How he had stood against an army to defend his family.

* * *

"Zj'amais eu aen ôte chance à tchiré sur lii Anglais," Alfred once sheepishly admitted after one too many beers.

* * *

We filed out of the church in a solemn yet festive procession, weeping tears of both joy and sadness from our eyes, as we waltzed slowly behind the pallbearers and the simple brown coffin draped in a flag of blue and white, and wound into that late November day. The sun shone bright and warm, its rays piercing the wisps of grey clouds, thawing that gauze of snow that had gathered overnight, and washing the cobblestone pathway in sunlight and meltwater. Crowded together, we watched the pallbearers load the coffin into the hearse, and then watched the hearse drive off. Alfred would be cremated. We planned to spread his ashes in the spring.

After the hearse left, we milled about in the courtyard, under the old stone-faced steeple, and greeted folks we'd not had the chance to see before the service. Danny and Isabelle whined with hunger and Monique whispered rumours of Bear Paws in the minivan. I hugged an endless series of matantes, menoncles, and increasingly distant cousins.

Voices reminded folks that lunch and tea awaited us at the legion hall, and a few of the older folks began to make their way toward their vehicles, but most seemed to be in no hurry. It was rare to see so many branches of the family, with all of its leaves, twigs, and smaller saplings, gathered like this. We rooted ourselves to the courtyard to prolong the moment.

"Make way! Le vieux a faim!" shouted J.P. Gauthier. "Pis moé itou!" he boomed, and laughed. He half-dragged his old man down the church steps and plowed through the crowd; we watched them push and shove like bulls in a cow pen, the old man's cane whipping like a switch. As they neared our circle, Dad held his arms up and stepped in front of the pair.

"Slow down," Dad growled. "Crisse, J.P., tu vas lui tordre la cheville."

J.P. blinked, his cheeks growing red.

Dad leaned in toward le vieux Gauthier, who sucked lips, and scrunched his cheeks. "Es-tu okay, Menoncle?"

The cane wobbled beneath the old man's hands.

"Hein?"

"Y t'a demandé comment ça va," J.P. boomed. "He asked if you're okay."

Le vieux sucked and smacked his lips and worked them up into a word. "J'ai mal au cul," he said, patting his bum. "Mes fesses sont endormies sur l'banc."

J.P. boomed and laughed, and reached out and smacked Dad on the shoulder. "See?" he said. "His ass fell asleep. Y'avait besoin d'une marche. We'll see you at the hall, eh."

Dad grunted. Muscle fired at the back of his jaw and he shifted, as though adjusting his weight from one foot to the next like a fighter before throwing a punch, but instead of striking out with his fist, Dad leaned forward and shouted in the old man's face. "Hey, Menoncle! C'tu vrai qu't'as volé la terre à papa?"

The question dropped like a grenade. *Did you steal Dad's land?* J.P. flinched, and stood transfixed, tongue flopping inside his fiery cheeks. Menoncles Frank, Roger, et Dave, et puis Matante Carole, Yolande, et Fred, and some of the others frowned in confusion.

"Pa'ce que c'ça qu'Alfred ya écrit," said Dad.

Like shrapnel, Dad's words seemed to sheer the old man's armour. Exposed, le vieux began to transform as though unburdened by the weight of a life-long ruse. His spine suddenly straight and rigid, wrinkles stretched taut over his brittle bones and his teeth grew large as his lips curled into a snarl. He slammed his cane firmly on the ground and glared at his nieces and nephews.

Dad nodded. He turned toward his brothers and sisters, and he told them about the letters we had found with Alfred's will, the letters that Alfred had exchanged with Mémère, and which described how Pépère had lost his land, how le vieux Gauthier had pulled a fast one on Alfred.

"Lui a triché," he said.

Working words through his clenched jaw, J.P. managed to huff and protest. "Fuck off," he said, his arm waving toward the bush east of town. "This old story again? Papa y'a acheté sa terre fair and square." He glared at the quiet crowd gathering around us. "This is horseshit. Let's go, Papa," he said, and he reached towards his father, but before he could grab hold of his arm, I learned forward and flicked his elbow.

Un pichenotte.

"Nice jacket," I said.

J.P. flinched again. "W-What?"

"Nice jacket," I repeated.

"Thanks," he croaked.

"What happened to your flannel?"

"Ah bin," he slowly grinned and glanced back at the church. "You don't wear flannel to a funeral. Come on, Pichenotte, you should know—"

"Funny thing that. We found a jacket that looked just like your flannel, dedans la cabine à Alfred, just a few days ago, right Papa?"

"That's right," said Dad.

Le vieux Gauthier frowned, eyes darting back and forth, trying to follow along.

J.P. coughed. "That's a nice story."

"Puait comme une chicoque," said Dad.

"Stunk like a skunk," I said.

"Fallait s'en débarrasser," said Dad.

Air wheezed through J.P.'s throat-locked, jaw-clasped lips. "W-What did you do?"

"Had to burn it," I said. "Behind the cabin."

J.P. stared, his cheeks quivering like bowls of red jelly.

"Found your flask too," I added.

"Dis-nous, mon homme, c'tu toé qu'ya fouillé la cabine à Alfred? Quessé tu cherchais? Quessé ta pris?"

"Mon ostie d'voleur," I muttered. "What did you take?"

Le vieux Gauthier looked over at his son.

"Voleur."

Les menoncles et matantes, the cousins distant and near, began to murmur around us, their voices rising like wind through the trees. Swirling through stone and grass and around bark and stump, coursing through the coulees and valleys beyond the horizon, and across the prairie in waves that echoed and reverberated in our bones. Our voices rising through time, old, and warm. Overhead dry leaves chattered.

"Voleur."

J.P. shook his head. "Non," he said. "Non." But his words seemed hollow, half-hearted—and they fell away like autumn leaves on the cobblestone path, swept up and carried away by the wind and the chorus. Cast out, they rattled along the surface of the stone-faced church, around the steeple, and into the blue.

"Voleur."

30.

Les vieilles chansons

BERNIE ELASTIC SCRATCHED AND SQUEALED OVER THE little boom box on the table next to the rye bread, cold cuts, Bothwell marble cheese, trays of fruits and veggies, cookies, and other desserts. Folks lined up to fill their Styrofoam plates. Les plus vieux went first, followed by les matantes et menoncles, and then mums with kids in tow. Plates loaded, they drifted back to their tables, or paused to greet and chat with some old face or friend they'd not seen in years.

Another table bristled with an assortment of beverages: hot tea and coffee, with cream and honey, a jar of white sugar, and packets of artificial, sugar-free sweetener for the diabetics. Juice boxes. Bottles of water. Canned soft drinks, regular and diet. A cooler filled with ice and beer tucked beneath the table care of Frank. Standing amid a circle of older cousins, I watched the line grow before the food table. We guarded the drink cooler.

"Eh, boy, t'un peu jeune là hein?" Marcel quipped as a boy with a paltry clutch of dark whiskers upon his chin casually reached under the table and lifted the cooler lid. The boy pulled his hand back and his cheeks flushed.

"C'est pour mon père," he said, whiskers trembling like his voice.

"Uh huh."

"C'qui ton père?" asked another cousin.

The boy's cheeks turned a deeper shade of red and he scooped a Pepsi off the table, then fled through the food line.

"Doit t-êt' un Gauthier," Marcel laughed.

Someone slapped me on the shoulder. I grinned stupidly and took a sip of my beer. I had been lauded all afternoon by folks who'd witnessed the exchange with J.P. and le vieux in front of the church. Folks, who had for so long only wondered, si c'était pas parenté, what they might have said given the chance, had burst like thunder against the mountain, like a downpour of cold rain. They showered J.P. and le vieux with sharp and scathing words in response to a lifetime of insults and resentment. Under the hail, J.P. and le vieux retreated from the courtyard, into the big Diesel truck parked up on the curb. Glaring out at the crowd of angry cousins, J.P. started up the engine. The truck coughed and sputtered, then the wheels squealed on the concrete and, vomiting smoky clouds of rubber and dust, it peeled off down the road.

At the hall, Dad explained to his brothers and sisters what we had found in the cabin. The mess, the jacket, the flask, la chicoque. Then he told them about the letters.

"J'm'rappelle de ça," one of them nodded. She remembered Mémère at the kitchen table, scratching paper in the candlelight.

"Pis la terre à Alfred?" another asked.

Dad shrugged. "Elle appartient à une compagnie d'gravel."

"Tabarnak."

"Y la louait juste."

"Sacrament."

The food-lines dwindled as everyone drifted with bulging plates toward their tables to sit and snack. The music wound down, but someone shoved a fresh tape in the cassette player, and it began to crackle with some old tunes. Laughter washed like waves across the hall.

Danny and Isabelle stuffed themselves with cheese while Mom urged them to eat the fruit on their plates. Monique shrugged, and turned to Dad, who stared at his plate. The untouched rye bread and meat. John glanced out at the crowd of tables around us, frowning as though searching for an overgrown path through the brush.

"What's up," I said.

"Oh, it's just—" he began, and paused, as if considering his words. "Everyone seems so happy, for a funeral."

Popping a piece of cheese into my mouth, I shrugged. "Just more comfortable like this, I guess." Then, after a moment, I added. "Besides, I think Alfred would have wanted it this way."

"So, Rich," said Monique, "Where's Becky? Didn't you tell her about Alfred?"

"Yeah, I did. We've been talking over the phone. She's got some papers to write, though. End of term, eh. She sends her love."

Monique nodded, but as I flicked some cheese across my plate with a finger, she began to frown. "What aren't you telling me?"

Music drifted over the table. One song ended, but then another started up. *Voulez-vous écouter chanter, une chanson de vérité—*

"He's thinking of moving to the city," Mom said.

"What?" I sputtered "How do you know?"

"About time!" Monique snorted.

"House isn't that big, Rich. We can hear you through the walls."

As Monique pressed, question after question, and I grunted and nodded occasionally in response, I began to smile in spite of myself. Although the notion of leaving and moving into the city caused the roots coiled through my guts to roil and constrict, I found comfort in the idea of return. Above all, I found comfort in the possibilities that lay before us, imagining what Becky and I might build together. As content as Alfred had seemed on that small plot of bush, it seemed suddenly to me to be inadequate, no longer what I envisioned for myself. Instead, the world had opened up and, for perhaps the first time I could recall, I wondered what it held.

Dad stared solemnly at the crumbs on his plate.

At the head of the table, Eddie Gauthier, J.P.'s older brother, towered over us. I flinched, and grew tense, until I noticed the way he stood, how he swayed gingerly, a quiet birch tree in a breeze, waiting for an invitation to speak. Dad glanced up at his cousin and blinked.

"Menoncle," Eddie said. Although they were technically cousins, the Gauthier children were all a dozen or more years younger than Dad, and had grown up calling Dad and his older siblings uncle and auntie. He grunted, and cleared his throat. Then thrust his hand out. Dad shook it. And Eddie nodded.

"I just wanted to apologize, eh, pour mon frère."

"Oh, it's okay, Eddie. No sweat."

"No, no," Eddie shook his head. "It's not okay." He pursed his lips and glanced at the wall as though scanning the horizon beyond it for the farm. "J'savais pas, you know. I mean, I figured Dad and J.P. had probably spent too much time alone, together, on that damn farm," he sighed and left the words hanging there, unfinished.

Dad stood and grabbed Eddie's hand, shook it again, and patted Eddie on the shoulder.

"T'es t'un bon homme, Eddie."

"Ah bin, tu vas me faire pleurer," Eddie said, and aggressively cleared his throat. "I'm going to grab a beer. You want one?"

"Non, merci. Prends soin, Eddie."

"Toé itou," Eddie nodded, and he drifted off toward the drink table.

Dad watched his cousin-nephew for a moment, then smiled, and sat quietly. "He always took after his mom, him," he said. "Gentle soul."

"Well," Mom said. "Maybe I'd better start cleaning off those tables."

The hall had cleared out some, with a few of the older folks going around shaking hands and hugging others before heading out. There remained a good number of people though, sitting and chatting at the array tables along the walls. Across the floor, Roger pretended to aim and fire a rifle. O-wah! You could almost hear Frank shout. Dave waved his hands and scoffed. 'Tante Jo laughed; Carole and Yolande slapped their knees and howled. And there were kids everywhere, squealing, chasing each other through the hall, darting around adults and crawling beneath the tables. They jumped and rolled and climbed, leaped off the stage, their boots thumping heavily on the floor.

"Laisse faire, for now," Dad said.

"Why don't you guys go play?" Monique said to Isabelle and Danny, planted on a pair of stackable blue chairs. They timidly eyed the other kids—their ever-distant cousins—shook their heads, and picked crumbs from their empty plates.

"Want more cheese?" John offered, tending his plate, with its small pyramid of cheese cubes, toward his children.

"Christ, John. They've had enough cheese," Monique said. "Any more will plug 'em up."

I tried not to laugh and had to cover my smile with a hand. Monique shot me with a glare, and I pretended to examine the ceiling.

Dad leaned forward and glanced down the table.

"Hey, you guys want to dance?" he said.

"Yeah!" Danny and Isabelle shouted.

"Okay. Come on," he said, and he led the kids onto the dance floor before the boom box.

Mom and Monique exchanged a puzzled look. Dad wasn't much of a dancer.

We watched as Dad pointed to Isabelle and Danny's feet, then pointed to his own shoes. He began to jig. Just a few slow steps at first, for Isabelle and Danny to follow, and stomp along. Then he got fancier. Quicker. Or, at least, he tried. His dance wobbled between une gigue and a free-wheeling stepdance, with his feet flashing wildly beneath him in loose tempo with the fiddle tune still scratching on the boom box. His energetic attempt made the kids laugh, and as Isabelle and Danny squealed in delight, other kids began to notice, to drift by, and gather around, toothy-smiles splitting their small, flushed, faces. They began to stomp along as well, in time with the tune, and Dad glanced at the growing crowd and missed a step or three.

"Can't stop now, Émile!" Uncle Dave shouted from across the hall, and his brothers, and sisters howled and laughed. And Dad kicked off again, hopping up and down, feet flashing under his legs; wasn't very traditional as his arms flailed for balance and he frowned in concentration even as his lips split apart in the biggest grin I had ever seen. I felt myself pulled to the floor and pushed my chair back, rose, and drifted into the growing circle. Cousins seemed to drift closer as well, feet itching, heads bobbing, their legs firing as though touched by gunpowder and fire. Kids squealed as their parents and grandparents joined in, and we hopped and flailed up and down—some for the first time!—our feet kicking, scratching, in flashes of colour on the pale floor. Our legs churned and our bodies grew warm. Sweat sprouted from our brows and leaked down our cheeks. And as we danced—my back flared, but succored by the vigour—I felt our collective dread, the sorrow and sadness, years of disappointment and despair, begin to drain out through our feet and our legs, and the drops of sweat drippings from our brows, and I spun with furious energy across the floor, and laughed as I thought of Alfred, and how, though we would never see him again, his presence was all around us. He had brought us together. As his music blared relentlessly from the cassette player, Alfred appeared at our sides in his ragged jeans, dusty camouflaged ballcap, sunglasses, and his knobby fingers flashing over the neck of a battered fiddle, imbued with sudden, fantastic talent, and his boots clattered in time on the floor, and so we danced, we danced. I cried, tears washing down my cheeks, and splashing upon the floor. The floor grew wet, fertile like the soil after the Red spills its banks, and the trees and the plants, the crops and the weeds, burst to life afterward in the hot coming sun, sprouting verdant and wild. I glanced up from my feet and saw Mom and Monique standing, clapping in time, and laughing, John still popping cheese cubes in his mouth, Dad holding Danny and Isabelle's hands as they hopped, and I laughed, and kicked my feet until they hurt. Alfred was with us, and so we danced. We danced.

Après la fonte

31.

Highwater

THERE WAS BUT AN ECHO OF SPRING MELT AND highwater in the fields and the ditches when we drove to Alfred's cabin. Tapered remnants and sinews of river water in the floodway. The sun sat skewered in the blue as we drove out from Winnipeg toward the bush line.

"Take the 501?" Becky said. "It's more scenic."

"Is it?"

"Well," she shrugged, and we stared at the flat, empty fields around us, the small bunches of trees around farmsteads, and the barren wind-breaks. "Quieter, at least."

Turning, I glanced in the sidemirror on my door, and saw Monique following behind us. We wound off the main highway, through empty fields, past solitary homes, barns, and batteries of grain silos, and miles of fence, and crossed into the brush, that short, stocky, wall of Manitoba bush. The pavement gave way to gravel and the rumble of ground-up rock popping beneath. Dust sprouted and clung to us like clouds of mosquitoes. Finally, we spotted the cabin through the thin and leafless trees, budding late after a long and cold winter. Dad's truck was parked out front. He stood outside by the cabin, and waved to us as we turned into the driveway. Mom stepped out of the truck as we climbed out of the Buick, and we gathered, hugged, and turned to see Monique's van pulling in behind us. The kids jumped out and ran toward us, while Monique shut their door, and John stretched, arms lifting in the hot spring sun. After we'd all hugged again and began to mill about the front, Dad grunted.

"Might as well," he said, and fetched the urn from his truck. He held it carefully, almost like a running back cradling a football. With his chin, he pointed toward the back, and we began to make our way.

The cabin had been cleaned out over the winter. We'd met a lawyer before Christmas and gone over the will, disposed of items according to Alfred's wishes—distributing knick-knacks to a host of nieces and nephews—and sold, gave away, or hauled to the dump furniture that no one wanted. Dad got the bulk: the tools, equipment, and blades, and the contents of that old chest, the old heirlooms. Matante Fred took his books and papers. Frank and Roger each got a gun: a rifle and a shotgun. Alfred willed me la grande. Dad's brothers and sisters, and some of their cousins, picked over the pictures and the stuffed animal heads on the walls. Monique got some money for the kids' education. In the end though, even as Alfred had frugally gathered and kept things over the years, there hadn't been much to distribute.

After we'd taken care of his things, we notified the gravel company. They still owned the land—Alfred had but leased a small plot—and they thanked us, and then told us that they would demolish Alfred's cabin later this spring.

* * *

The first time I saw Alfred's cabin, it looked like a sunrise. Bright yellow walls, glowing upon the ground. At least, the first time I remembered. I was seven or eight years old. My parents had dropped me off on their way to Grand Forks with Monique. I knew Alfred, but I had never spent any time alone with him, and I stood nervously outside as my parents drove away. After he took my hand and gave me a tour of his yard, we ventured into the house, and I sat quietly on the couch, trembled, and glanced at the frightening things on the walls— the severed deer heads, and the twisted racks, and dusty spider webs. Alfred offered to cook something to eat, and I nodded, but otherwise sat unmoving as I waited. Alfred began to whistle, off-key, happily enough, and I began to warm up, and I quietly fetched my backpack, rifled through it, and pulled out my Game Boy.

Tetris. I played the shit out of that game.

Alfred fried sausage on a pan and glanced over at me peering into this small, light-grey, box, pumping out Russian-themed MIDI music and random beeps.

"Quessé qu'c'é ça?"

"Game Boy," I said.

"Hein?"

"Un Game Boy," I repeated.

"Ah, okay," he nodded. "Pis, quessé qu'ça mange en hiver un Game Boy?"

I paused and looked up at Alfred, looming over a hot stove, with a greasy spatula in hand, and I shrugged. "Des batteries."

Alfred laughed and shook his head. "Tabarouette," he said. And he piled up the sausages on a plate with some potato fries et des galettes. "Okay, mon homme. Viens manger."

* * *

Becky stood in the yard, waiting, as I drifted around the corner. She waved and pointed to the back, where I saw John and the kids at the line, the others only flashes of colour through the burgeoning trees. Dad shouted that he'd found the trail, overgrown, littered with fallen aspen, but navigable. The kids yelled—hiyaa!—and swung makeshift branch-swords at the low-hanging limbs, and the twigs, and the husks of desiccated leaves.

"Watch out," Becky warned as I approached. "Still a bit wet around here," she said.

The ground sunk underfoot, squishing, and squirting water with every step.

"I've seen worse," I said, and as I reached Becky, I grabbed her hand, and I pointed to the old open-face woodshed—it was old now, but I had built that thing with Alfred.

"Water rose up from the swamp way back there," I said. "And it came through the trees and lifted that thing up off its foundation, and nearly pushed it into the cabin there."

Becky glanced at the trees, and woodshed, and then the cabin, and I could see an eyebrow lifting, in the corner, a small frown spreading across her forehead.

"It's true!" I swore.

"Uh-huh."

"Look," I said. "You can still see the highwater mark at the base of the trees." I pursed my lips and glanced back at the cabin. "We even had to sandbag, you know. Back in '97. Stayed up all night guarding that dike. Alfred and me. Kept his cabin dry."

Becky smirked and shook her head, I couldn't tell if she truly doubted me, or was egging me on, somehow getting me to think, and talk about Alfred, and what he had meant to me. What he still meant to me. And so, I laughed and waved her look away.

"Rich!" Monique yelled, her voices ricocheting through the woods. "Get over here!"

"Come on, Rich," Becky said, and she pulled me along, toward the voices, while my eyes remained anchored to trees, fixed upon the high-water mark.

The ceremony was simple. After Mom recited a short prayer au bon Dieu, and we shared a few brief words about Alfred, we stood behind Dad as he uncorked and upended the urn. Ashes spilled out in a clump, caught the wind, and spread across the forest floor. After a moment, John corralled the kids, and started back toward the cabin. Monique placed a hand on Dad's shoulder, then followed her husband. Mom glanced at me and Becky. They turned, and started back up the path. I sighed, and stared up and squinted at the sunlight streaming through the naked tops of the trees, and I listened to the wind rattle the branches. Was that Alfred?

Dad turned, touched my arm, and I looked down, smiled sadly, and nodded. Together we walked up the path.

* * *

Through the night, we laboured. The pump motor coughed and whined, and water gushed over the dike. Wind raked through the yard, and pushed the water toward the cabin where it burst in cold showers, again and again, against the dike, like rain driven sideways. Sandbags slumped, and shifted underfoot, and we braced the dike with plywood and two-by-fours. We bailed water as though in a leaky canoe, tossing bucketfuls over the bags.

The pump motor gave out again. Swamped.

But Alfred would not give up. And even as his back flared with pain, firing acid down his legs and up his spine, and he cried out, he kept bending down and filling his bucket, then tossing that water over the dike. And I stood next to him and followed, bucket after bucket, in an endless and mesmerizing stream, until as light cracked through the trees, and the sun bilged slowly over the horizon, we saw that the highwater had passed.

fin

Acknowledgements

I gratefully acknowledge that this novel draws on research supported by the Social Sciences and Humanities Research Council.

This project began as a creative thesis for my MA in the Department of English and Film Studies at the University of Alberta, and I wish to thank my supervisor, Thomas Wharton, and my readers Albert Braz and Pamela Sing, for their keen insights, comments, and support, which proved invaluable as I revised the manuscript (and concurrently wrote my PhD dissertation).

Thank you kindly to my colleagues, mentors, professors, and friends in the Department of English and Film Studies for their great encouragements, support, readings, and many conversations at the Sugar Bowl (and other watering holes): Brittney Blystone, Anita Cutic, Amanda Hooper, Alison Brodie, and Sahar Charradi, as well as Jordan Kinder, Ben Neudorf, Sarah McRae, Ana Horvat, Chelsea Miya, and William Owen. Thank you in particular to the creative writers who gathered sporadically like cats to read each others work:

Mackenzie Ground, Kaitlyn Purcell, Uchechukwu Umezurike, Jason Purcell, Mahdi Kashani Lotfabadi, and others whom I may have forgotten! Special thanks to the EFS By-Weekly Creative Writing Group: Conrad Scott, Leslie Robertson, Kat Cameron, and Lianna Ryan, for their persistent readings of my revisions in progress! An equally big thank you to Matt Cormier, Stephen Webb, and Keighlagh Donovan for reading the finished manuscript.

Un gros merci aussi au gens du Manitoba, les amis, la famille, la parenté, les connaissances, and folks from Ste. Anne, Richer, and Ste. Geneviève, and down the highway in Winnipeg. Un gros marsi to Cindy Flamand of St. Ambroise for reading early versions of the novel, and, with Charlene Bergen and Serena Suderman, for teaching me some "dirty" words in Michif! Finally, as always, thank you to Lisa Bergen!

Lastly, thank you to the folks at NeWest Press for their support, enthusiasm, and professionalism, and in particular, to my editor, Smaro Kamboureli, for the wonderful conversations, insightful readings, and the many suggestions that greatly improved this novel! Merci.

Typeset in Adobe Caslon Pro and Kawai Craft Regular

Matthew Tétreault (he / him) is Métis and French-Canadian from Ste. Anne, Manitoba. He is the author of *What Happened on the Bloodvein* (Pemmican Publications, 2015), a dark, but humourous collection of interrelated short stories set in southeast Manitoba. Matt holds a PhD in Métis literature and literary history from the University of Alberta, and he received a Governor General's Gold Medal for academic excellence. His dissertation traces the literary history of the Red River Métis. In between academic and creative writing projects, Matt plays guitar, video games, and poker for pocket change. He recently moonlighted as the "farm boss" on his in-laws' ranch in St. Ambroise, where he, his wife, daughter, and his old cat, Major Tom, landed upon their return to Manitoba. *Hold Your Tongue* is his first novel. He lives in Winnipeg.